Trick Me Twice

Copyright © 2020 by Becca Steele

All rights reserved. No part of this book may be reproduced or transmitted in any form or by any means, electronic or mechanical, including photocopying, recording or by any information storage and retrieval system, without written permission from the author, except for the use of brief quotations in a book review.

Editing by One Love Editing

Proofreading by Sid Damiano

Cover illustration by Seaj Art

Becca Steele

www.authorbeccasteele.com

This is a work of fiction. Names, characters, businesses, places, events, locales, and incidents are either the products of the author's crazy imagination or used in a fictitious manner. Any resemblance to actual persons, living or dead, or actual events is purely coincidental.

TRICK ME TWICE

USA TODAY & WALL STREET JOURNAL BESTSELLING AUTHOR
BECCA STEELE

AUTHOR'S NOTE

The author is British, and British English spellings and phrases are used throughout.

For Ivy

Man is least himself when he talks in his own person. Give him a mask, and he will tell you the truth.

OSCAR WILDE

RAINE

HALLOWEEN

"This is an emergency broadcast announcing the commencement of the annual Fright Night. When the siren sounds, let the games begin. Good luck to you all."

As the unnecessarily dramatic, robotic voice faded from the speakers, smoke began swirling through the night air, and the sound of a siren blared all around me. Strobes lit up the area in sharp flashes, illuminating the surroundings for milliseconds at a time before plunging us back into darkness.

Beyond the rides and food stalls, in front of the haunted house, stood a group of masked, hooded figures, dressed in black. The masks glowed with neon LED lights, creating sinister slashes over their eyes and mouths. Most of the guys had green, yellow, or orange masks, but the three centre figures had red, purple, and blue masks.

I immediately knew who they were. The three kings of Alstone High.

Kian, Xavier, and Carter.

The guy in the blue mask seemed to stare right at me, and it felt like my heart stopped. Without a shadow of a doubt, I knew it was Carter. I edged closer to the chain-link fence, trying to stay out of his sight.

The sirens suddenly stopped.

His attention was locked on me.

He ran.

I did, too.

ONE

CARTER

ONE WEEK EARLIER

I owned this school. I was untouchable.

Sauntering down the hallways of Alstone High with my group of friends, aware of the envious looks thrown our way, even the teachers fawning over us. Most of them, anyway. We were at the top, and Kian, Xavier, and I ruled them all.

And that was the way it was going to stay.

Until one girl ruined it.

"See me after class, Mr. Blackthorne." My English Lit teacher thumped my desk as he slapped my essay down on it. D. Fuck. If I didn't keep up my grades, my spot as football team captain was gone. Even worse, I'd have no hope of getting into Alstone College. A degree from there opened more doors than one from Oxford or Cambridge, and if I was going to follow in my dad's footsteps, I needed to take my place there next year. I gritted my teeth. This was the only class I was struggling in, and it had to be with the one teacher I couldn't control.

Tearing my gaze away from my paper, my attention shifted to the girl sitting at the desk under the window. Raine Laurent. Plain Raine. Mousey-brown hair scraped back in a tight ponytail, a school uniform that should really be burned, it was so ill-fitting...she had "future librarian" written all over her.

My eyes strayed from the small smile playing across her lips to the paper she was clutching in her hand, and resentment burned through me. How did she get an A, *again*, and I could only manage a D? Again?

As the bell rang for the end of the class and everyone piled out, I reclined back in my seat, casual and indifferent to everyone's eyes, but inside I felt my future slipping from my grasp.

"Another D. I expect better from you, Mr. Blackthorne. Your entire future is in jeopardy if you don't buck your ideas up." Clenching my jaw, I remained silent, tuning out Prof. Patel's rant as he laid into me. I focused again in time to hear him say, "I expect a B or above for your next assignment, or you can kiss goodbye to any hope of getting into Alstone College. You may have a provisional acceptance, but remember, confirmation is entirely dependent on your grades."

When I still didn't comment, he leaned across the desk towards me, holding his thumb and forefinger up in front of my face, his voice hard and uncompromising. "You're *this* close to failing. This is your final warning. Do I make myself clear?"

"Yes, sir." I forced the words out.

"Good. You're dismissed." He retreated to his desk, and I got the fuck out of there.

The hallway was already empty, most people having left since it was the end of the school day. I headed for my locker to dump my books before I headed over to the field for football training.

Rounding the corner, I saw Raine, closing her locker. Fucking great. The only person around, and the last person I wanted to see. An image flashed in my mind: Raine, holding her A-graded paper, a smug smile on her face.

The simmering anger burned. I stalked up to her, smacking the books out of her hands so they fell to the floor with a crash, and then before I knew what I was doing, I had her pinned against the lockers with my hands planted either side of her head.

Her harsh intake of breath sounded loud in the corridor, her chest rising and falling against mine. Without any conscious thought, I lowered my hand and wrapped my fingers around her throat.

We both froze for a moment.

What the fuck was I doing?

Her pulse was racing under my grip. Instead of dropping my hand like I meant to, my thumb stroked down the side of her neck.

Her skin was so fucking soft.

I watched with fascination as her chest expanded with a breathy sigh that she desperately tried to stifle. Her hazel eyes widened, her pupils dilating, but she brought up her hands to push me away, swallowing hard under my grip. She placed her palms flat on my chest, barely even putting any effort into her movements. Even if she had, I easily held her in place with my body weight. She was fucking tiny—she didn't stand a chance against me.

With an effort, I focused on the reason for my anger and reminded myself that this girl was the cause of misery in my life.

"What's your fucking deal, Laurent? Sitting in class with that smug little smile on your face, thinking you're so much better than the rest of us. Do I need to remind you of your place?"

Her heart-shaped mouth tightened into a thin line, and she stilled.

Tension grew heavy in the air as she held my gaze. Why wasn't she backing down?

"Anything you want to say?"

A gleam of defiance entered her eyes, but she remained silent.

I released my grip, and she slumped backwards with a harsh exhale.

"Get out of my sight." Stepping over her fallen books, I strode over to my locker and slammed my thumb on the fingerprint sensor. Behind me, I could hear Raine scrabbling around to pick up all her shit, and then she fled, leaving me alone with my thoughts.

D. Fuck.

RAINE

"Let me help you with that."

Standing next to one of the honey-coloured stone pillars outside the front entrance of Alstone High, I paused in the process of picking up my backpack. My stomach flipped at the low drawl, and not in a good way. I turned my head to see Carter Blackthorne, self-proclaimed king of the school, eyeing me with arrogant disdain. The football god with a muscled body that shouldn't be allowed on an eighteen-year-old, expressive eyes that reminded me of autumn leaves, all browns and golds, depending on the light, and mussed, chocolatey hair falling across his forehead. He was undeniably hot, and he knew it.

Looks weren't everything, though, especially as far as I was concerned. As well as his general arrogance, lately he seemed to get some kind of sick pleasure from tormenting me when no one else was around to witness it, and I had no idea why. I kept my head down and tried to stay out of his way, other than Mondays, when it was unavoidable.

Unlucky for me, we were sort-of neighbours, and ever since my uncle had divorced my aunt and left us to fend for ourselves more or less, she and Carter's parents had struck up a friendship. They lived in a huge mock-Tudor mansion on the corner of one road, and my aunt's and my smaller house was also on the corner of my road, meaning our houses were perpendicular to one another.

Carter seemed to take personal offence at their friendship—I guess we weren't his kind of people, or something. Or at least, I wasn't. I wasn't rich or popular or outgoing, and I didn't care about impressing the in-crowd. I remained invisible to most of them, but Carter? There was no avoiding him. Especially not now.

"I'm good, thanks," I bit out, swiping my bag from the floor before he could grab it. My head was a mess, thanks to our earlier interaction at the lockers, but right now, my strongest emotion towards him was anger.

"What's the matter, Laurent? Too high and mighty to allow me to carry your bag now, huh?"

"I'm perfectly capable of carrying my own bag, thank you." I turned my back on him.

That was my first mistake. He spun me around, ripping the bag from my hands, inserting himself into my personal space without a second's hesitation.

"It wasn't a fucking question, *Plain Raine*."

I set my mouth in a flat line, refusing to let him see how he affected me, even though every part of me trembled with awareness at his presence. His body heat made me suck in a breath, his hard muscles pressing into my breasts, his black-and-green football uniform a dark contrast against the crisp white of my school blouse. He was all hot and sweaty from his training, and that should've been enough to make me take a step back, but no. Instead I found myself breathing him in, mesmerised by the rise and fall of his chest, the way he stood tall and unyielding, feet planted on either side of mine, as he looked down at me.

His eyes. There was no warmth in those autumn depths as he took me in. "Come on."

Sighing, I followed him towards the car park. There was no point in refusing.

Why? Why did he have to be my neighbour? Why did I have to be on his radar, now? All exacerbated by this completely ridiculous arrangement that meant I had to rely on him for a lift home—to say it was torture for both of us wouldn't be an exaggeration.

It had all started last month, at the beginning of our final year at school. I'd mentioned in passing to my aunt that the after-school drama club was looking for students to work on costumes and set design. The next thing I knew, my aunt and Carter's mum had come up with this plan which forced us into riding back from school together since he had football training after school on Mondays. So, while I was grateful that I got to be a part of the drama club and do something I loved, my one highlight of the week was always tainted by the fact that I knew I'd end up in some kind of confrontation with him.

It was clear that Carter's parents felt some sense of duty towards me—pity, even. I hated being a charity case, but I sucked it up so I could get to do something I loved, and with the threat of his allowance being cut, Carter had to play chauffeur to me every Monday. We were both bitter about it, though.

The drive home was silent. My mind replayed the moment when he'd held me against the lockers earlier. The dark look in his eyes as he'd effortlessly gripped my throat, the fear, immediately followed by the completely unexpected jolt of lust and excitement that had shot through me, shocking me into silence... The entire duration of drama club had flown by in a blur as I struggled to process my thoughts and my reaction to him.

I'd *liked* what he'd done to me.

What was wrong with me?

I couldn't take my eyes off Carter's hands flexing on the steering wheel, the way he held the tension in his body, his jaw set as he stared straight ahead. The low autumn sun streamed through the windows, the trees either side of us a riot of rich browns and golds, but the beauty didn't penetrate the darkness surrounding us inside the car.

We turned onto my road, and Carter pulled up at the bottom of my driveway. Looking out of the windscreen, I noticed the front gates were closed, which meant my aunt was out at work. I sighed. Not that I wasn't used to spending time alone, but I could've used some company, a distraction from the thoughts running through my mind.

"Problem?"

I jolted out of my thoughts at Carter's impatient tone. "No problem." Swiping my bags from the floor, I fumbled for the door handle. Then I paused, briefly closing my eyes and taking a deep breath to steady my voice. "There is a problem, actually."

His gaze swung to mine, and he raised a challenging brow. "You..." I swallowed. "Why do you hate me so much?"

The darkness surrounding us grew thick and suffocating, reflected in his eyes. He reached out his hand to my face, and then he suddenly gripped my jaw, his fingers digging into my skin.

"You know what my feelings are towards you? Indifferent. In order to hate you, I'd have to care about you. You're nothing to me. Insignificant."

Nothing to me. Insignificant.

I should have been glad of his words, but to my horror I felt tears pricking my eyes, and my lip trembled.

Tearing away from his grip and yanking my door open, I fled the car.

He roared away from my front gates, turning the corner and disappearing from sight before the first tear fell.

That night, my dreams were haunted by emotions and memories I'd done my hardest to suppress. Even though I'd put my past behind me, Carter's words had pierced through to the part of me that was still a small, scared little girl who felt worthless and unloved.

TWO

CARTER

"Listen up." I was in the cafeteria with my best mates, Xavier and Kian. "Why don't we make Fright Night more interesting?"

After the annual tradition of trick or treat pranks got way out of hand and ended up with the tragic death of a student, this year the county council had organised a massive Halloween carnival they were calling Fright Night, in the vague hope we'd hang out there rather than terrorise the locals. Everyone expected Kian, Xavier, and I to plan something, and we weren't going to disappoint.

"What you thinking?" Kian turned to me, interest sparking in his eyes.

"What if we add some stakes to this game?"

As I outlined my idea, identical devious smiles spread across their faces.

"I can't fucking wait." Kian rubbed his hands together.

As he and Xavier began arguing over mask colours, my attention was diverted by a lone student entering the door—Raine Laurent. Anger burned through me as the memory of what had happened yesterday overtook my mind.

I rolled to a stop in the garage next to my dad's Bentley. That meant he was home. Which meant my English teacher, who just so happened to be one of his old school friends and golf buddies, must've contacted him about my grade. Fuck. I'd hoped I might be able to fly under the radar, but I guess not.

Sure enough, when I entered the kitchen, there he was.

"Carter." So much disapproval dripped from that one word.

"I'll try harder."

"That's not good enough. This is the third time this has happened." He stayed calm and collected, too composed to show any outward signs of anger, but it was all there in his clenched jaw and the frustrated hand he was running through his hair. "Need I remind you that your future is at stake, here? I can open some doors for you, but without that degree, you're not going to last five minutes."

"I know."

He continued as if I hadn't even spoken. "Why can't you take a leaf from Rainey's book? Her grades are impeccable."

And there it was again. Raine fucking Laurent. Both my mum and dad thought she was so fucking perfect, kissing her ass and going on about how clever and amazing she was all the time. The constant comparisons were nothing new, but every time I was compared to her and found wanting, it fucking stung.

"Maybe I could speak to Pam, see if Rainey can give you some tutoring," he mused.

My stomach rolled, and I gritted my teeth. "Not a good idea, Dad. She'll be way too busy with her own schoolwork."

"I'm sure she wouldn't mind—"

"No. I promise I'll do it, Dad." Fuck. That.

"You'd better. This is your last warning." Turning his back to me, he called out for our housekeeper. *"Joan?"*

I took that as my cue to leave. I'd just reached the door, Joan entering the kitchen and giving me a small smile, when my dad's voice stopped me. "Don't forget the school rules— you're off the football team if you don't improve your grades."

There was no way I was getting kicked off the team. We were already fucked with Kian's suspension, and I was the captain. If I was gone, too, the rest of the team would be screwed, with no hope of winning the championships. Why did my dad have to be buddies with someone who had the power to take away the one thing I loved? And why did he have to constantly compare me to Raine Laurent?

"Got to get my books from my locker. I'll be back," I muttered, sliding out of my seat and stalking over to Raine before anyone could reply.

Her eyes widened as I neared her, and she glanced around wildly as if she was looking for an escape. I suppressed the sudden, unexpected urge to wrap my hand around that little throat again. What the fuck was wrong with me?

"Outside, now." I continued stalking towards the doors, knowing she wouldn't want to cause a scene in front of the other students.

Hearing a muffled curse behind me, I smiled to myself as I turned to face her.

"What do you want?" She stared at me defiantly, but she couldn't disguise the shake in her voice.

"This way." The last thing I wanted was for people to think I was showing an interest in her, and I checked around me to make sure no one was paying us any attention. Satisfied we were in the clear, I gripped her arm, dragging her down the opposite corridor. She stumbled, trying to keep up with my pace as I rounded the corner and came to a stop under the stairwell.

As soon as we were there, I let go of her, pushing her up against the wall and planting my hands on the wall behind her head. I was thrown for a moment at the feel of her small body against mine, before I gathered myself and spoke the words I'd dragged her aside to say. "I want you to find another way home from school on Mondays."

She stood completely still, staring at me with wide eyes, her pupils dilated with an intoxicating combination of apprehension and arousal. Eventually, she took a breath and spoke, her voice practically vibrating with tension. "I-I can't. What will I tell my aunt and your parents? How am I going to get home?"

"Not my concern." As I leaned into her, the scent of apples and caramel invaded my senses.

"I can't." Her mouth set in a stubborn, flat line.

Pressing my body into hers, I lowered my mouth to her ear. "You will. I don't care how it happens, I don't want you in my car again." She didn't need to know that her presence made me feel out of control, that she got under my skin like nothing else, and I hated it. The best thing for both of us was for her to stay as far away from me as possible.

Her chest rose and fell beneath me, her breathing rapid against the side of my face. Drawing back, I waited until her eyes met mine, before I continued. "And you need to stop sucking up to my parents."

"I'm not," she whispered, lowering her gaze.

"You are." I laughed. "You know, they only praise you because they feel sorry for you. You'd have to be completely naïve not to realise that they don't mean any of the things they say to you. Don't forget your place, Raine Laurent. You're insignificant. Nothing." The cruel lies fell easily from my lips, and she stiffened beneath me, a tiny, pained whimper escaping from her mouth before she clamped it shut.

Glistening tears gathered on her lashes. One fell, and my eyes followed it down her face to her cheekbone. Before I knew what I was fucking doing, I gripped her chin in my hand and licked away the tear, the saltiness bursting on my tongue.

She let out a shocked gasp, and another tear fell.

"Why?" she managed to say. "Why?"

She didn't deserve an explanation from me, and I didn't have one to give her. "Because I fucking can."

Back in the cafeteria, I pushed all thoughts of Raine Laurent from my mind. What had just happened between us, I had no fucking idea. I'd lost all rationality when it came to that girl. All I knew was, my dad needed to get off my back, and she needed to stay well away from me.

The boys didn't seem to notice anything amiss, and we fell into an easy discussion about the logistics of our plan for Fright Night. Preparation was key—it was no good going in without any idea.

Once we had everything together, we headed outside to join some of the football team before the rest of our lunch break was up.

My ex-girlfriend, Anastasia, was hanging out in the quad area with Imogen and their little group of friends. She caught my eye, tilting her blonde head at me hopefully, and I gave a slight shake of my head. Yeah, she was hot, but way too high-maintenance for me. If she thought there was a chance we'd be getting back together, she had another think coming. I'd been there, done that, and I had no intention of repeating myself. Playing the field was much easier—no commitments, no burden of having to constantly take the other person into account when making decisions. It sounded selfish, but my only goals this year were to stay at the top where I belonged, graduate with the grades I needed to get into Alstone College, and to keep my spot as football team captain. If we could win the football league this season, even better.

I noticed Xavier glancing over at Imogen when he thought no one else was looking, and I rolled my eyes. These were two people who were in serious fucking denial about wanting to get back together. They'd broken up at the beginning of the summer, and Xavier had been a miserable fucker ever since.

Not that it was my problem to sort out. My attention turned to the football game we were playing after school on Wednesday against our biggest rivals.

"You think we can beat Highnam Academy? Blount's got a serious chip on his shoulder after the last match. I wouldn't put it past him to try something sneaky."

"I've got it covered," Preston Montgomery III, one of our strikers, assured me. "You concentrate on holding him back, and I'll do my thing."

"Shame I won't be there, making us all look good by scoring the goals. Hope you're up to the task," Kian muttered under his breath, glaring in Preston's direction. I let it go, because I knew how frustrated he was about being suspended from the team and Preston getting all the praise in the meantime.

We'd be stuck without Preston, though. New to the school this year—he'd transferred from the USA, and other than his irritating habit of referring to football as "soccer," he was a talented player who worked well with the rest of the team. I just hoped that when Kian was back from his suspension, he'd get over this grudge he was holding against his teammate.

"I'm more worried about Cameron." Xavier finally tore his attention away from Imogen. "When he crosses the ball to Blount, they're unstoppable." Despite his input, Xavier wasn't actually on the team—for some reason, aka his thing for Imogen, he'd joined the drama club this year. Even though he was a decent player, he'd easily given it up for a chance to prance around on a stage with her. I didn't get it, but whatever. No one would dare to question him either—his uncle was a huge TV producer, married to a former supermodel, and his whole family always seemed to be hanging out with celebrities. Meaning, everyone at school wanted to suck up to him.

"With Carter running the show, no one can get past us." Chris, another of my teammates, grinned at me.

As everyone began talking tactics, my mind wandered to my English class. If I didn't get my shit together, I wouldn't be running the show for much longer.

THREE

RAINE

"You're quiet. Even more than normal." My friend, Lena Drummond, peered at me as we sat in front of the large monitors in the computer lab during our free period on Wednesday.

We'd only become friends this term, when we'd been partnered together on a project, in our shared Economics class, and while I kept everyone at arm's length, there was something about her that I was drawn to. I wished I could let her in, but I found it so difficult to open up. Something I was working on, but the fear of being hurt was always there. The fear of rejection. Carter's words came to my mind again. *Insignificant. Nothing.*

Sometimes, I wished Lena's don't-give-a-fuck attitude would rub off on me. She was so confident, so uncaring of what people thought of her. Even now, she flouted the strict dress code rules with her heavy eyeliner, black painted nails, and fishnets with boots instead of the usual tights and shoes the rest of us wore. She could get away with it, though, being school royalty. Her family pretty much ran our town, along with the Lowry and Cavendish families.

She was untouchable, even to Carter Blackthorne and his friends.

I opened up my file browser, navigating to the folder with my partially completed essay. Next to me, Lena opened up a complicated-looking screen, covered in numbers. "I'm fine."

She raised a brow at me, clearly not believing my words. "Try saying that more convincingly, and I might believe you."

"It's nothing, really. Just a run-in with Carter. Nothing I can't handle."

"Carter? As in, Carter Blackthorne?"

"Yeah."

Turning her head to stare at me, she frowned. "Really?"

I nodded.

"What's his problem with you?"

"Nothing I can't handle," I assured her, refusing to allow my voice to tremble.

"Boys are more trouble than they're worth," Lena muttered, almost to herself. "If he gives you any trouble, tell me, okay?"

"I will. Thanks." Grasping for a change of subject, I gestured at her computer screen. "I don't get how you understand that."

"Ha. Numbers are easy to me. Maths, computers, whatever. Give me a needle and thread, though, and I wouldn't have a clue where to start."

"You have creative talent, too, though. You have your own style. You always look great. Me, on the other hand?" I pointed to myself. "Well..."

She turned her full attention to me. "That's because you use your uniform to hide away. To make yourself less noticeable. Me? I don't give a fuck. I'm not hiding anything."

I gaped at her. "You noticed that?"

"Raine, no offence, but I had no clue you even existed until this year. You're a pro at making yourself invisible."

"I..." What could I even say to that? How could I explain the voices inside my head, constantly telling me that I wasn't enough? That I hid away so no one would have a chance to hurt me? To make me feel less?

It could be blamed on any number of things—my parents passing away, being shuffled between temporary places before my aunt adopted me, the kids in those places who'd singled me out as an easy target when I'd turned up at their school, an outcast in uniform that never quite fitted. I bore no physical scars from that time, but the emotional ones had taken a lot longer to heal. Wherever the blame lay, I'd learned over the years to keep to myself, and now, that was my comfort zone. I felt safe when I slipped under the radar and stayed in the background. It was my armour, my protection against being hurt.

Lena studied me closely, her lips pursed in thought. "I've had an idea." Her eyes gleamed with a challenge. "Do you trust me?"

I stared at her for a long moment, before I made my decision. "Yes." My voice was a cautious whisper.

A huge smile spread across her face. "It's time to step out of the shadows and into the light." My stomach flipped at her words. What was that supposed to mean? She turned back to her computer but kept talking. "Does this hiding away extend outside of school hours? Like, do you ever meet up with anyone outside of school? Do anything social?"

My cheeks grew hot. "No."

"Hey, I wasn't trying to make fun of you. It's okay that you haven't. I just get the feeling you're hiding, rather than doing it out of choice? Am I right?"

Wow, she was direct. And completely correct. "Yes." I sighed, lowering my gaze. "I guess...I'm used to keeping to myself. I don't know how to be any other way." I couldn't add the rest of it, couldn't voice my fears aloud, but that was enough of an explanation for Lena.

"Okay. We're going to try a few things. Get you more comfortable being around people."

"Why are you doing this?" Why would she want to help me?

She smiled, turning back to face me. "Because...let's just say that I know what it's like to hide away. And I can read you, and I know that underneath that cautious exterior the real Raine Laurent is dying to come out to play."

"What do you have in mind?"

"Fright Night. You're coming with me."

Fright Night? Was she serious? That was going to be a huge event—all the local schools had been issued invitations, and I was pretty sure almost all the students in my classes would be there.

I stared at her for a moment, before I managed to gasp out the words. "But...but that's a huge event!"

A satisfied smile played across her lips. "Exactly. That's why it's perfect. There'll be so many people around, it'll be easy for you to blend in. Doing this, you get to be around people out of a school setting without the pressure of attention on you. Trust me, you can handle this."

I stopped and thought for a minute. She was probably right, and maybe with her there as a buffer, it would be okay. I groaned under my breath. "I don't know what...I want to say yes, but I guess I'm scared." If I was truthful with myself, I knew I needed to stop hiding away all the time. Why couldn't I have Lena's confidence? Why was I still so hung up on my past that I couldn't move on?

"I know you are, but this will be good for you." She placed her hand on my arm, squeezing it briefly. "I promise you'll have fun."

I didn't really have an excuse. I was only going to be spending the evening home alone, anyway. Again. It was rare that my aunt and I both had an evening at home together these days, where I wasn't busy doing homework or sewing costumes and she wasn't working another overnight shift at the hospital birth unit where she was a senior midwife.

"Okay," I said finally. Turning back to my computer screen, I mumbled, "I hope I don't regret it."

"You won't regret it," Lena promised me. "You get to be in disguise, too, so you don't even have to worry about people recognising you if you don't want them to."

My fingers paused, mid-type, and I twisted in my seat, giving her my full attention. "A disguise?"

"Costumes," she elaborated. "It's Halloween. You do know most people will be wearing costumes, right?"

Right. "Oh, yeah."

"No need to sound so enthusiastic." She rolled her eyes, grinning at me. "I think you should make something. Use your talent for costume design."

"Hmm. I guess I could. So you want me to come up with something that disguises me? Why don't I just wear a full body suit?" I smirked at her. "Ooh, I could go as a hot dog."

"Did you actually make a joke?" A proud smile spread across her face as I shrugged, then nodded. "Yay! This is a breakthrough. You're becoming comfortable enough to joke around me." The smile disappeared as she narrowed her eyes at me. "But you are not going as a hot dog. Think of a sexy disguise."

I laughed. Sexy was just about the last word anyone would use in relation to me. "Fine. I'll see what I can come up with. What's your costume?"

"Harley Quinn, or an approximation, at least. It means I can mostly wear my own clothes." She shrugged. "You know me. I'm not one to conform."

For the hundredth time, I wished I had her attitude. How freeing would it be to be yourself, completely? "That's true," I agreed. "Okay, so I need a costume. I don't have much time, but I'll see what I can put together. Anything else I need to know?"

"Nope. Nothing I can think of. I'll meet you by the main park gates beforehand, and we can take it from there."

"Okay." I returned my attention to my screen, scrolling back to the beginning of my essay so I could read through everything I'd written so far. As a group of people entered the room, Lena leaned towards me, lowering her voice.

"You need to have fun. I mean it. This is your last year at school, and you don't want to have regrets."

I sighed. "I know, and I'll try."

"Good." Her voice was satisfied. "I'm glad you're coming."

"Me too." *I think.* How had I been talked into this? Lena was right, though. This was my final year. And if I couldn't do this, how was I going to manage when I was at university at the other end of the country?

Engrossed in my work, I didn't notice the large body sliding into the seat next to mine until the scent of spiced cedar hit my nostrils. Lena remained oblivious on my other side, headphones on, tapping at the calculator next to her keyboard as she chewed on the end of a pen.

"Done with your essay already? It's not even due until Monday."

I jumped, swinging my head to face Carter so quickly that my ponytail flew around and smacked me in the side of the face. He smirked, and I felt my cheeks heat. Counting to ten in my head before I replied, I wrestled my thoughts under control, the mix of apprehension and awareness that I felt at his presence churning uncomfortably in my stomach.

"Some of us like to be ahead of the game," I said primly, turning back to my screen.

Out of the corner of my eye, I could see his lip curl, and he opened his mouth to say something, but suddenly another body was sliding into the space between our seats, breaking the connection between me and Carter and allowing me to breathe. I looked up to see Dylan Rossiter smiling down at me, and I returned his smile with a relieved one of my own.

"Hey, Raine. I've been looking for you. Would you still like a lift home after drama club on Monday?" He stared down at me, his soft brown eyes full of warmth. Dylan was also in the drama club, where he worked on set design and helped out behind the scenes. After Carter had left me crying in the hallway yesterday, Dylan had caught me wiping away my tears, and, concerned, had immediately asked me what was wrong. Not wanting to get him caught up in Carter's drama, I gave him a vague explanation of needing to find a way home from drama club on Mondays, otherwise I may have to drop out. He lived in the opposite direction to me, but he'd told me that he might be able to sort something out.

"I'd love one." I eyed him hopefully.

"In that case, I've got you. Wait for me after drama club."

"She doesn't need a lift. She's coming with me." Carter's voice came from behind Dylan, his tone daring me to disagree.

"But you— But I—" I spluttered, caught off guard. What was he playing at? He'd made it crystal clear that he wanted me to find another way home on Mondays.

Dylan's face fell and he glanced at Carter, taking in what was probably some kind of threatening expression on his face, before turning back to me. He mouthed *sorry*, then mumbled, "Oh, okay. If your situation changes, let me know." Then he fled the room, leaving me staring at Carter in disbelief.

"What was all that about?"

Carter stared at me silently for a moment, before he turned his back on me, leaning over to talk to his friend Kian, who was sitting on his other side.

A frustrated huff escaped me, and I glared at the back of his head. What was his problem?

FOUR

RAINE

Adjusting my costume, I attempted to suppress my rising discomfort as I eyed myself in the mirror. In the end, I'd put together this particular outfit because it was the exact opposite of everything people would expect from me, and therefore, I'd hopefully be able to remain incognito if I ran into Carter and his friends—or anyone from Alstone High, for that matter. I was banking on the fact that other local schools were attending, and no one would imagine that I would show up. Plus, the whole idea of me attending the event was to push me out of my comfort zone, and this was most definitely set to do that.

The mascara I'd applied somehow made my lashes look long and lustrous, framing my hazel eyes and making them appear bigger and more intense, and the toner I'd put in my hair earlier had made it look darker, richer, redder, rather than the usual light brown. Supposedly the toner washed out easily—I hoped so anyway. I didn't want anyone to see me like this at school on Monday. Shaking my hair free of its ponytail, I picked up my curling wand, and half an hour later it hung in soft curls down my back. After slipping on the green fabric mask that covered my eyes, I was ready.

The Uber that I'd splashed out on roared away, and I turned my attention to the huge wrought-iron gates leading into the two-hundred-acre space of greenery and sports facilities that made up Parton Park, where Fright Night was already underway. I stopped dead outside the gates, taking it all in. Rides and stalls in bright neon colours were set up in large clusters throughout the grassy open area that was normally used for casual sports games and summer picnics. A large Ferris wheel stood tall at the near end, and at the far end where the grassy area ended, before the skatepark area began, stood a haunted house, the entrance a huge, sinister-looking gaping mouth. Sweeping lights illuminated the huge space, and thumping music boomed from speakers all around us. A steady stream of people moved in through the gates, and the scent of popcorn and candy floss hung heavy in the air.

Despite myself, a smile tugged at my lips. Maybe this was going to be fun, after all.

I spotted Lena, aka Harley Quinn, near the gates, loitering by a shooting stall where you could win a prize if you managed to shoot a set of moving targets. Looking as edgy and gorgeous as she always did, she was watching a guy dressed as Captain America take shots at the targets over and over again, each time coming close but missing. Every now and then, he'd glance over at her with a flirty wink, but she remained impassive.

After having my ticket scanned at the gate by a guy

dressed as a skeleton, the bones made from some kind of glow-in-the-dark material, I made a beeline for the shooting stall. Sidling up to Lena, I spoke in her ear. "Got your eye on Captain America?"

"No way." She snorted, still staring at him. "I'm counting how much money he's putting into that game. So far he's paid twenty-five quid and hasn't managed to hit any of the targets yet."

"I'm sure those games are rigged," I mused.

"Probably." She turned to me, and her jaw dropped. "Fucking hell, Laurent! You don't even look like you!"

"That's the point." I couldn't help smiling at her reaction, even as I shuffled awkwardly from foot to foot.

"You look fucking hot. Stop fidgeting."

"I can't help it, I feel weird," I admitted. "I'm not used to this. Any of this."

Her blue gaze assessed me, and she nodded. "I get that. I know it's hard for you."

"How are you so confident?" Maybe she had some tips.

"Honestly? I literally don't give a fuck what any of these people think of me. You should try it sometime. It's liberating."

"I wish I could." I sighed. "Remember, you're school royalty, though. You're a Drummond. Not only that, you're badass."

"I am," she agreed with a smirk, propping her hand on her elbow and posing with her baseball bat, before she laughed and rolled her eyes. "Not really. I just don't care what people think. Wanna play one of the games before we meet up with the others?"

"Yeah." I smiled, relaxing at her words, grateful she was easing me into tonight's celebrations. I had so much trouble letting anyone get close to me, but I wanted to let

Lena in. I needed a friend. Someone to confide in, to be myself with.

"I never lose at these." She tugged me across to the hook-a-duck stall, waving to a couple of her friends that were standing nearby drinking bright blue slushies. I recognised them from my Economics class, but there was no recognition in their eyes as they casually scanned me.

The girls and the game were both forgotten as the music suddenly cut out and all the lights dimmed. A hush descended over the entire park, as from the PA speaker system, a sinister, crackling voice announced a five-minute countdown.

"Countdown for what?" My heart was suddenly thumping way too fast, and I swallowed hard.

"Halloween games, probably. I think Carter and his friends were planning something for tonight." Lena waved an unconcerned hand. "Come and meet my friends."

Carter? I was just about to ask her to elaborate on the games comment when a loud, insistent beep sounded from somewhere near her waist, and she dug her phone out of the pocket of her jacket.

"Shit," she muttered, her face falling. "Raine, I've gotta go. I'm sorry."

"*Go?* You can't leave me all alone here!" I was panicking.

"Fuck, this is the worst timing," she muttered. "Listen to me. You've got this. Join the fun, be somebody else for the night. Look how dark it is now—no one will have a clue it's you. I didn't even recognise you to begin with. You'll be fine." Her eyes met mine, and she stepped closer as her voice softened. "I'll introduce you to my friends before I go, okay? I won't leave you alone if you're not happy."

No. I could do this. I was here, and I was going to at

least try to stay. I attempted to channel her confidence. "I'll stay for a bit. That's all I can promise at this point. Don't worry about introducing me. I kind of like the thought of staying anonymous." As I said the words, I realised I meant them. There was something liberating about no one knowing who I was. I could be whoever I wanted to be tonight.

She studied me closely, then, seemingly satisfied, flashed me a quick smile. "Good. Stay safe, and call me if you need me, okay?"

I nodded firmly. "I can do this." I watched as she slipped away through the gates, leaving me standing alone next to the stall. Taking a moment to get my bearings and plan what I was going to do next, I headed over to the chain-link fence that ran down the side of the part of the park we were in.

My newfound confidence evaporated as soon as it had arrived. I was suddenly too hot, despite the fact that "skimpy" didn't even cover the costume I was wearing. Leaning my head back against the cold metal of the fence, I closed my eyes, breathing deeply, trying to calm my racing heart.

This was ridiculous. Something like this shouldn't be so difficult. Why was I so awkward? Why did I find it so hard to be around most other people?

A new determination filled me. Enough was enough. I was going to be a normal, sociable human being for one night in my life. I was going to mix with everyone else and have fun, even if it pushed me out of my comfort zone.

Taking a deep breath, I opened my eyes.

For a split second, time seemed to stop. My whole body stilled, poised on a knife edge, waiting for the cut.

Then, it happened.

"This is an emergency broadcast announcing the commencement of the annual Fright Night. When the siren sounds, let the games begin. Good luck to you all."

As the unnecessarily dramatic, robotic voice faded from the speakers, smoke began swirling through the night air, and the sound of a siren blared all around me. Strobes lit up the area in sharp flashes, illuminating the surroundings for milliseconds at a time before plunging us back into darkness.

Beyond the rides and food stalls, in front of the haunted house, stood a group of masked, hooded figures, dressed in black. The masks glowed with neon LED lights, creating sinister slashes over their eyes and mouths. Most of the guys had green, yellow, or orange masks, but the three centre figures had red, purple, and blue masks.

I immediately knew who they were. The three kings of Alstone High.

Kian, Xavier, and Carter.

The guy in the blue mask seemed to stare right at me, and it felt like my heart stopped. Without a shadow of a doubt, I knew it was Carter. I edged closer to the chain-link fence, trying to stay out of his sight.

The sirens suddenly stopped.

His attention was locked on me.

He ran.

I did, too.

FIVE

CARTER

"Ready?" Kian's voice was muffled behind his mask. Looking around at the circle of guys, I grinned.

The introduction, in the style of an announcement from *The Purge*, crackled from the speakers, and I was fucking ready. Waiting for the sirens to sound so I could collect my prize.

My focus zeroed in on a girl leaning against the fence, staring in my direction, and my breath caught in my throat.

Fuuuuck.

I recognised the costume—the villain Poison Ivy. Those curves, though? Should be illegal. Full, perfect tits, a tiny waist, flaring out to hips that gave her the very definition of an hourglass figure. My gaze trailed over her toned legs and waves of reddish-brown hair that fell down her back and shoulders. Her lips were full, too, and her eyes, although partly hidden by the mask thing she had on, were sparking with the challenge. Her costume was basically a leotard, covered in green leaves, and she had on tan knee-high boots covered in some kind of green material.

I'd never seen anyone so sexy in my life.

I was temporarily stunned.

"She's mine," I hissed to Xavier and Kian, indicating my head in her direction.

"Fuck you, Carter." I felt Kian's glare from behind his mask, but I'd seen her first. "Fine. I pick...her," Kian relented after it was clear I wasn't about to change my mind, pointing towards another hot as fuck girl, dressed like an angel.

"Done. I pick her." Xavier pointed towards the Dodgems where his ex-girlfriend stood with a group of her friends, and I knew both Kian and I were rolling our eyes behind our masks.

"Wait for the siren." I raised my voice so the others could hear me. "When it stops, go for whoever you want, except those three." I pointed out the three girls we'd chosen, knowing no one would dare to disagree.

The siren sounded, and I was ready.

Smoke permeated every corner of the carnival, thanks to our earlier planning. The boys split off, a blur of dark figures with neon masks, and I grinned. As the sirens stopped, my gaze was drawn to Poison Ivy. *Ready or not, here I come*, I mouthed from behind my mask, watching her eyes widen as I took off, running straight at her, needing to reach her before anyone else did. Despite my declaration that she was off limits, I knew it wouldn't work that way in reality. I could feel Kian hot on my heels, his eyes on my girl, rather than his.

Even from a distance I could see her freeze, her gaze locked on mine. My blood was pumping through my veins, and I fucking loved it. She stood paralysed as I drew closer, and then she finally moved.

The chase was on.

She darted behind one of the stalls, running headlong

down the side of the chain-link fence. This was almost too easy. I drew back a little to give her a chance to get away—I needed the chase, and catching her would be so much sweeter when she gave in.

I watched her look wildly around her, no doubt trying to find a hiding place.

"You can run, but you can't hide," I called, and I saw a shudder go through her body. Fuck, yes.

She rounded the back of the funhouse and down the other side, getting caught up with a group of girls being chased, coming the other way. Now I'd lost sight of her. Fuck.

There was a flash of green next to the Dodgems, and I increased my pace. She was running blindly now, desperate to get away. Out of the corner of my eye, I saw Kian run at her, and she made an abrupt turn, darting around two guys in green masks. A huge figure dressed as a clown appeared in her path, leering at her, and she scrambled back, then flew towards the gaping mouth marking the entrance to the haunted house.

"She's fucking mine," I shouted, lunging at Kian, and he pushed back at me.

"Not if I catch her first."

We stared at each other for a minute, neither of us backing down. Then I pushed away from him and tore inside the haunted house after my prey.

RAINE

It was so dark in here. Screams came from all around, echoing off the walls, as I crept through the maze of corridors. A glowing skeleton lunged at me, and I jumped back in fright. The sound of delighted laughter followed me as I spun, running blindly down another corridor.

A creepy-looking clown loomed over me, lit by a single bulb swinging from the ceiling, and I shrieked in terror, scrambling to get away. *Another* clown? Seriously? If there was one thing I hated above all, it was clowns. It reached out an arm towards me, its white painted face stretching into a huge distorted grin, exposing rows of bloodstained teeth.

It's only make-up, it's only make-up, I chanted in my head, desperately trying to convince myself that it wasn't real. Taking a deep, shuddering breath, I twisted and ducked under its arm, racing down another corridor, desperate to find a way out of this maze.

A dead end.

I felt a breath on my neck. "Boo," someone whispered, and then a body was pressed against mine, pinning me in place, and I screamed for my life.

"Keep screaming, baby. It makes me hard." The pressure of my captor's mask against my skin disappeared as he lifted it away from his face, and then cool metal slid across the side of my neck, combined with the soft warmth of lips.

Bile rose up in my throat. *Kian*. His lip piercing was a dead giveaway, combined with the fact that I felt a base, instinctual fear as he held me in place. What would he do to me, here in the dark?

Overcome with terror, I screamed again.

Suddenly, his weight was gone, and I was gripped around my stomach and forcibly dragged back down the corridor.

"You're not playing fair." I heard Kian's voice from behind me.

"Fuck you. I picked her first."

Carter. Carter was the one holding me. For one second, I breathed a sigh of relief, before my brain caught up with what was happening.

Oh, fuck. I was in so much trouble.

He dragged me down a narrow corridor and into a wider space, where a single light illuminated a witch stirring a fake cauldron. The witch watched us pass, not bothering to do anything, even though I was clearly struggling. "Help!" I called out. She cackled, before her attention was diverted by a giggling girl running past, hotly pursued by a guy in a mask with yellow LEDs.

Carter's hand clamped over my mouth, and I felt the first tear fall, trickling under the fabric of my mask and onto my cheek. He gave a low growl of pleasure as he felt the tear run onto his finger, and I inhaled sharply. Who enjoyed making someone cry? There was something seriously wrong with him.

I continued to struggle against him as he spun me around and pushed me into a small alcove. It was pitch-black in here, other than the glow from his horrifying mask, and my heart rate spiked to new levels. Spots danced in front of my eyes. Was I about to pass out?

I couldn't even scream, because his hand was still over my mouth. I gasped for breath, unable to get enough air into my lungs as he pressed his heavy body against mine.

"Shhh. It's okay," he soothed, still holding me in place.

I whimpered as his body pressed closer. "You're so fucking sexy," he whispered.

Another tear trickled down my cheek. My head spun, as the fear and adrenaline spiked with a shot of pure lust, utterly unwanted. My mind was confused, and my body didn't know what on earth was going on. I closed my eyes, trembling in his grip as he angled his head closer to my ear, his mask scratching against my cheek. "Give me all your tears, baby."

My eyes flew open in time to see him pull down his hood and push his mask onto the top of his head. He scrutinised me closely, and in the blue glow I could just about make out his eyes, darkened with lust.

His jaw tightened and he swallowed hard, pulling back enough to give me some breathing room. "Do you want me to let you go?"

I stared at him for a long moment, warring with myself, before I slowly shook my head. I thought I detected a glimmer of relief in his eyes as I acquiesced, but I might have imagined it.

"Good decision. I'm gonna make you feel so good, I promise. Don't scream, okay?" His voice was breathless. How was I affecting him like this? If he knew it was me, what would he do?

I nodded, and he slipped his hand from my mouth to my throat. He squeezed. A choked cry escaped me, as he licked the track of my tear, slowly, decadently.

He placed a single kiss on my cheek, and then his mouth was closing over mine, paralysing me with his touch. He nipped at my bottom lip, then again. Then kissed me. Again.

His lips. They were so soft against mine.

Somehow, I found myself kissing him back, and his tongue slid into my mouth. Sparks exploded behind my eyes. The fear and adrenaline had found an outlet and flowed straight from me to him, a perfect electrical circuit.

Excitement coursed through my body as I melted into him, lost in the feel of his lips on mine.

I kissed him harder. He made a low noise of approval, sliding his free hand up my body, onto my breasts. Panting, he broke the kiss, and I moaned as he eased down my leotard straps, exposing me to him. The darkness gave me a false sense of confidence, knowing that he wouldn't be able to make out much.

"I wish I could see you properly." He dragged his thumb over my nipple, circling it, sending more sparks coursing through me. Then his mouth was on mine again, and my hands were somehow going around him of their own accord, and I was pulling him closer, feeling him grind his hardness against me. He smiled against my mouth, and I was shaken. He'd never smiled at me, not once. Of course, he didn't know it was me.

He used his hand on my throat to tilt my head, and then he was sliding his teeth down my neck, down, down to my breasts, and he sucked my nipple into his mouth, biting, licking, worshipping my body. So *this* was what people talked about. This was what it was like to be with someone who knew what they were doing. The clumsy fumbles I'd had with my...summer fling, if you could call it that, were nothing compared to this. I was so wet, and he'd barely even touched me. I'd wondered if there was something wrong with me, that I hadn't been able to get turned on by Ralph, but my body was having no such trouble with Carter Blackthorne.

His hand moved in between my legs, and he growled. "Mmmm."

The sensations he was sparking inside of me were indescribable. A soft moan fell from my lips as he eased my leotard aside, before pushing a finger roughly inside me. I tensed for a minute, but the pain never came. "Ca—" I bit my lip, hard, to stop myself from saying his name. If he knew it was me, he'd stop. And I didn't want him to stop.

I licked my lips, tasting the blood from where I'd bitten it so hard, as he added another finger, his thumb working at my clit. He kissed me harder as he played my body expertly. He wasn't soft or gentle, but I'd never been so turned on in my life. I could feel the wetness sliding down my legs as his fingers pumped in and out of me while his thumb continued to stroke over my clit.

Tugging my lower lip between his teeth, he bit me softly as he curled his fingers inside me. A huge shock wave of pleasure hit my body, sending me soaring and leaving me gasping for breath.

I was coming all over his hand. The symphony of shouts and screams in the background faded into nothing as I came apart.

For him.

The first orgasm I'd ever had that wasn't self-induced and it had to be from my tormentor.

"Your little pussy dripping all over my fingers is so fucking hot," he groaned, his voice lowered to a husky rasp. "Taste yourself." Then without missing a beat, he was shoving his fingers into my mouth, and I almost gagged as they hit the back of my throat. "Taste," he said again, then withdrew them slightly, and I was able to swirl my tongue around them. The idea of tasting myself—it had never even occurred to me before, but something about Carter's rasped instructions... I obediently licked and sucked his digits while he praised me, telling me how sexy I was and how hard he was for me.

This was...he was on another level. My body responded

to his actions and dirty words, and the taste of myself on my tongue...I never wanted him to stop.

For a moment, I allowed myself to think the unthinkable. Was this how it would feel if he was mine? As soon as the thought had crossed my mind, the fear, which had temporarily faded away thanks to his skills in making me forget, returned in full force. Once he found out who I was, I was in so much trouble. What was he going to do to me when he found out? I needed to escape before that happened. If I could manage to get back outside, I could blend into the crowds and sneak away.

"I can tell how good you'll be at sucking my cock." His hoarse words against my ear sent a whole different kind of fear through me. A delicious fear. I'd never given anyone a blowjob before, and here I was, about to experiment on Carter Blackthorne.

My trembling hand went to his jeans, but he stilled it. "Not yet. We've got all night."

All night? A shot of panic zipped through my body.

No! No, I couldn't be stuck with him for a whole night. He'd find out who I was, for sure.

SIX

RAINE

Carter tugged his mask back down over his face and put his hood over the top. I could feel the heat of his gaze slide across my body as he adjusted my leotard, pushing the straps up so my breasts were no longer exposed. He paused a moment, before gripping me firmly and spinning me around so my back was to him. As he walked us both through the maze of the haunted house, I could do nothing but stumble along in front of him, his hold on me was so tight.

An exit sign flashed up ahead, and I breathed a sigh of relief. As we staggered out through the door, slamming it on a guy running at us with a chainsaw in his hands, I attempted to twist away from Carter, scared of what he'd do to me when he found out who I was.

My struggles only made him tug me harder against him, and I hissed. "I love your fight. Maybe even more than your fear." I could hear the excitement in his tone as he picked me up and swung me over his shoulder like a sack of potatoes, sending all the blood rushing to my head.

He stalked down to the side of the haunted house

before putting me down, still holding me against him, his hand around my throat again.

I stared up at him, his eyes unreadable behind his mask as he looked down at me.

"Your heart's beating so fast. Scared?"

I nodded. There was no denying it. Although I could guarantee that he had no idea that the majority of my fear had nothing to do with the way he held me helpless against him, and everything to do with what would happen once he found out who I was.

He laughed, pleased. *Psycho.* "Good. Now, are you gonna tell me your name?"

No. I couldn't. "Let's stay anonymous," I suggested, my voice barely above a whisper. Would he recognise my voice?

He studied me, then shrugged, releasing his grip on my throat. His whole demeanour went from imposing to relaxed, and it threw me. "If that's how you want to play it. Can you at least tell me what school you go to? I know it's not Alstone High, because I *definitely* would have remembered you."

My relief at his words combined with an undercurrent of disbelief. While I was glad that he seemed oblivious, how could he not know it was me? Then again, even Lena hadn't recognised me to begin with, and there was no way anyone would suspect I was here. "No. Not Alstone High," I managed.

"In that case, we should make the most of tonight. Come on." He stared at me for a moment. "Don't want you being caught on camera."

What?

He tugged me away from the haunted house, his grip tight on my wrist, but not bruising as it had been previously. We weaved between stalls and ended up outside a small red-and-white striped tent, completely out of place among the neon glow of the other rides and stalls. A chalk sign on a stake outside simply said "Fortune Teller." Pushing the canvas aside, Carter ducked through the flap of the fortune teller's small, dimly lit tent, nodding to the heavily made-up woman inside. Tight black curls tumbled around her lined face, her fingers heavy with ornate rings as she shuffled the cards in her hands. She nodded back, throwing him a wink, her eyes glittering in the flickering candlelight as she took me in with her shrewd, dark gaze. We passed her in a flash, round behind a curtain into the back area.

"Aunt Marie." Carter voiced his reply to my unspoken question as he knelt down, rummaging in a duffel bag. "Not really my aunt. She lives in the old Cutler house, the one they say is haunted? Me and my friend Kian used to go trick-or-treating at hers on Halloween. We were sure she was a witch. One time we..." He trailed off, muttering "never mind" under his breath. "Anyway, she's alright once you get used to her. She let us leave our stash in here tonight."

Stash?

He handed me a bundle of fabric. "Put this on."

I shook it out to see a dark hoodie.

"Shame to cover that gorgeous body, but if you're coming with me, I'm not gonna risk you." He helped me into it, his touch surprisingly gentle as he zipped it up. It hung almost to my knees, huge on me. I shivered as his hands brushed over my collarbone, and then his masked face was next to my ear. "I can't wait to see you on your knees for me, later."

I was in so much trouble.

He reached for my mask, and I shrank backwards. "No."

"I'm only gonna swap it for a mask like mine," he reassured me, holding up the full-face mask that was in his hand.

Biting my lip, I quickly grabbed the mask from his outstretched hand and spun around, giving him my back. I ripped off my own mask and pulled the other one over my head, then stuffed mine into the pocket of the hoodie, before I turned back to face him.

"How is it you still manage to look hot in this massive hoodie with a mask covering your face?" He fiddled with the button to turn on my mask's LED lights, and then everything before me was suddenly lit up with a blue glow. I stifled a snort of laughter. He'd never used the word "hot" in relation to me before. As quickly as the thought appeared, it was immediately replaced by a rush of guilt at the knowledge I was purposely withholding my identity.

Thankfully, he silenced my uncomfortable thoughts by continuing, "Take this." A cold metal canister was thrust into my hand, and I slid it into my pocket. Carter lifted my hood up over my head, then linked his fingers with mine.

The warmth of his large hand encompassing my own...it sent butterflies racing through me. I pushed down the feeling before the guilt could rise up in me again. We made our way back out into the main area of the tiny tent, and Aunt Marie stopped Carter with a hand on his arm as he brushed past her. He spun to look at her, but it wasn't him she was facing.

It was me.

Her hypnotic eyes bored into mine, and it was like she could see into my very soul. She beckoned me closer, and my body obeyed before I even realised what I was doing.

"Two halves, so different, yet the same. Trick him once, and you have much to gain.

The gain will not come without a cost. Can you hold on when hope is lost?"

At her foreboding, low chant, a whole-body shiver ran through me, and I froze in place, unable to tear my gaze away from hers. She moved her hand from Carter's arm to my own, her long, blood-red talons gripping me firmly, and pulled me closer. Her voice dropped to a whispered warning.

"Are you willing to pay the price? Trick him once, but don't trick him twice."

My heart sped up, thumping in my ribcage.

"Stop scaring her," Carter hissed to Marie, breaking through the heavy, claustrophobic atmosphere that was holding me captive. She turned her eyes to his.

"Beware the one who seems—"

He raised his hand and sighed. Loudly. "Enough with the cryptic messages." As he tugged me out of the tent, he whispered, "You get used to her. She always speaks in riddles."

His assurances weren't enough to take away the icy tendrils of fear that had wrapped their way around me, embedding themselves in my soul. She'd seen straight through the mask, straight through *me*. Her words were a clear message, one I couldn't ignore.

As Carter led me away from the carnival, towards the area behind the skatepark, next to the graffitied wall by the subway where a group of masked, hooded figures waited, the warning she'd given me played through my mind, over and over again.

Are you willing to pay the price? Trick him once, but don't trick him twice.

SEVEN

RAINE

We reached the others. Only a small group, and there was no sign of the two guys in the red and purple masks—Kian and Xavier. I let myself relax a little. I doubted Kian would have even been aware of my existence, but Xavier did, since I'd been the one sewing his costumes in drama club. Although, now, with the mask covering my entire face and the hoodie swamping my body, I was pretty sure it was even harder for anyone to see through my disguise.

"You know the rules," Carter announced. I listened, fascinated, as he continued. "Video or photograph your evidence, and upload it to the drive using the password you were given. Avoid any identifying features. No faces. Tag your evidence with your codes." He glanced around at the group before muttering to himself, "Where the fuck are Kian and Xavier?"

"What about the girl?" someone called. Everyone's attention swung to me, and Carter stepped closer, his arm curling around my waist protectively.

"She's with me."

"I thought all the girls were being taken to the cove? Those were the rules," another guy challenged.

"She's with me," Carter repeated, his grip on me tightening as he squared his shoulders. "Anyone got a problem with that?"

I held my breath. There were general mutters, but no one came out and said anything.

"Okay. Three hours. Meet at the cove." Everyone split off, and I was left standing there with Carter's arm still around me.

"What's going on?" I ventured, keeping my voice low.

"Just a bit of friendly competition. First, we picked the girls we wanted, now—"

"You picked the girls you wanted?" I barely managed to get the words out.

"I know where your mind's going, and it's not like that. No one was taken against their will or anything."

Hadn't he taken me against my will?

It was as if he knew exactly what I was thinking. "Remember, I asked you if you wanted me to let you go, and you said no." His arm tightened around me. "Believe me, most girls would jump at the chance at being caught by one of us." A low chuckle escaped his lips. "I can guarantee that you were the only one who really put up a fight."

His hand ran up and down my back, and I relaxed under his touch. "Now, we get to do something to win bragging rights."

"Bragging rights? And where did the girls go?" The questions fell from my lips before I could stop them, and I could only hope he wasn't paying attention to my voice.

"Yeah. Bragging rights. As for the girls...they got taken on a nice little ride to the same place we'll be going later. An all-night party."

"I can't stay out all night," I whispered. Technically, I could, but I wasn't about to. Carter started to say something, but I cut him off with another question. "Why didn't you send me away with the other girls?"

He fell silent, then when he eventually spoke, his voice was full of confusion. "I don't know?" He pulled me closer. "I hadn't planned on keeping you with me. There's something about you, though. Something addictive."

"You don't even know me." I curled my body into his.

"Maybe that's part of the fun," he murmured, before he let me go.

A bolt of longing hit me. How I wished he'd show this side of himself to me in the outside world. I mean, I knew there had to be a nicer side to him, otherwise he wouldn't be so popular, but I'd only ever been the recipient of his hate. I swallowed the lump in my throat at the thought that once he found out who I was, it was game over.

Needing a minute, I turned back towards the carnival, the lights blinking on and off enticingly and the sounds of music, laughter and screams filling the air. I sighed before I even realised what I was doing.

Carter's head whipped around in my direction. "Shit," he muttered. "I'm taking you away from all the fun, aren't I?"

I stared at him in shock. "N-no. I'd rather be here with you. I've just...I've never been to anything like this before," I told him truthfully.

He took my hand again and began tugging me back towards the carnival. My mouth fell open in stunned disbelief as he said, "Pick something. We have time."

Once I'd convinced myself that I hadn't been hallucinating and he was actually serious about taking me back, a huge smile spread across my face. Not that he'd be able to see it. I looked around me, at the rides and stalls illuminated by the lights cycling between colourful flashing neons to white strobes, then back again. What to pick? "Nothing with clowns. They freak me out."

I hadn't realised I'd said that aloud until he laughed. "No clowns. Got it. Anything else?"

"What would you pick?" As time went on, I grew bolder in speaking to him. He hadn't recognised my voice yet, so I was more or less sure that I was in the clear.

"Me?" He seemed surprised that I'd asked. "Other than getting you back in the haunted house again?" His voice dropped to a low rasp as he pulled me closer.

"Something different," I murmured. I didn't think I'd survive another go inside there.

"Maybe that." Letting go of my hand, he pointed towards the same shooting game that Captain America had been trying his luck at when I'd first arrived. "But we can do something else, if you want to go on the rides."

I looked to the left of the shooting game to the neon blue Ferris wheel, standing tall among the other rides. "Do we have time for two things? The big wheel might be fun."

"Really?" I heard the scepticism in his tone. "Are you sure?"

"Never mind. It was only a suggestion." I turned away from the Ferris wheel and began walking in the direction of the shooting gallery.

Carter stopped me with a hand on my arm. "If that's what you want to do, we'll do it." Before I could say another word, he dragged me towards the wheel. We stopped at the bottom, staring up, and I heard him swallow hard. A sudden thought struck me. Was the fearless Carter Blackthorne afraid of heights? No. I dismissed that thought as soon as I'd had it. Something told me that there was a story behind his reluctance, though.

"We don't have to do this," I murmured softly, going up on my toes so I could speak in his ear.

"We do." Without another word, he paid the man in the booth, waving away my offer of payment. He led me over to the car, and I slid inside. The attendant clicked the bar into place, and Carter tugged me into his body. "Good thing you're so tiny," I heard him say under his breath as he sprawled out in the cramped space. The ride juddered to life, and he clutched the bar with the hand that wasn't around me. We ascended slowly as the other cars filled, and I heard him groan quietly as we got higher, his leg bouncing restlessly.

"Are you okay?" I ventured.

"Fine," he muttered brusquely, and I shrank back. He huffed out a breath. "It's nothing. Just a stupid fucking… never mind."

"Tell me," I commanded softly, tentatively placing my hand on his thigh, his powerful muscles tense under my palm.

"When I was a kid, my dad made me read this story in the paper. No idea what his thinking was behind it; he said he wanted to warn me of the dangers, but why he had to make me read it, I don't know. Whatever. It was an article about a local boy dying at a fairground. He was on a big wheel, and he fell from the top and snapped his neck. I think he'd been fucking around in the car or something, standing up. For some reason the story stuck in my head, and I had nightmares about it for about a month straight. Never been on a big wheel since. Stupid, right?"

I hadn't been expecting that. For someone like Carter,

so confident and untouchable, to admit to any kind of vulnerability—honestly, I was at a loss for words.

"No, it's not," I said finally. I was totally out of my depth here. My hand squeezed his leg lightly. There was something strangely intimate about being here with him in this swaying car. It felt like the rest of the world didn't exist. Just us, here, suspended in the air, hidden behind our masks. I decided that distracting him might be the best option. "Tell me about the cove. You said the girls were being taken there?"

"You're not from around here?"

I bit my lip. "No," I lied through my teeth. Of course, I knew about the cove, not that I'd ever been there.

"Down the coast, past the pier and the beach, there's a cove at the bottom of the cliffs. Most of the tourists don't know about it. There's a party there later. Exclusive. Select."

I deflated a little. Of course. Only the elite, hand-selected by Carter and his friends, would be invited. "You're coming with me," he added, oblivious.

Before I knew it, the ride was coming to a stop at the bottom. The bar lifted and I climbed from the car, my feet a little unsteady, and Carter took my hand again. "That wasn't as bad as I thought it would be." I could practically hear the smirk in his voice as he continued. "Of course, I did get to have a hot as fuck girl draping herself all over me, distracting me from the thought of plummeting to my death."

I didn't even know how to respond. I was so out of my depth tonight, I couldn't even see the bottom. The whole evening felt completely surreal, like I'd fallen into a dream. Thankfully, he didn't seem to require a response from me because he continued talking. "Want to take the masks off for now? I want to see your face."

"Not yet." I shook my head frantically. "Later."

"If I didn't know better, I'd think you were trying to hide something."

There was suddenly so much suspicion in his voice, and I panicked, trying to come up with a good enough reason to keep them on. "Isn't the whole point to remain anonymous? So no one knows who we are?"

"Yeah." His voice hardened. "We're taking them off when we go to the cove, though, okay?"

"Okay," I agreed softly. I needed to leave before that happened. Before he found out who I was.

I should have left already, or even better, come clean, but I didn't want to stop. He'd said there was something addictive about me, but the Carter Blackthorne I was experiencing tonight? The guy who flipped between scarily domineering and sweet, who'd given me an orgasm in a haunted house of all places, then shown me his vulnerable side? I was already addicted to him, and I couldn't even explain why.

"Watch this." I snapped out of my thoughts to see that we were now standing in front of the shooting gallery, and Carter had a gun lined up, pointing at the moving targets. With the same confident, practised ease he always seemed to have, he fired three shots in quick succession.

"You got one hit," the attendant told him in a bored voice.

"*One?* This thing is fucking rigged."

I stepped closer, sliding my hand up his arm to try and ease the tension. "I was impressed."

"Really." The disbelief in his voice was clear. For

someone like Carter, I guess it was disappointing. I didn't care, though.

"Really." I glanced idly at the shelves of prizes. "Did you win anything?"

"Sorry, you only get prizes for hitting three targets," the smirking attendant informed us.

Carter bristled, looming over the attendant, who shrank back, the smirk dropping from his face. "This is fucking ridiculous."

"Come on, let's go." I tugged at his arm, needing to get him away before he did something stupid. He glanced down at me, his eyes barely visible behind the lights of the mask, but I could see the way his expression softened slightly, and he let me pull him away from the shooting gallery. The lights faded behind us as he took control and quickly moved us through the crowds, away from the carnival, past the skatepark, towards the subway and the graffiti wall that marked the edge of the skatepark.

The sounds of the carnival were replaced with the noise of the occasional car rumbling down the road over the subway, and the wind whistling through the trees. We came to a stop, back in front of the wall again. Reaching into the pocket of my hoodie, Carter pulled out the canister that he'd given me earlier. "Are you in the mood for some art?"

Art?

"Why?"

He grabbed another canister from his own pocket, and gestured towards the wall. "Want to add to this?"

"Are we allowed to?" I whispered.

"We can do whatever we want. Tonight, there are no rules."

EIGHT

RAINE

I stared up at him, his hooded figure towering over me, the glow of his mask giving him a sinister, otherworldly vibe. But somehow, I felt...happy. Excited, even. Who knew that a mask could be so freeing? "Let's do this." I examined the wall, at the colourful images and words spanning the length. There was space at the far side, where the writing had faded, and I headed towards it.

I felt Carter's presence at my back, and when I came to a stop in front of the wall, I heard him inhale sharply, followed by a clatter as the canisters fell to the floor. His arms came around me from behind, and he gripped my throat with one of his huge hands as he pressed his body against me. This time, I felt no fear. Only an intense rush of desire, that intensified when he tightened his grip.

I arched back against him, a soft moan escaping my lips.

"You want me, don't you?" His voice held no hesitation—he knew exactly what he was doing to me. I nodded, and he pressed closer. "I can't wait to have you. To leave my marks all over your skin, hearing you gasp for breath as you come all over my cock."

I gasped right then, vivid images making my knees go weak. This shouldn't have been turning me on, but it was, and my head was spinning. No one had ever...I'd never even *heard* anyone speak the way he did before. Yes, my sexual experience was extremely limited, but I didn't think I was that clueless. I already knew there was another side to Carter Blackthorne, based on the way he treated me, but this...this was so unexpected. My nipples hardened beneath my leotard, and I pressed my body back against his. He was hard already, and we were both breathing heavily. What was he doing to me?

"I need your number. And your name." He released his grip on my throat, sliding both his arms around my waist. "There's something about you, something different to the other girls I know. I already know I want more than just tonight."

His words had the same effect as being doused with a bucket of icy water. Tears filled my eyes, again. I trembled in his grip, the guilt spiralling through me as I struggled to compose myself. I was so close to blurting out the truth at that moment, I had to bite my tongue, hard, to stop the words spilling out.

Thankfully he seemed to sense I was at my limit, as he released me and bent down to swipe the cans from the floor. Grateful for the distraction, I took the can he handed to me and faced the wall. "What do we paint?" My voice thankfully came out steady.

"Whatever we want." Shaking his can, he pulled off the lid and aimed it at the wall. Directing the black paint in a steady stream, his artwork gradually took shape. It was simple as far as art went—the outline of a mask, identical to the ones we both wore. I studied it carefully, then rolled my own canister to check the colour.

"Let me help." I uncapped mine, and went over the black slashes he'd already painted, highlighting them in neon blue to symbolise the glow from the lights. "I can't believe I'm doing this. What kind of influence are you having on me?"

"Don't you like being my little deviant for the night?" His tone was amused. He stopped what he was doing and turned to watch me as I finished up highlighting the mask. Gripping his phone, he took a quick photo of our joint efforts, then continued to stare in my direction as I sprayed the last couple of lines. "You look so fucking hot doing that."

I laughed self-consciously, no clue what to reply to him. My artwork complete, I dropped the canister to the floor and stepped back to look at it critically. If only I had more colours...I could have done something truly amazing.

"I really want to kiss you right now." Carter suddenly pounced on me, and I was powerless to stop him.

I really wanted to kiss him, too.

He pulled me around the side of the wall. Behind it ran a narrow gap, all along the length of the wall, between the wall and the vertical bank that led up to the road. It was just wide enough for a person to squeeze through.

I tried not to think about exactly what was crunching under my feet as Carter tugged me into the tight space, moving deeper behind the wall. "No cameras here. No one to see who we really are." He reached down and pushed my mask up on top of my head.

No light, either. My shaking hands went to his neck, and after pushing up his own mask, he bent his head to mine. I felt his hot breath on my lips, and then he kissed me.

This kiss was different. This time there was no fear, no dominance on his part, only two people who were in complete agreement. He explored my mouth, and with every stroke of his tongue, I fell further under his spell.

The glow of a bright torch suddenly illuminated the space we were in, shining on Carter's face. "Hey!"

We both startled at the loud bellow, Carter tearing himself away from me and slamming his mask back down over his face, and I scrambled to follow suit. Even in my panic, I couldn't help feeling grateful that the light had been pointing at his face rather than mine. As soon as the thought entered my head, the same rush of guilt that had been surging through me on and off all evening returned with a vengeance.

Carter grabbed my hand and pulled me down the other end of the wall, away from the security guard. I stumbled after him, feeling more crunching under the soles of my boots. We exited at the other end, and he led me down into the subway. Weak strip lights flickered along the walls, and the air was stale and foul.

"When I say, you run. Through the subway, make a left, and keep going. First alley you get to, go down it. My truck's parked at the end. Wait for me." He was so calm, his voice sure as he instructed me on what to do. As he was talking, he was pulling out a cylindrical object from his pocket, which he lifted into the air. "Go. I'm right behind you," he hissed, then tugged the pin out of the top of the cylinder. Thick blue smoke began pouring from it as he held it in the air.

I didn't wait any longer. I ran, flying through the subway, hearing a faint clatter and a shout from behind me as Carter threw the smoke grenade in the direction of the security guard. The ground began sloping upwards, and I emerged, breathless, onto the pavement by the side of the road.

I looked to the left, where Carter had told me to run. Tugging the hoodie and mask off as quickly as I could, I dropped them in a pile by the subway exit, next to a streetlamp.

Then, I turned right.

As I turned, the bird perched on the streetlamp took flight.

Behind me, I heard the heavy beat of wings and the harsh, warning caw of the raven.

I sat up in bed with a start, my heart pounding. Glancing over at my phone, I saw it was almost three in the morning. A soft breeze caressed my overheated skin, and dread rolled through my body as the realisation hit me.

The window was open.

I fumbled for my bedside lamp, flicking the switch, and in the dim glow, I saw a shadow detach itself from the wall. With a shriek, I dived under my covers, my whole body shaking with fear. Then the covers were ripped off me, and Carter was there, a dark, savage look in his eyes.

The relief at the fact that it wasn't a murderer or killer clown was immediately doused by the complete and utter rage pouring off him, smothering me in his darkness.

"Wh-what are you doing here?" My voice came out hoarse and shaky, and I licked my lips nervously. He stayed silent, and then he slid onto the bed, as smooth and graceful as a jungle cat, crawling up to me.

"Do you know what I did tonight?"

Oh, shit.

"Where do I start?" His hands pinned my shoulders down so I was helpless to move. If anyone heard him speaking without actually seeing what he was doing to me, they'd think he was discussing the weather with his conversational tone. But his eyes...his eyes promised retribution for what I'd done.

"Let me see..." he continued. "I met a girl. A girl who, in my mind, was a stranger." He paused, licking his lips briefly. "I asked her if she attended Alstone High. Do you know what she said, Raine?"

I whimpered.

"She said she didn't. Then, I asked her if she was from around here. She said no."

Shifting on top of me, he lowered his head, his nose grazing over my cheek. I was immobile, the fear keeping me paralysed. "I thought things were going well, but she disappeared on me. All that I had left of her was this." His hand disappeared from my shoulder, and I felt it slide down my side, before a piece of green fabric was waved in my face.

My mask.

"Something seemed familiar. I kept thinking, do I know this girl?" He dropped the mask next to my head, and his large hand returned to my shoulder, his grip bruising. "Then I looked at the photo I took of her when she was defacing the wall. Her boots looked familiar. Couldn't think where I'd seen them before. Something about her voice, too. I drove around instead of doing the Halloween pranks I'd been planning for fucking months, turning it over and over in my mind. I suddenly thought of something. Caramel apples."

"W-what?" I whispered.

He put his face to my hair and inhaled deeply. "Caramel apples. I should've known." Drawing back slightly, his gaze returned to mine again, black and suffocating. "The hair colour threw me, until I saw you lying here.

Oh, yeah, that and the fact that *you kept fucking lying to me.*"

"I'm sorry." A cry tore from my throat as he pressed his weight onto my body, making all my breath escape from my lungs as he crushed into my ribs.

"You will be." His dark promise slithered through me, sending tension coiling through my gut.

"Wh-what are you going to do to me?" My voice was weak and breathless.

"Why didn't you say anything?"

The first tear fell. "I'm sorry. I know it was wrong. I was...I was afraid of what you'd do to me if you knew."

"You're lying." His eyes followed the movement of my tear as it fell. Then he shifted, and I gulped some much-needed air into my lungs. "Tell me why."

My eyes closed, and in a trembling voice, I admitted the truth that I hadn't even allowed myself to think. "I didn't want you to stop."

Another tear fell.

"Look at me."

My eyes flew open, and he stared at me for a moment, his face illuminated by the glow of the lamp, then lowered his face, and his lips were on mine, hard and furious.

I froze in shock for all of two seconds, before I kissed him back.

His mouth was punishing, slamming against mine, savage and raw. He attacked me with his lips, and I met every single assault, moaning into his mouth, my legs hooking around him of their own accord as he sent fire racing through my veins.

"You want me, don't you?" His voice was a low growl as he moved to nip at my neck, and I sighed, allowing the quietest *yes* to escape.

He stilled above me.

Suddenly, his body weight was gone, and he was looking down at me with total and utter contempt. His eyes were hard and unforgiving, and his harshly spoken words fell like acid rain on my skin.

"You can want me, but you can *never* have me. Watch your back, little trickster."

NINE

RAINE

From the minute I awoke, I hadn't been able to shake the overwhelming trepidation that had stayed with me ever since Carter had come into my bedroom and told me that he knew who I was. He hated me before, but now, he actually had reason to. I'd never dreaded school like I did this morning. I really needed to speak to someone, but I guess I felt a sense of guilt surrounding everything that had happened between me and Carter. Guilt for the way I'd tricked him, lied to him, and made him think I was someone else.

As I turned the corner and the gorgeous, golden stone buildings of Alstone High came into view, my gaze was immediately drawn to a familiar figure, slouched against the wall with his arms crossed over his impressive chest. I noticed the moment he saw me because he straightened up, the distant expression on his face replaced by a hard, dark look.

My stomach flipped, and my steps slowed.

"Everything okay?" Lena eyed me with concern. She'd been picking me up on the way to school every day since we'd been paired on our project, and I'd started to look forward to our random morning conversations. She'd asked me how Fright Night had gone, both via text and again this morning, but all I'd told her was that I'd left early. I owed her the truth, but I was working up the courage to tell her.

"Yeah, fine." I gathered myself, and as we ascended the steps, I did my best to ignore Carter, despite his dark gaze boring into me. We drew level with him, and I held my breath. One more step, and I'd be inside the doors, free.

Then I felt the hand on my elbow, and I was dragged against his torso. I gave a squeak of fright, losing my balance and accidentally elbowing him in the ribs. He made a low, angry noise in his throat.

"Raine?" Lena had suddenly noticed I wasn't next to her anymore. I did my best to school my expression into one of unconcern, although from the look in her eyes, I didn't think I succeeded.

"I'm fine. I'll catch up with you later, okay?"

She frowned, but at my pleading look, headed inside with a sigh, only after she'd shot a pointed look at Carter and drawn a finger across her throat. Her theatrics made me smile, despite everything, although the same couldn't be said for Carter.

"I've been waiting for you." Five innocuous words, but spoken in the low, sinister tone Carter used, sent icy shivers down my spine. He held me in an iron grip, my back against his torso. People were throwing us strange looks as they passed, no doubt wondering why Carter, king of the school had me, a nobody, pressed up against him.

"Little trickster."

His lips were tickling my ear, and I had a sudden, inexplicable urge to laugh. A smile tugged at the corners of my lips before I could stifle it.

"Something funny?" The grip on my torso tightened. He pulled me behind the columns at the top of the steps, into the shadows away from prying eyes.

"N-no," I stammered. My brain was going haywire. I took a deep, cleansing breath, and then my nose was suddenly full of cedar and spice. Why did he have to smell so good?

"Remember how I told you to watch your back?" His low, threatening tone sent prickles of fear through me.

"I said I was sorry." Gathering my courage, I met his eyes. The gold flecks blazed like fire as he stared down at me. Yeah, he wasn't going to be forgetting what I'd done anytime soon.

"Too little, too late."

"Yeah? You hated me already, what difference would it have made?"

"I already told you that to hate you would mean I actually cared enough to form an opinion," he said in a bored voice.

"It sounds like you care now." What was I saying? Goading him was the worst idea. Yet, somehow, the words kept spilling from my mouth. "If anything, I should be the angry one. You threatened me, intimidated me, and made me scared to say anything. I don't like you, Carter."

I was breathing heavily by the end of my rant. This boy. I hated speaking up, didn't answer back, but there was something about Carter Blackthorne that riled me up.

His eyes sparked, and he leaned down, his breath hot on my ear. "You don't like me? What about when you kissed me? Let me touch you?" Lowering his voice even further, he moved so his lips were touching my ear, every single part of me tingling with awareness. "What about when you came all over my hand?"

I had nothing to say to that. My fists stayed clenched tightly at my sides, and I turned my head away from him.

"You can keep lying to yourself, but I can see straight through you. Watch out, Laurent. You like to hide in the shadows, but soon, everyone will know your name."

He tore himself away from me, leaving me slumped against the wall, my heart pounding. What had I done?

The whispers started during my Economics class. People threw curious glances my way, smirks and low taunts heading in my direction. Lena slid into her seat next to me, brow furrowed. "What the fuck is going on with everyone today? Why are they all looking at you?"

I shrugged, staring down at my desk. "No idea."

"If anyone's said anything about you, I'll fuck them up," she said fiercely, which got a smile out of me. I had no doubt she'd actually do it, either.

"Hey, Imogen! What's going on?" Lena stared over at Imogen Lang, a challenging brow raised. If anyone knew what was happening, it was her. Beautiful and popular, she was part of Carter's group, but unlike the other girls, she was actually nice to everyone. I'd never even heard her say anything bitchy about anyone.

She glanced at me, then back at Lena, biting her lip. "Maybe you should check your phone."

"You do it, I can't look," I muttered.

Lena blew out a breath and pushed her blonde hair behind her ears, before picking up her phone.

She was silent for a while, and then she spoke, the

words spat from her lips like bullets. "I'm. Going. To. Kill. Him."

Oh no. No. "Tell me," I whispered.

"Quieten down, everyone! Today we'll be studying the economic repercussions of the collapse of the Lehman Brothers." Our Economics teacher, Mr. Hicks, looked pointedly at me and Lena, and I shut my mouth. When he turned to his laptop to begin his slideshow presentation, Lena slid her phone over to me.

It was open at the social media gossip account for students of our school. An account I avoided wherever possible. The only drama I was interested in was the drama club.

There was one new post. Almost all the posts were anonymous, but this one had been posted by Carter Blackthorne himself, giving it instant credibility in the eyes of the students reading it.

WHAT HAS RAINE LAURENT BEEN
UP TO?

The question was written over an image taken in the gym changing rooms, if the background was anything to go by. Slightly unfocused and grainy, it depicted a girl with hair more or less identical to mine, her head level with the crotch of a guy that I vaguely recognised from the football team. The first thought that ran through my head was, who was giving him a blowjob in school? Then, I gritted my teeth as the outrage hit me, followed by nausea churning in my stomach.

"Seriously? Is he for real?"

"What the fuck is his problem?" Lena hissed.

"Silence! Miss Drummond, this is your one and only

warning." Mr. Hicks gave her a stern warning, and she rolled her eyes but stopped talking.

I opened her phone to a new message and started typing furiously. I couldn't get her involved. It wouldn't be worth my time. If she put pressure on Carter, or tried to, he'd just fuck with me out of school, or in places Lena couldn't reach.

Don't do anything. Please. Let me handle this.

She read it with a frown and shook her head.

Please. I need to fight my own battles.

"I guess I can understand that," she whispered. "But say the word, and I *will* fuck him up."

Her impassioned promise on my behalf sent a flutter of warmth through me, dulling my outrage, and I couldn't help a tiny, grateful smile at her determination. "Thanks."

"Miss Drummond, Miss Laurent." My head flew up to see Mr. Hicks, his mouth set in a flat line. "See me after class."

Great.

The rest of the morning I did my best to ignore the whispers that followed me everywhere, the attention almost unbearable. People who had never given me the time of day before were openly staring, gossiping about me as if I was the latest source of entertainment. As my discomfort grew, so did my anger at Carter, until I felt like I was about to explode.

When lunchtime rolled around, I hid away in the huge library, and instead of heading to the English class that I shared with Carter in the afternoon, I stayed tucked into a tiny alcove in the archives. I tried to bury myself in my textbooks, but after my phone buzzed for what felt like the hundredth time, I finally gave in and opened my notifications.

I shouldn't have looked.

Texts from unknown numbers, and comments on the AHS gossip site photo...all negative.

> Who the fuck is Raine Laurent?
> Didn't realise he was that desperate
> Hope he didn't get an STD from her diseased mouth
> WHORE
> I'd give you a tenner to suck my dick
> If you want a real man, text 06817332111

The afternoon seemed endless. I didn't make it to any of my other classes, remaining hidden among the books. As soon as the bell rang to announce the end of the school day, I gathered up my things and escaped to the theatre. Being pretty much in charge of costume design, and getting close to the dress rehearsal stage, I had to be on hand for alterations, and I still had to finish sewing the additional outfits for the lead characters.

Dylan paused, paintbrush in hand, to throw me a sympathetic glance, giving me a hesitant wave from his position balanced precariously on a ladder in front of a partially painted backdrop on the stage. I returned his wave, continuing on to the backstage area and into the room where the costumes were kept. Sinking down into the seat in front of the large drafting table, I finally took a breath. Being in the one place in this school that I loved soothed me, and I felt myself relax in tiny increments as I lost myself in my needlework.

"Hold still..." I mumbled through a mouthful of pins, as I carefully tacked the fabric around Imogen, our lead actress. I finished pinning it into place then stepped back, eyeing her critically. "Hmm. I think maybe I'll bring the hem up another inch. What do you think?"

She eyed herself in the full-length mirror, all shiny jet-black hair, porcelain skin, and small, delicate features. Her brows pulled together. "Hold it up?" Even her voice was sweet. How she'd managed to gain queen bee status in our school, I'd never know. I suppose it didn't hurt that her parents were diplomats, her older brother was a professional footballer for Manchester United, and her best friend Anastasia Egerton's family were peers. Ana's dad was an actual earl, or something. Rumour had it, the royal princes had attended her last birthday party, although I had no idea if that was true or not.

"There." I lifted the fabric, and she nodded.

"That looks good to me. Thanks." Her dark eyes flicked to mine for a moment. "Are you okay? After the...thing this morning?" Her tone was careful.

"I'm fine," I assured her, willing myself to believe my own words. She gave me a sceptical look, but she didn't push it. There was nothing she could do, anyway. In fact, her best friend, Anastasia, was Carter's ex-girlfriend.

"For what it's worth, I could tell it wasn't you in the picture. I'm sure that if people looked at it closely, they'd be able to see that."

"Maybe." I shrugged uncomfortably and cast around for a change of subject. "Are rehearsals going better, now? I don't get to see much, being backstage."

"I think so." She seized onto the change of subject, her expression opening up. "I'm channelling Johanna and constantly reminding myself that this is only acting, and Xavier isn't Xavier, he's Anthony." A sigh escaped her lips. "I won't deny, though, kissing Xave again, after everything? That's going to be difficult."

I was surprised she'd been so open with me. "Yeah," I agreed, not that I'd know. From all I was aware of, she'd had a bad breakup with Carter's friend Xavier at the end of the last school year. I had no idea of the details, but you could feel the tension between them every time they were in a room together. They were both talented actors, though—Xavier, surprisingly so, since he'd never shown any interest in drama until this year. Hopefully their acting skills would be enough to get them through, even though the play called for them to pretend to be in love.

Anyway, not my problem. If it wasn't a situation like now, where I had to forcibly spend time with them, I'd stay as far away from Carter and his friends as possible.

"You're all finished," I told her. "I'll get those alterations done ready for next time." After making a note on my clipboard, I unpinned her, and she disappeared back into the auditorium.

"Why is he so obsessed with you?" I spun around to find Xavier Wright eyeing me, his gaze contemplative. My cheeks heated. I couldn't deny it, I'd had a bit of a crush on him. Not anymore, but at one point I couldn't even look at him without feeling all hot and flushed. He was absolutely gorgeous. Tall, dark, and handsome didn't even come close. And his smile? Girls more or less swooned when he directed it at them. Imagine Tyrese Gibson's smile and multiply it by ten, and you still wouldn't be close.

I realised I'd been staring at him without saying anything when the corners of his lips curved upwards. "Still tongue-tied around me, huh?" He shook his head. "I just don't get his obsession," he muttered to himself. Then he stepped closer and cocked his head. "We doing these costumes, or what? I don't have all day."

Ah, yeah. There was a hint of that asshole behaviour. One of the reasons I'd quickly managed to get over my little crush on him. That, and the fact he was in Carter's inner circle. "Y-yes. Could, you sit down, please." I cleared my throat. "You're mostly done, but I need to measure your head for the hat."

He nodded, crossing to the chair and sprawling back in it, all long limbs and lithe, graceful lines. I grabbed the measuring tape from the workbench and came to stand next to him. "Keep your head still, please." I carefully wrapped the tape around his head, idly admiring the swirling pattern shaved into the back, then returning my attention to the task at hand. "Hmm, your head isn't as big as I thought."

My annoying habit of vocalising my inner thoughts reared its ugly head, as I realised when he swung his gaze to meet mine.

Amusement glinted in his dark eyes. "What's that supposed to mean?"

I guess I'd have to explain myself. "You know. You have a big ego." I quirked my lips at him with a shrug, desperately trying to play it cool, although inside I was anything but. Attempting to joke around with anyone popular was so far out of my comfort zone, I didn't even know why I was trying.

He stared at me in silence for a moment.

Then he gave me his signature blinding smile, and my heart skipped a beat. "That ain't the only thing that's big about me, baby."

Now I was at maximum embarrassment levels. I fled into the safety of the costume racks, hearing his amused laugh behind me.

Fuck my life.

TEN

RAINE

After waiting on the front steps for twenty minutes, I finally concluded that Carter had already left. I didn't know why I'd expected him to wait for me after everything that had happened after the weekend. By this point, the student car park was empty, and the only people left were the cleaning staff. Scrolling through my phone, I debated between calling Lena or booking an Uber. It was a five-mile walk home, and part of the route was on a busy main road with no safe path to walk along, so that wasn't an option. My thumb hovered over Lena's name. Why was it so difficult to ask for help?

"I heard someone needed a lift." A huge, matte-black SUV pulled up at the school entrance gates. An older guy with tousled, dirty-blond hair and a huge grin was in the driver's seat, his inked arm casually resting on the window frame. As I stared at him, suddenly tongue-tied, his grin widened and he pushed his sunglasses up on the top of his head, revealing bright blue eyes that were sparkling with amusement. "Hey, Lena. I think your friend here's been struck dumb by my good looks."

"Fuck off," I heard from inside the car, and then Lena was leaning around him to give me a smile. "Ignore my brother. He...gets a lot of female attention, so he automatically assumes everyone wants him." She rolled her eyes. "Anyway, get in. We'll take you home."

"I didn't know you'd be with someone when I called you. I can get an Uber." I grimaced as I realised I was probably interrupting their plans.

"You're not getting an Uber. Get in." Lena gestured to the door, and with a sigh, I climbed into the car, collapsing against the cool leather seats. Lena turned to face me. "Raine, meet my brother, Cassius. Cass, this is Raine. My friend, *not* one of your groupies."

Cassius laughed and winked at me in the rear-view mirror, and I felt my cheeks heat.

"Hi," I managed.

He threw me another wink, before he started the engine and smoothly manoeuvred away from the school. After I'd given him directions, I sat back again, blowing out a heavy breath.

"You want to tell me why you were stranded at school? Wasn't Carter supposed to be taking you home?" Lena kept facing forwards, which I was thankful for because I found it easier to reply.

"I haven't been totally truthful about what happened at Fright Night. I...I messed up." To my horror, my voice wobbled, and tears filled my eyes. Cassius glanced at me in the rear-view mirror again, his aviators hiding his eyes, but the smile disappeared from his face. He murmured something in a low voice to Lena, and she nodded before twisting to face me.

"Do you want to talk about it?"

I nodded, biting my lip to try and hide the trembling. Fuck. This whole thing had hit me harder than I thought.

"Okay. Hang on for a minute, Cass is going to take us somewhere we can talk. He'll leave us, unless you want him to stay?"

"It might be good to get a guy's input," I found myself whispering, before I even knew what I was saying. Why not add to my humiliation? Although, it could be a good thing. Lena's older brother was popular, hot, and experienced with girls. Maybe he could give me some advice from a man's point of view. Maybe.

Lena gave me a reassuring smile and a single nod, before turning back to face the windscreen, and I closed my eyes, concentrating on my breaths to steady my nerves.

Exiting the car, I took a deep breath of the fresh sea air, then followed Lena and Cassius down to the beach alongside the pier. We took a seat on the large rocks that butted up against the sea wall. The waves lapped at the shore, Chaceley Rock with its abandoned lighthouse stood silhouetted on the horizon, and boats heading back from a day's fishing dotted the water. Seagulls circled overhead, and as the sun moved lower, I sighed, a little of the day's stress disappearing.

"Tell us what happened." Lena touched my arm.

I let the entire story pour out, purging it from my system. I told them everything, not holding back. Tears fell as I spoke, but it felt so good to get it all out. By the time I came to a stop, the tears were running down my cheeks and my throat was raw, but I felt free.

"Let's wipe those tears away, babe." Cassius gently smoothed his thumbs across my cheeks, then squeezed my arm gently. I found myself relaxing. There was something about him, about both of the Drummond siblings. There was no judgement from either of them, just concern and acceptance.

"I'm sorry I wasn't straight with you." I turned my gaze to Lena. "The whole thing...I just felt so..." Trailing off, unable to articulate my feelings, I shrugged helplessly.

"First of all, do you like Carter?" Lena studied me closely.

"Yes," I admitted, my voice small. "Stupid, right?"

"We want who we want." Cassius gave me a shrug as if to say, *what can you do?*

"Um, Raine?" Lena interrupted whatever else Cassius was about to say. She waved her phone under my face. "Did you check the gossip account again?"

"No. I try to avoid looking on there. Especially after today."

Her phone was thrust into my hand, and I stared down at the screen.

There was an image of a masked Carter, holding my hand and leading me towards the Ferris wheel. The accompanying caption said:

WHO'S THE MYSTERY GIRL WHO MANAGED TO CATCH CARTER BLACK-THORNE'S EYE?

Oh no.

I examined the picture closely, but there was no way to tell it was me. My face was completely obscured by my own mask, and no one would believe I was at Fright Night anyway.

A sigh escaped me as I handed the phone back to Lena. "What am I going to do?"

"Here's how I see it, yeah?" Cassius' eyes met mine, his

expression thoughtful. "From everything you've told me, it sounds like he's into you, but for whatever reasons, he doesn't like the fact, and he's pissed off that you tricked him."

"I didn't mean to." Balling my fists at my sides, I prodded the sand with the toe of my shoe, feeling the crunch of tiny stones and crushed shells under my foot. "I just...I know it was wrong."

"I know." He gave me a reassuring smile. "People like Carter, though, they like to have the upper hand. Not only that, they're stubborn as fuck, so it can take a while for them to realise what the rest of us already knew." He turned to Lena and rolled his eyes. "Remind you of anyone?"

She snorted, nodding her head.

"Anyway." He leaned forwards, swiping three small pebbles from those scattered in the sand below us. Placing them on the rock next to me, he pointed towards them. "Three things you need, right?" He picked up one of the pebbles, handing it to me. "You need to stop his dickhead behaviour towards you." Another pebble was handed to me. "You need to find out for sure why he doesn't want to like you." His eyes gleamed as he passed me the final pebble. "And you have to get him to admit that he wants you. Gotta fight fire with fire."

"What does that mean?" I ran my thumb across the cool, smooth surface of one of the pebbles, eyeing him curiously.

A huge, blinding smile spread across his face. "We're gonna make him jealous."

I stared at him.

"How are we going to do that?"

"Leave it with me."

ELEVEN

RAINE

Tuesday brought more of the same. Another photo appeared on the AHS gossip account, this time of the same girl with a different guy from the football team. The first I'd heard of it was when I opened my locker and found a printout of the photo that had been slipped inside, along with a phone number written in biro. As soon as I'd found it, I navigated straight to the gossip account, knowing that the image would be there as well.

Why was Carter doing this to me? My behaviour didn't warrant this kind of reaction.

All day I was propositioned by guys, hearing whispered insults wherever I went, "slut" being one of the nicest. Not to mention the increasing number of texts from unknown numbers, and yet again, the hateful comments on the AHS gossip account photos. Every single time I opened my phone I had another alert.

Do u swallow?
Touch anyone else from the football team & there will be consequences

How much for a BJ?
Meet me round the back of the library at lunchtime
UR A SLUT
I hope u choke on a dick and die, whore
Did she pay them to let her suck their dicks?

The library and the costume storage room became my two places of refuge. Despite Lena urging me to stay strong, the weight of all the attention was almost too much to bear.

I was in the bathroom between classes, washing my hands, when Anastasia Egerton entered. As I turned from the sink, intent on making my escape, she stalked across the bathroom to me. Shoving me backwards, she stared down at me, her lip curled with disdain. "Working your way through the football team, are you? Is that how you're paying your way through school?"

I threw out my hands to avoid smashing into the wall, more shocked by her words than her actions. "How did you know?" My voice came out as a shaky whisper. I hadn't realised that she knew anything about me, let alone my financial situation. Too late, I realised that my reply had sounded as if I'd admitted to being the one in the photos, even though I was referring to her second question.

"Everyone's seen the photos. And Carter told me about your uncle leaving you high and dry."

Wait, Carter had *told her*?

She must've read the confusion and hurt on my face, because she rolled her eyes and muttered, "I saw you in his car a few weeks ago, and I asked him about it."

Great. My aunt had wanted to keep the news of her messy divorce quiet, knowing how people would gossip, and now, thanks to Carter, the gossip queen of Alstone High knew.

I'm not working my way through the football team, by the way. I didn't say that aloud, though. There was no point wasting my breath.

Moving around Anastasia and racing for the exit, I'd just reached the door when her voice sounded again, the threat in her tone clear. It was as if she'd heard my unspoken reply. "The pictures don't lie, Raine. Remember your place. And don't even think about trying to make a move on Carter. He'd never be interested in someone like you. He'd never be that desperate."

Except he *had* been interested. And I'd ruined that, and he hated me, and now he was punishing me for it. At Anastasia's muttered "pathetic," I'd had enough. Running from the bathroom, I flew through the corridors, escaping to the safety of the auditorium.

As I entered the backstage area, Dylan and Joey paused in the middle of their set construction to stare at me, before exchanging concerned glances.

"Hi, guys," I managed, rushing past them as quickly as I could and entering the costume storage area.

Footsteps sounded behind me, and Dylan and Joey were crowding into the doorway. I groaned under my breath as I sank into my seat and rested my head on the cool wooden surface of the table in front of me.

"What's going on?" Joey spoke up. He worked on set construction with Dylan, but unlike Dylan, I hadn't really ever spoken to him.

Raising my head, I glanced between the two of them, biting my lip as I picked up a roll of sewing tape from the table.

"You can trust him." Dylan seemed to sense my thoughts. "If this is anything to do with Carter, just know that Joey here likes him probably even less than we do. We, as in me and you," he added with a small smile.

"He's not wrong. I hate the way that Carter, Kian, and Xavier lord it over everyone else. Their whole group of friends, in fact."

Dylan nodded, then lowered his gaze to the ground. "We're not good enough for people like them." The bitterness in his voice was unmistakable.

Rolling the tape in my hands, I found myself telling them the story, or at least the part about the gossip that was being spread about me. They were outraged on my behalf, and after I'd spilled everything, I felt like a weight had been lifted.

"Carter is bad news, Raine. If you want my opinion, I think it's best to keep your head down and stay out of his way." Dylan patted my shoulder sympathetically, glancing over at Joey.

Joey leaned back against the wall, crossing his arms. "I agree. People like Carter Blackthorne thrive on attention. He'll eventually get bored if he doesn't get a reaction from you."

I could only hope that they were right.

When I woke up the following morning, my bedroom window was open, and a black mask with glowing blue LED lights was on my desk.

TWELVE

RAINE

After the mask had appeared, and with Dylan and Joey's advice echoing in my mind, I made it my mission for the rest of the week to stay as far away from Carter as possible.

Wednesday was another day filled with snide remarks and more repulsive texts and comments, but by Thursday, the gossip seemed to be dying down. People were bored, hungry for new drama. Other than the dwindling texts and comments on the photos that I did my best to ignore, I managed to make it through the rest of the week without incident. A photo appeared on the AHS gossip account on Friday morning showing one of the teaching assistants in a *very* compromising position with a student, and just like that, I was forgotten as the new gossip spread like wildfire.

Forgotten by most people, anyway.

On Friday night, my phone buzzed with a message as I lay on my bed, Netflix playing on my laptop as I sketched out a rough dress design in my sketchpad. Placing the pad down, I grabbed my phone, and almost dropped it in shock as I saw who the message was from.

Carter: Enjoyed your time in the spotlight, Raine? Your moment of notoriety?

As much as I hated his harsh words, my heart skipped a beat at the sight of his name on my screen. My fingers hovered over the keypad as I debated how best to reply—I didn't want to antagonise him, not when the gossip had finally died down.

Me: Please leave me alone. I've stayed out of your way
Carter: Out of sight but not out of mind

What was that supposed to mean? Eventually, I sent a simple response to see if he'd elaborate on his words.

Me: ???

After waiting for over fifteen minutes with no reply, I rolled onto my stomach and pulled up the conversation thread again, staring at his last message to me, before I closed it with a sigh. My eyes strayed to the Fright Night mask, taunting me from the corner of the room where I'd thrown it.

Before I knew it, I found myself reopening the conversation thread and texting Carter again.

Me: Did you leave that mask in my bedroom?

This time, he responded instantly and my stomach flipped as I read his response.

Carter: Yes. A reminder of what you did and how I won't forget it. You can't escape me, little trickster
Me: Breaking into my bedroom is a criminal offence
Carter: You sure about that? Who are you going to tell?

There was nothing I could reply to that. Whatever I said, I knew the outcome wouldn't be good. Instead, I turned off my phone and attempted to lose myself in my drawings.

On Monday, walking into school with Lena, no one looked twice at me. In fact, it was back to normal. I was my usual, invisible self. Could I dare to hope that Carter had given up? Even lunchtime, which was the one time of the day I was dreading, was fine. It was an unseasonably warm day, and I sat outside in the courtyard with Lena and her friends, aware of Carter's presence but successfully ignoring him for the most part.

I actually attempted to join the conversation instead of letting the conversation flow around me, like I normally did, and managed to hold up a conversation with Sammy, a girl in my textiles class, for almost twenty minutes, discussing the costumes I'd been making for the school production. Who knew, after the initial five minutes of awkwardness, I was surprised to realise I was actually having a good time.

"That wasn't so hard, was it?" Lena whispered, nudging me as we headed back into the school building after lunch.

"No. No, it wasn't." A smile spread across my face.

"Ready for later?" We stopped by our lockers, exchanging the books we needed.

I closed my locker with a bang. "As ready as I'll ever be. Are you sure your brother doesn't mind? I'm sure he's got loads more important things to be doing."

Lena smirked. "My brother lives to interfere with people's lives. Trust me. He wants to fuck with Carter just as much as you do."

"If you're sure. I'm not convinced that any of this is a good idea, but I guess it's too late to change the plan now."

All the air left the hallway as cedar and spice hit me, and my world shrank as my eyes met a pair of brown and gold ones. A dark look appeared on his face as he held my gaze silently, and then he stalked in my direction. I held my breath as he brushed past me, and that small movement, combined with the look he'd given me, sent a chill down my spine.

"Do you think he's given up?" I whispered to Lena, once he was gone, already knowing the answer.

"People like Carter don't give up that easily."

At the end of the day, I found out exactly why he'd been so quiet.

THIRTEEN

RAINE

"Raine? A word?" I glanced up from my sewing machine with a start to see Mrs. Whittall, head of the drama department, standing over me with pursed lips.

"S-sure," I stammered, taken aback by the severe look on her face. After gathering up my things, I followed her out of the backstage area and into her small office next to the auditorium. She indicated the seat across from her desk, and I collapsed into it breathlessly.

Taking a seat opposite me, she opened the drawer and pulled out a familiar red metal box with a number 5 stamped on the lid. The cash inside was used to purchase materials for the costumes needed by the drama department.

"I was counting up the receipts earlier, when I noticed that they didn't tally with the amounts in the cash box." One long fingernail tapped on the lid. "Not just by a small amount, either. Over four hundred pounds is missing."

I gaped at her in horror. "Wh-what?"

She sighed heavily, placing the box back in the drawer before returning her attention to me. "Only a small number of trusted students have a key to this room. *You* are the only student who is aware of the combination that unlocks this particular cash box. The only person, in fact, other than me."

Was she implying—surely not!

"You don't think it was me, do you?" My voice was shaky.

"Is there something you want to tell me, Miss Laurent?"

"No. It wasn't me, I swear! I would never." Nausea rose up in my stomach.

Her voice softened. "Raine. I'm aware of your...change in circumstances. If you're in financial trouble, there's help available. You don't have to resort to theft."

"I didn't take the money, though!"

She shook her head sadly. "I'm afraid that I don't believe you. You're a talented costume designer, with no prior instances of bad behaviour, and for that reason I'm giving you a chance. Hand over your key and return the missing money to my office, and we'll say no more about it. You'll no longer be trusted with a key, but you can continue with the drama club."

"B-but this isn't fair! I don't have it!" Frustrated tears filled my eyes as I looked at her helplessly.

"Then you can leave. And don't come back until the cash is returned. All four hundred and twenty pounds of it."

"Please..."

"Miss Laurent. Don't make this any worse for yourself."

With a cry, I fled the office, running straight into Dylan, who was passing by with a pile of scripts in his hand. We tumbled to the floor, papers flying everywhere.

"I'm so sorry!" I cried, picking myself up and starting to gather up his papers.

He sat up, rubbing his stomach where I'd crashed into him. "I think you winded me."

"I'm so sorry," I said again, my voice wobbly.

"It's okay. Are *you* okay?" He looked at me with concern.

"Not really."

After gathering up the rest of the scripts, he took my hand and tugged me to my feet, then released me. He patted my arm gently. "Do you want to talk about it?"

The story came pouring out. Poor Dylan—this was the second time he'd had to listen to me upset and ranting. When I'd finished, his expression had morphed from concern to shock and now outrage on my behalf.

"I can't believe Mrs. Whittall would do something like that. You're the nicest, most trustworthy student in the entire drama club. How could she even think for one second that you'd take the money?" He paced in front of me, deep in thought. "You don't think it was Carter, do you?"

Yes. "I-I don't know. But I'm not going to take it lying down. The photos were bad, but this? This is on another level."

His brow furrowed. "What does he have against you?"

That, I had no answer for.

I managed to hold it together as I walked through the silent school building. Outside, though, standing with the sun warm on my face but ice around my heart, it hit me. A choked cry escaped my lungs as I tried to stop the tears from falling, but it was no use.

"Something happen, Laurent?" Carter was suddenly there in front of me, his football uniform covered in mud and a satisfied look on his face as he watched me falling apart in front of him.

A current of rage snapped through my veins, and just like that, I snapped.

"You did this!" I screamed and swung at him. My hand connected with his jaw, swinging his head around to the side.

His mouth dropped open, and he blinked, incredulity spreading across his face as he raised his hand to his face.

"What the actual *fuck*, Raine? Do you know how many people have dared to slap me without my permission?" His voice was steel.

I didn't answer him, frozen in shock that I'd hit him.

"None. Zero." He crowded me against the wall, trapping me in place with his huge body.

"You deserved it." I was shaking with anger beneath him, welcoming the burn as it chased the sadness away. "You've taken away the one bright spot in my week, the only thing that meant something. Do you know how important drama club was to me?"

He ignored my words, his hand still rubbing across his jaw. "Don't you dare raise your hand to me, again. I told you to watch your back, Raine."

"Watch yours." I glared at him through my tears, breathing heavily.

"What are you gonna do? You have no power in this school." His mouth was so close to mine, his breath hot on my lips, and I jolted as I felt his hardness press against me.

With an effort, I managed to smother the spark of lust that shot through my body and focused on my task. "Really?" The familiar purr of an SUV sounded behind Carter, and it gave me a sudden burst of confidence. "We'll see about that."

Before Carter had a chance to react, I tore myself away,

darting under his arm, and skipped down the steps towards Cassius.

Leaning against the door of his car, he watched me coming towards him with a huge grin on his face. "Babe!" he exclaimed, lifting me into his arms. "Arms around me," he hissed in my ear, and I complied, laughing into his neck as he carried me around to the passenger side of the car. "You should see his face."

He set me down, and I climbed into the SUV on shaking legs. "Bye, Carter," he called out of the window as we drove away. I didn't dare to look, instead staring straight ahead. The euphoria from managing to shock Carter faded as I filled Cassius in on everything that had happened.

"You think he's behind the missing cash?"

I nodded. "I'm sure of it. He practically admitted as much. It would've been easy enough for him to get a key, too. He's Carter Blackthorne—there's nothing he can't get when he puts his mind to it. Other than a decent grade in our English class, that is."

"Fucker," he muttered. "I'd bet anything that there's something incriminating in his house. You need to get there and investigate."

"How exactly am I going to do that?"

He glanced over at me before returning his eyes to the road. "Invite yourself over next time he has a party. Wait until he's been drinking, then sneak up to his room and do a bit of sleuthing."

"It sounds like you have personal experience with this," I commented, and he laughed.

"Yeah, you could say that."

"I don't know that I have it in me to invite myself to one of his parties," I admitted. "What I might be able to do is invite myself over with my aunt, though. Sometime when he's not there. Then maybe I could sneak away and see if I can find anything." My brain whirled, thinking up plausible scenarios for inviting myself round his house.

We lapsed into silence as Cassius turned onto my road. Pulling to a stop outside my house, he turned off the engine. "Homework. Get to Carter's house, get evidence, and keep getting under his skin. You got him to crack today. Don't lose that momentum." Turning to me, he eyed me critically. "Remember what I said about fighting fire with fire? From a purely objective point of view"—he winked at me—"you've got a banging body, but you're hiding it away. Lena said you've got skills in costume design. Put them to good use."

"Ugh. I don't want to draw any more attention to myself."

His expression turned serious. "Listen. You've got to stop hiding away. You can't go through life hiding in the shadows. Maybe it's time to step into the light."

I stared at him. "Has anyone ever told you how much you sound like Lena? That's the exact same advice she gave me."

"She learned from the best." He shrugged, then grinned at me.

"If you say so."

FOURTEEN

CARTER

My head was a fucking mess. "Do you know anything about Cassius Drummond seeing a girl from our school?"

I felt Kian's stare, but I kept my attention on the road.

"Cassius? Why are you interested? Wait, it's not Ana, is it? Do you want to get back with her?"

"Fuck, no."

"Good. That girl might be your type on paper, but she isn't right for you."

"Truth." We'd never really had much in common, and we both knew it. Not that Anastasia had admitted that to herself. She still wanted me. Wanted the prestige of being my girlfriend. Too bad for her, I wasn't interested in a trophy girlfriend.

Not anymore.

Kian was silent for a minute, scrolling through his phone, before he spoke again. "Nothing on his socials about anyone from school. You want me to check with Weston?" He named Cassius' best mate, who had been our football team captain until he left to go to Alstone College.

"No. I was just curious because I saw him at our school earlier, picking up one of the girls." I played it casual, gritting my teeth at the image that was burned into my mind. Raine, jumping into his arms, both of them looking way too fucking happy.

"Who?"

"Raine."

"Who's that? Wait—Raine Laurent? The girl you're always talking about? What's your obsession with her, mate?" His tone became sly.

"I'm not fucking obsessed." My grip on the steering wheel tightened. "She's my neighbour, and a fucking pain in the ass. That's it. Just having a hard time believing she'd be hanging out with Cassius Drummond."

"Hold up." His thumb swiped over his phone. "No pics... Ah. She's been tagged in a few." He studied them closely. "Oh, yeah. I remember her now. She's been hanging out with Lena Drummond lately. Can't say I ever remember seeing her around school before that."

Yeah, that's because my little trickster liked to hide herself away.

"There's your answer, then." He tapped on his screen. "She's Lena's friend, so that's how she knows Cassius. He was probably doing her a favour."

A favour. It hit me then. She knew I wasn't going to be giving her a ride home, so she must've arranged for him to pick her up. I still couldn't believe she'd dared to slap me, but the outrage had faded as soon as I'd seen her go to Cassius, replaced by a feeling I definitely didn't want to associate with her.

"She's not his type," Kian continued. His words conjured more images—Raine, wrecked after the orgasm I'd given her. Kissing me. Distracting me on the big wheel. If

Cassius had seen her the way I had...if *anyone* else had seen her the way I had, they'd want her, too. It wasn't such a stretch to imagine Cassius being interested, after all.

"Did you ever hook up with Halloween girl again?" Kian suddenly asked. When people had asked me about it after the picture of me holding her hand had been blasted on the gossip account, I'd brushed it off, telling everyone she was from out of town and she was a one-night hook-up. Everyone accepted my explanation—why wouldn't they? I was surprised Kian had brought her up, though, since we'd both been chasing after her to begin with. At least he didn't seem to be holding a grudge.

"No," I said shortly and changed the subject. "You want to go to the bowl this week? I need to blow off some steam."

"If you want."

I glanced over at him, brows raised, before turning my gaze back to the road. "No need to sound so enthusiastic." He was always down for a fight. Both of us had our moments when it all got too fucking much, and fighting was the best way to relieve the tension. Anyone could fight at the bowl—it was only for fun, and Kian fought there way more than I did. So to see him so unbothered about it all, yeah, that was really out of character. "Blowing off steam in other ways, are you?" Come to think of it, he'd been a lot more mellow this last week. He'd even patched things up with Preston, something I never thought would happen.

"Yeah." He grinned.

"Who is she?"

He fell silent and eventually said, "I'm not ready to talk about it, yet."

"Alright." I wasn't about to push him, not when I had things I wasn't ready to talk about, either. Glancing over at him, I steered the conversation to safer topics. "Did Mack get back to you about the warehouse?"

"Yeah, I forgot to say. We can pick up the keys after school on the Friday and take them back on the Sunday."

"I can't fucking wait for this." We shared a grin. "Party of the year, for sure. Everyone's gonna want to be there."

"Yep." His tone was satisfied.

We pulled up outside the Cutler house, and after I'd parked on the overgrown driveway, I looked over at him. "I'll wait here. See you in a few."

"Fuck off. If I'm going in, you have to." He narrowed his eyes at me. "She likes you better, anyway."

"Only because I pretend to like her tea."

"Whatever. You coming?"

With a groan, I got out of the car, sliding my keys into the pocket of my jeans, and we started up the path to the front door. A creaking gothic structure, all painted in black, it was exactly the house you'd imagine someone like Aunt Marie to live in. People said it was haunted, but I was more or less certain that the only things haunting it were the spiders living underneath the floorboards on the rickety wooden porch.

"Boys!" Aunt Marie was standing in the doorway. How did she always know we were coming? Looking at her now, dressed in some flowing black dress with her wild black curls around her face, it was easy to see why we'd thought she was a witch when we were kids. The reality was that she was an artist, a successful one at that, and her "fortune telling" was nothing more than being exceptionally good at reading people. She loved playing up the witch angle over Halloween, though, scaring the local kids.

We followed her into her cluttered kitchen and took a

seat at the oak table. Kian smirked when I got stuck with the chair with the wobbly leg, and I glared at him.

Aunt Marie busied herself at the ancient stove, pouring water from the whistling kettle into the teapot, then carried it over to the table. "Tea?" Without waiting for a reply, she began setting out cups and saucers in front of us. I picked at the fleck of dried paint on the side of my cup before leaning back in my seat, careful not to put my weight on the wobbly chair leg.

Marie's soft murmur filled the quiet kitchen as she lifted the lid from the pot, swirling the tea inside with a spoon. "One hides behind a mask. One has a secret. Beware the false one. You will lose your heart if you do not heed the warning signs."

Kian and I exchanged glances. "Which one of us was that aimed at?" I asked, although I knew I wouldn't get a reply. She never explained her riddles and I'd given up on trying to figure them out.

"Raine!"

The loud croak made both Kian and I jump. There was a flurry of wings, and Picasso landed on the table in front of me. He cocked his head, staring at me with one beady eye. "Raine!" He hopped closer. "Raine!"

I glared at the raven. I couldn't fucking get away from Raine, even here.

"Picasso." Aunt Marie snapped her fingers, and he hopped to her shoulder, like some giant black parrot.

"Is he implying it's going to rain?" Kian glanced out of the window at the clear skies, and then eyed the bird distrustfully.

"I don't think he was talking about the weather," I muttered under my breath.

Aunt Marie ignored us both, deciding the tea was

steeped enough, and began pouring it into our cups. I picked mine up, steeling myself against the bitter liquorice flavour.

Fuck. It was disgusting.

Kian didn't even bother attempting to drink his, clicking his fingers at the raven. Picasso obediently flew down and buried his head in the cup. I rolled my eyes at Kian and tapped at my watch.

He nodded, flashing five fingers. "Where's the table you want me to move?" he asked Aunt Marie, breaking the silence. She stood, and he followed her out of the kitchen, while I was left alone. Idly, I scrolled through my phone, attempting to ignore Picasso's pointed looks. Somehow, I found myself scrolling through Raine's social media. Kian was right—there were hardly any photos of her other than a few she'd been tagged in, where she wasn't the main focus.

"Raine!"

"Shut up."

Fucking raven.

FIFTEEN

CARTER

The raven had been taunting me, but that was nothing compared to the effect of seeing Raine in person, *in my house*. She'd been avoiding me at school all week, so I hadn't seen her. Not that I'd been looking...or checking her social media accounts.

Lies.

Coming to a halt at the bottom of the stairs, my eyes went straight to her. She stood in the foyer with her aunt and my dad, lashes sweeping down, her gaze focused on the floor rather than on me. The familiar burn of anger hit me as I saw her standing there, but it was almost smothered by the need pulsing through my veins. I took her in. Her long, thick hair, hanging down her back instead of up in a ponytail, a black dress that clung to her curves, and down to those boots. The same boots she'd worn at Fright Night. How could I hate and want someone so much? Why the fuck couldn't I want someone else? *Anyone* else. Someone my dad didn't see as perfect, someone who hadn't lied to me and pretended to be someone she wasn't.

Eventually she raised her eyes to mine, and the hurt in

them, directed straight at me, was clear. It was almost enough to make me feel bad for what I'd done. Almost.

My dad cleared his throat, giving me a pointed glance. Gritting my teeth, I straightened up, slipping on the same polite mask I used around Raine and her aunt, and pasted a smile on my face. So this was why he'd cornered me earlier and instructed me to dress smartly.

"Pam. Raine," I greeted. "This is an unexpected surprise." Unexpected and fucking unwanted.

Speaking over me as usual, my dad placed a hand on the small of Raine's aunt's back. "Pam, come on through. Delia's just—" He was interrupted by the loud chime of the doorbell, and a smile spread across his face. A smile that filled me with apprehension.

I soon found out why. Our housekeeper, Joan, appeared with Sanjay Patel in tow. As in, Professor Patel, my English teacher.

"Carter." He didn't look all that pleased to see me. Unsurprising really, since we both knew that I was only in his class thanks to the pressure from my parents. Neither of us wanted me there.

"What's going on?" I addressed my dad. He ignored my question, instead introducing Prof. Patel to Raine's aunt and making a point of saying how Pam was single. Looking more closely at Raine's aunt as she stood there giving Prof. Patel a coy smile, it suddenly dawned on me. This was a set-up. Glancing over at Raine, I saw she looked as uncomfortable as I was, wringing her hands and grimacing. Good.

"Carter. Sanjay mentioned that your essay is due next week. I don't need to remind you how important it is that you keep your grades up." I was aware of the deathly silence that suddenly filled the space. How fucking dare he call me out like that in front of everyone? But he wasn't finished.

"I've spoken to Pam, and we've agreed that Raine will study with you tonight. Maybe her good influence will have an effect." He gave me a smile that was completely fake, his eyes daring me to disagree with him. "You may as well make a start now. You can study in your bedroom. The door is to be kept unlocked. Do I make myself clear?"

"Sounds great," I managed. "Raine?" It wasn't worth disagreeing with him. Even though he never got physical with me, he liked to tear me down with his words. That was even worse in a way—he had a way of getting inside my head, twisting me up.

Turning on my heel, I headed up to my room, assuming Raine would follow. I heard the sound of her boots on the wooden stairs behind me, and my jaw clenched. Those boots...she must've known they'd be an unwanted reminder of our time together. And now I had to spend time with her in my fucking bedroom, my one safe space.

I pushed the door open, and she followed me in. As I turned to face her, I saw her eyes darting around everywhere, taking everything in. Her gaze landed on my bed, and she pulled her lip between her teeth, a faint blush appearing on her cheeks. She cleared her throat, tearing her gaze away.

"Carter?" She spoke in a soft, hesitant voice.

"Stay the fuck away from me." The burning anger and betrayal I'd felt ever since she tricked me had intensified, and as much as she'd avoided me, I'd also avoided her, because I was at the point where I didn't trust myself not to completely lose control. I needed to blow off steam, but my partner in crime, Kian, had been distracted all week, and Xavier didn't like to get his hands dirty. Meaning, I had no outlet for the rage inside me.

She ignored my warning growl, swallowing hard and

stepping closer. "What am I supposed to do? Your dad's expecting us to study."

What was she supposed to do? Well, my dad would have plenty to say if we didn't study, and no doubt Raine would be happy to tell him if we hadn't done any. Although...maybe I could persuade her, now she knew what I was capable of. Then again, I did need to get a good grade on this essay to keep my spot as the team captain.

Mind made up, I pointed towards my desk. "Sit there and don't fucking touch anything. Don't even move. I'll be back." Before she had a chance to say anything, I left, heading back downstairs to pick up my bag from the hallway where I'd dumped it earlier. I paused, hearing my name mentioned. Moving closer to the door to the formal living room, which was slightly ajar, I waited, listening.

"He's just not interested in putting the effort in. He can't be bothered to try. It's pure laziness on his part." My dad's words had me balling my fists at my sides, my jaw clenching so tightly that it was giving me a headache. "I hope Raine will be a good influence on him. You must be so proud of her, Pam."

"She works hard."

Typical comment from Pam.

"She's very conscientious. A girl that Carter could only dream about ending up with one day. If only he would pick someone like Raine as a girlfriend, instead of those brash, in-your-face girls that he seems to bring around."

"Carter is only concerned with the superficial. You know this," my dad responded to my mum.

A throat cleared, and my dad spoke again. "Apologies, Sanj. We shouldn't be discussing this with you here."

Their conversation turned to other subjects, and I

moved away, suppressing the rage. Fuck, I needed to burn it off. I pulled my phone from my pocket.

Me: The bowl. We're fighting. NO EXCUSES

Kian responded instantly.

Kian: OK. I'll text when I've set it up

I blew out a heavy breath. Knowing that I had an outlet for my anger helped to dull it to a low simmer. I responded with a thumbs up gif, then headed back to Raine. Pushing the door open, I saw her slam my desk drawer shut, and she spun around to face me with guilt written all over her face.

"What are you doing?" In two strides I was standing in front of her, staring down at her. I gripped her chin in my hand. "Answer me."

She stared up at me, her eyes wild and afraid.

"Stop giving me that look, Raine," I growled.

"What look?" Her voice came out as a shaky whisper.

Releasing my grip on her chin, my hands went to her waist, and I effortlessly lifted her onto the edge of my desk. Placing my arms either side of her, I lowered my head to look directly into her eyes. "That look you're giving me right now. That look that makes me want to do bad things to you."

Her mouth fell open. She swallowed hard, but she held my gaze. "You don't deserve to do bad things to me, Carter. Not after what you've done."

I lifted my hands from either side of her, pushed her legs apart, and stepped in between them. This was a bad idea. Really, really bad. She made no move to stop me, frozen in place. I needed the rage back. "I don't deserve to? What about what you've done, huh?"

"Me? I think it pales in comparison to what you've done." Her voice shook, but she bared her teeth at me.

"First the slap, now talking back to me. Do I need to remind you of your place, Plain Raine?" At the same time as I growled the insult, I pressed my hips into her, unable to stop myself. Her breath hitched. My eyes lowered to her heart-shaped mouth as she licked her lips, preparing a comeback.

"You keep saying that, but I know my worth," she hissed through gritted teeth. Her chest rose and fell sharply, her eyes darkening as her anger overtook her fear.

I leaned forwards. My mouth went to her neck, inhaling the scent of caramel apples, then moved up to her ear, and she stiffened beneath me.

"Shut up." Bringing my hand to her neck, I wrapped my fingers around her throat, feeling her pulse thumping wildly.

Her soft gasp as I gripped her made me smile, but she soon recovered.

"Go on, squeeze." She taunted me with her words. "Does it make you feel good to know you can choke me? Leave bruises on my skin? Overpower me just because you're bigger than me?"

"Raine..." My grip tightened.

"Do it."

Those two words snapped the final thread of my control.

SIXTEEN

RAINE

His lips crashed down on mine.

No.

No, no, *no*.

I shoved at him, scraping uselessly at his chest through his T-shirt. Tearing his mouth away, he released his grip on my throat and grabbed my wrists, pulling them away from him and managing to twist my left wrist in the process. I cried out at the sudden pain and lunged forwards, pulling his lip into my mouth and biting down as hard as I could.

"You fucking—" he shouted, finally releasing me, his hand flying to his lip.

"Can't handle a bit of blood?" Where all this newfound confidence was coming from, I didn't know. It had taken him pushing me over the edge by framing me with the theft to do it. I held on to it with both hands.

He stood, towering over me, blood dripping from his lip and running down his chin, as I cradled my wrist, both of us angry and unwilling to back down. Time crawled to a halt as we stared at one another, neither of us wanting to be the first to break the connection.

Hurried footsteps sounded in the corridor, and Carter's eyes widened. For once we were on exactly the same page.

"Bathroom!" I hissed urgently, and he nodded, diving for his bathroom door and slamming it shut behind him. I fell into his desk chair, yanking open the lid of his laptop and pressing a button to wake up the screen.

"Everything okay? I heard a shout." Carter's dad poked his head around the door, peering suspiciously around the room.

Clearing my throat, I placed my hands in my lap so he wouldn't see them shake. "Everything's fine, Mr. Blackthorne. Carter stubbed his toe. He's in the bathroom. Would you like me to pass on a message?" I couldn't meet his eyes.

"No, no, that's fine. Thank you, sweetheart. His voice grew soft. "Thank you for doing this for him. I hope that you will be a good influence on him."

"I'll try," I managed. My throat was so dry all of a sudden.

"Good. Well, I'll leave you to it." He backed away and left the room, closing the door behind him. I collapsed back in the chair, before springing to my feet. Now I wasn't hypnotised by Carter's eyes, I needed to check if he was okay. Why, I couldn't say.

Holding my breath, I knocked on the door of the bathroom but didn't wait for a reply before I entered the small en suite room, decorated in white tiles with black accents. Carter stood at the sink, his eyes meeting mine in the mirror briefly before he turned his gaze away. Taking a step closer, I saw that his lip was still bleeding, although he'd wiped away the blood on his chin.

Without taking another second to think about it, I ripped off a couple of pieces of toilet paper from the roll on the wall, folded them into a square, and dashed the square under the tap to dampen it slightly. I hopped up on the counter next to him, and when he remained staring straight ahead, I grasped his chin. "Let me..." Reaching out, I pressed the makeshift compress to his lip. He growled under his breath but let me touch him. "You need to move closer." Frustrated, I pulled at his jaw, and I thought I saw a hint of a smile appear, before it vanished. He moved closer, though. In fact, too close. Standing to the side of me, but his hard thigh was pressed against my leg, and his nearness made my heart race. Now he wasn't looking at me like he hated me, the feelings that I'd been suppressing returned in full force.

I sucked in an unsteady breath. "I think...um...just hold it on yourself." Hopping off the counter, I barged my way over to the sink. My wrist was starting to throb a little now—not much, and in actual fact I didn't think he'd even meant to twist it, but I didn't want to risk it swelling or anything. I turned the tap on, holding my fingers under the water until it became icy cold, then placed my wrist under it with a sigh of relief.

"Did I hurt you?" I'd been so engrossed in my wrist that I hadn't even noticed Carter move, and now he was behind me, peering over my shoulder. He was still holding the tissue on his lip, but his other arm came around me, and he gently cradled my wrist under the running water. His touch set all my nerve endings alight, and I couldn't help pressing back just the tiniest bit, my back up against his hard body.

"Not really," I whispered, not wanting to ruin this moment with a return to animosity.

"I didn't mean to." I felt him swallow hard against me, and then he was speaking again, his voice so low that I had to strain to hear it. "I go so fucking crazy around you, Raine. You're no good for me. I don't trust myself when I'm around you." His voice grew even lower. *"I don't like who I am around you."*

His words really, really hurt. More than anything he'd said to me in the past. Because I knew he believed them to be true. Was there any point in me saying how I felt around him? How I'd realised that I could stand up to my biggest tormentor without backing down, and that was something I'd never imagined I was capable of? My childhood bullying had left me retreating into my shell, making myself invisible, and I'd never fought back. Yet, with him, I'd managed to stand my ground. And being with him that night, anonymous and masked, I felt freer than I ever had in my life.

I couldn't articulate any of it, though.

"I see." I bit my lip, willing the tears away.

Releasing my wrist with a heavy sigh, he took a step back, and then he was gone. I remained where I was for a while, just trying to compose myself. Trying to make sense of the emotions whirling around inside me. Eventually, I straightened up, splashing some water on my flushed cheeks, and re-entered the bedroom.

Carter was sitting on his bed, his laptop open in front of him and the textbook next to him. He cocked his brow in a silent invitation, his expression carefully blank. I made my way over to him, tugging off my boots and arranging myself cross-legged on his bed. His bed was huge, so I didn't have to sit too close. The atmosphere between us was weird—it was like we'd reached some kind of fragile, temporary truce, and neither of us wanted to say or do anything to break it. My earlier, hurried search through his desk drawers had turned up nothing, and I decided to put my search for answers on hold for now. I was drained, in all honesty. Ever since Fright Night, actually, ever since this school year had begun, I'd been unable to fully relax, knowing he was there, ready to attack me with his words and actions.

"Okay." I broke the strained silence. "Have you started working on the essay yet?" Carter shook his head, and I sighed, pulling his laptop towards me. I opened up the web browser, navigating to the CliffsNotes website. "Do you use this?" Tapping at the screen, I glanced over at him. Sprawled casually on the bed, the top two buttons of his shirt undone and his hair tousled where he'd been running his fingers through it, he looked so good that I lost my train of thought as I trailed my gaze over his body before returning to his face. He raised his eyes to mine, reluctant amusement sparking in them.

"You were saying?" His lips tugged into a smile when I stared at him mutely, lost in his eyes. Ugh. This wasn't like me. Or at least, not with anyone else.

Clearing my throat, I forced my mind to concentrate. "I asked if you use this website."

"No."

"There's your first problem." Shuffling closer to him, I angled the screen so we could both see. "This website breaks it all down for you. It explains all these different concepts..." I typed the name of the play we were studying, *Macbeth*, into the search bar and then scrolled through the results. "See? If I'm not sure what something means, this is the first place I go."

Leaning forwards, he was quiet for a moment, staring at the screen. "I thought CliffsNotes was for people that weren't...y'know. Clever or whatever."

I rolled my eyes at him. "Just because someone doesn't understand something straight away, it doesn't mean they're not clever. There's no one way of learning that's right for everyone. Sometimes it takes looking at something in a new and different way for you to understand it."

"Yeah," he mused, a slight frown on his face.

"And just between us," I added, "Professor Patel can be a little dry in his teaching methods."

"That's a fucking understatement," he muttered, collapsing back against the headboard. We lapsed into silence, as I navigated to the summary of Act 1, scene 5. I opened his copy of *Macbeth* to the correct page, my eyes skimming over the familiar words. Familiar, because I'd already completed our assignment.

"Read this scene, and then we'll go through it," I suggested softly, handing him the book and indicating where he should begin.

"Read it with me," he countered. "You do the Lady Macbeth parts."

I groaned, my cheeks flushing. "I-I can't."

"You can." His voice was insistent. "We're not in class, there's no one else here. It's just you and me."

"Fine." My cheeks flushed, again. He flashed me a satisfied smile, and I sighed. "Give me the book, then."

Instead of handing me the book, he reached for my arm, tugging me closer before releasing me. Our legs were touching, and goosebumps popped along my arms. Somehow managing to ignore his presence, I began reading. "They met me in the day of success…"

I lost myself in the words, my self-consciousness vanishing almost as soon as it had arrived. When I paused for breath, I became aware of Carter watching me intently, an almost puzzled expression on his face. "What?"

He shrugged. "Never thought I'd see the day where we were in the same place and you weren't irritating the fuck out of me."

"Except for Fright Night," I pointed out, and his eyes darkened. I gritted my teeth, prepared for a backlash. Why had I brought that up?

"Are you seeing Lena's brother?" he suddenly asked, ignoring my comment.

"Huh?" My gaze flew to his. He'd schooled his features into a blank expression, and his voice was casual, so I couldn't tell what he was thinking.

"Never mind."

"No, I'm not." Despite Cassius' idea to make Carter jealous, I couldn't lie to his face. Not after I'd tricked him once. The fortune teller's words echoed inside my head again. *Trick him once, but don't trick him twice.* Why I was even thinking about that, I couldn't say. It wasn't like I believed in any of that kind of thing. Something about the way she'd spoken to me, though, and the intensity on her face...it had meant that her words had become imprinted on my brain.

Carter nodded, dropping the subject, and returned his attention to the page. "Carry on."

"It's your turn."

The next hour flew past, as we read the rest of Act 1 and went through the CliffsNotes summary. I asked Carter questions, and he responded with thoughtful answers, making notes on his phone as we worked through it.

Before I knew it, there was a soft knock at the door, and Carter's mum appeared. "Time's up." She smiled at me, before her attention turned to Carter. The smile dropped from her face. "I hope you behaved and listened to Raine. Your father and I expect at least a B on this assignment."

Next to me, I felt Carter stiffen. I met her gaze head-on with a sudden need to defend him. "He's going to do fine,

Mrs. Blackthorne. He's incredibly intelligent. There's a lot of points he came up with that I didn't even consider."

"I'll believe it when I see it," she said. "Come on, sweetie. I'll show you out. Your aunt's waiting downstairs."

"Bye, Carter," I murmured softly after pulling on my boots. He ignored me, his gaze fixed on his laptop screen.

With a sigh, I left the room.

SEVENTEEN

RAINE

Coming back to the park brought back all kinds of memories of Fright Night. Lena led me past the darkened café and large grassy area to the skatepark where tall floodlights illuminated a huge scooped-out bowl, with ramps and pipes surrounding it. The graffiti wall ran all along the back of the area, and my eyes were immediately drawn to the corner where Carter and I had painted our artwork, although I was too far away to see it.

"Welcome to the bowl." Lena gestured with her arms out. "I come boarding down here when I can. But Sundays are fight night."

"Fight night?" I stared down into the empty bowl. "Do you fight?"

Lena shook her head. "No. Not here. Only martial arts training." A small smile appeared on her face. "The people who fight here can be a bit...crazy."

"I didn't even know something like this existed."

"It's an open secret. I think most people know about it, but we don't really talk about it. Don't want to attract the interest of the wrong people, if you know what I mean."

"That makes sense." Coming to a stop in front of the large bowl, I turned to her. "So, what are we doing, anyway?"

She smiled, tugging me to sit on the rim of the bowl, our legs dangling over the side. "We wait for everyone else to show, then you're going to see some of the fights in action."

Kicking at the side of the bowl with the heel of my trainers, I eyed her suspiciously. "And how exactly is this supposed to make me more confident?"

"You're way out of your comfort zone, right?"

"Yep." Leaning back on my elbows, I stared around me. "I feel like that's happening more and more lately. Ever since I met you."

She laughed, pleased. "That's the first, and most important reason. I'm pushing you to do things because I know you have it in you, Raine. You have that confidence deep down inside you. And the more you do things that make you uncomfortable, the more confident you'll feel." She paused. "At least, that's the theory."

"Okay..." I glanced at her. "So pushing me out of my comfort zone was the first reason. What's the second?"

"Have you ever seen a real fight in action? Some of these guys are hot. And watching them fight? Yeah, I think you're gonna love it. And you might even pick up some tips."

"Tips on finding a hot guy?"

"No. Fighting back."

"Oh." We fell silent as the area began to fill, crowds milling around and people sitting all around the edge of the bowl like we were. Suppressing my discomfort, I decided to question Lena in an effort to take my mind off the increasing numbers of people surrounding us.

"Do they do this for money?" I tried to think back over the little I knew about fights—which was pretty much zero.

"No. Mostly for bragging rights, or to settle a grudge, or just because they're psychos who like to fight."

I laughed. "Psychos, hey? So which of the fighters do you have your eye on?"

Her expression became distant. "None of them." I sensed there was more to it, but I didn't push. I was quickly learning that while she was friendly and open in certain areas, there were parts of her she kept locked up so tightly, that I knew I'd never be able to penetrate them. Not unless she chose to share those parts with me. "Hey, look. The first fight is about to start."

I watched as two guys in sweatpants and dark T-shirts slid down the sides of the bowl and met at the bottom, then stood waiting. After a moment, a guy with a whistle appeared at the top, and the crowd fell silent as he introduced them.

"Fight one! Joshua versus Ricky! First to tap out loses!" The two guys shook their wrapped hands, then the whistle guy blew his whistle, and they began to circle each other.

Lena kept up a running commentary the entire time. "The guy with the whistle is Mack—he organises most of the events. Joshua is really powerful, but he's quite slow. Ricky, he's small but deadly."

I flinched as Joshua swung at Ricky with a brutal jab to the ribs. "Ouch. That looked painful."

"That was nothing. Keep watching." The anticipation in her voice was clear.

Nothing? The next second, I saw what she meant. Ricky lunged forwards, lightning fast, striking at Joshua with a series of jabs that had him staggering backwards. He followed it up by sweeping Joshua's legs out from underneath him, sending him crashing to the floor. Lena let out a cheer, and then her attention went to a guy standing across from us, watching the fight intently. She stiffened, ducking behind me.

I followed her gaze, frowning as I tried to make out his features from under his hood. His face was shadowed, but his sleeves were rolled up, revealing tattoos that snaked up both arms.

"Who's that, and why are you hiding?" I turned to her.

"Shh. Keep your voice down." Her own voice was low. "That's Zayde Lowry. Remember him from school? He was in my brother's year. One of his best mates, in fact."

I stared at Zayde with new interest. As he turned his head slightly and the floodlights hit his face, I could see the dark, almost feral look in his icy eyes. "Ah. I remember now. There's something scary about him," I mused.

"Yeah, you wouldn't want to get on his bad side," she agreed. As Zayde melted away into the crowd, she breathed a sigh of relief. "I didn't want him to see me, in case he told my brother I was here. Cass is alright, as far as brothers go, but he can be kind of overbearing sometimes."

"That makes sense. So if Zayde's one of your brother's best friends, you must know him quite well, then?"

"Kind of, I guess. They all hang out in the same group. Like they did at school, if you remember. My brother, Zayde, and Caiden and Weston Cavendish." The last name fell from her lips on a sigh, and I narrowed my eyes at her.

"Anything you want to share about any of those names you just mentioned to me?"

"Nope."

"Hmm." Unconvinced, I raised a brow at her, and she stuck her tongue out at me. Laughing, I returned my attention to the fight. I'd somehow managed to miss the end, but the whistle guy had slid down into the bowl and was holding Ricky's hand up in the air, to the sound of cheers.

"Okay, we have a break for a couple of minutes before the next fight." Lena leaned back on her arms, completely at ease in this place. Me, I still felt way, way out of my comfort zone, but as I looked around, I realised that no one was looking at me like I didn't belong. People were milling around, talking and laughing, and despite the fact that we were all here to watch people fight, the whole atmosphere was friendly.

"I like this," I decided.

Lena stared at me with a smile. "I'm glad to hear it. Any reason in particular?"

"It seems like there's no hierarchy here. Everyone seems like they're on an equal footing, you know?"

"Yeah. I mean, don't kid yourself, there's a lot of rivalry, and things can get nasty, but you're right in the respect that everyone's on the same level. Money and status don't matter here, for the most part. It's all about the fight."

"If only it could be like that at school," I mused.

"Yeah. But there's always gonna be a hierarchy in school, you know? That's just the way it is. And the ones on top can be the worst. Some people just like to make themselves feel better by putting others down." She rolled her eyes, and it was clear she was referring to Carter and his friends.

"Yeah, I—"

"Speak of the devil, and he will appear. Look." She leaned forwards, gripping my arm as she stared into the bowl intently. I followed her gaze to see *him*.

Carter. In the bowl with Kian.

"Oh, no," I groaned. "Why can't I escape him?"

Lena laughed. "Guess I forgot to mention that this is one of his favourite hangouts."

"You forgot. Really." I stared straight ahead as I spoke, unable to tear my eyes away from Carter. A tight black T-shirt stretched across his chest, and he was grinning at Kian as they shook hands before stepping apart. Kian lifted his hand, doing something to his mouth.

"What's he doing?"

"Taking out his lip ring I think."

"Oh." Looking at Carter, I thought back to the night before last, when we'd made some progress. Maybe. I hadn't updated Lena on the whole situation with him, mostly because I knew she'd have an opinion, and I wanted to work things out on my own. It was something I felt like I needed to do. And I was going to confront him, once I gathered the courage.

My thoughts were interrupted by the sound of the whistle, and they began to circle one another. "Why is he fighting Kian?"

"Who knows. They seem to do it a lot. Probably just blowing off steam." Lena shrugged, unconcerned, and I returned my attention to Carter.

The previous fight had been...interesting, sure. But this? "I see what you mean about hot guys fighting." My mouth was dry, and I squeezed my thighs together, trying to suppress the building ache.

"Yeah. Especially when you're attracted to them, huh? This is exactly what I was talking about earlier." She smirked at me, and I huffed.

"Shut up."

"You and I both know it's true. There's no point denying it."

"Fine, yes. I am attracted to him, and I wish I wasn't." I

sighed. "Not with the way he acts." *Except for Friday night*, I added silently.

"Yeah. He's a dick with poor taste in girls. You're worth five hundred Anastasias." Lena's words were fierce, and I smiled.

"I'm sure there's something good about her."

Lena snorted. "Not that I've seen. She's a bitch. She lives to make other people's lives hell."

"I'll take your word for it." Tugging the hood of my hoodie up, my eyes tracked Carter as he sent a wrapped fist flying towards Kian's jaw. Kian responded with a swift jab to Carter's ribs, and I saw him wince, then grin.

"Not everyone is as nice as you." Lena threw me a wink.

"Oh, I know that." I attempted a joke, and she beamed at me.

"Ha ha." Our attention returned to the fight, and I was mesmerised as I watched Carter and Kian exchange a flurry of blows, which seemed never-ending. "They're so evenly matched. It's almost pointless for them to fight," Lena murmured.

"Maybe that's the point," I suggested. "Equal bragging rights at school, if that's why they're doing it."

"Yeah. That, and it reminds people who's in charge." The whistle blew again, and the whistle guy slid into the bowl as Carter and Kian both separated, panting. The three of them conferred for all of thirty seconds, and then whistle guy held up both of their hands, to a mix of cheers and boos. I assumed the boos were from people who'd wanted to see one winner.

A sigh came out before I could stifle it, as I watched Carter rip off his T-shirt, using it to wipe over his face. My eyes roamed over his body, glistening with sweat, all his muscles pumped and defined. And the veins on his arms…

Lena interrupted my very thorough perusal. "Need a tissue for the drool?" She started cracking up, and I buried my face in my hands.

"I'm so stupid, aren't I? Lusting after him, when he acts like such an asshole, and I know nothing can or even should ever happen between us?"

"You're not stupid. And I wouldn't be so sure about nothing happening. Why don't you go and talk to him?"

I recoiled. "What? No! No way."

"Comfort zone." Lena gave me a challenging look. "If he treats you like shit, I want you to stand up to him. Don't let him bully you. He wants you, and he doesn't like that fact, and he's taking it out on you. Yeah, you tricked him, but he needs to get over it. And you—you need to learn to stand up to him, show him you won't take it anymore."

"You're right." My voice was barely above a whisper.

"Go. I'll be waiting. If you need me... No. You can handle this."

I hoped she was right. Clambering to my feet, I glanced over to see him over the opposite side of the bowl, and I began to push my way through the crowds towards him.

By the time I made it over to the other side of the bowl, he'd managed to acquire a girl under each arm, and my stomach sank as I saw who the girl on the left was. Anastasia, his ex-girlfriend. I took a step back. I couldn't go up to him now, not while she was there. The whole football team looked like they were there, too, surrounded by girls. Intimidated wasn't even the word for it. I was way out of my depth.

Stumbling backwards, I almost fell into Preston, one of the team strikers, who was eyeing Kian with concern. "This wasn't a good idea," he muttered. "Either one of you could've been hurt."

Kian's reply was lost to me as Carter's head lifted and his eyes met mine. They widened, pure shock falling across his face as he took in the sight of me standing there. I took another step back, then another, and I turned and fled, pushing through the crowds and escaping to the relative safety of the graffiti wall.

"Raine." The low voice stopped me in my tracks, and I turned to see Carter staring at me. "What are you doing here?" He was still breathing heavily, amped up from his fight, his hair wet from the water he'd tipped all over it. He'd never looked sexier, and I suddenly found it difficult to get any air into my lungs.

"Carter." That was all I could say, before he was right in front of me, his hands sliding into my hair and tilting my head upwards to meet his eyes. We stood, frozen in time, in this dark corner of the park.

"Raine," he repeated, lowering his head.

"Having fun with Anastasia?" As soon as the words escaped me, I clamped my mouth shut. There was no way he hadn't noticed the thinly disguised jealousy in my voice.

Drawing back, he studied me intently for a moment, the silence between us growing uncomfortable, before he gave a heavy sigh. "Ana's my ex for a reason, Raine. Whatever you think you saw, you're wrong." He closed his eyes briefly, his lashes sweeping down, before he focused on me again. "You shouldn't be here. Are you following me?"

"I didn't even know you'd be here," I said truthfully. "When I saw you fight, though..." I trailed off, realising I'd admitted too much, and he smiled as he slid his hands to my back, pulling me closer.

"You like watching me fight?" I buried my face in his chest, unable to answer, and he laughed softly. "Don't be shy, now." His voice lowered as he ran his hands down my back. "Tell me. Did it make you wet for me?"

My breath hitched at his words, and when he unexpectedly slid his hand down between my legs, I gasped, pushing my hips into him.

"Fucking jeans. I want to feel you." He rubbed the palm of his hand against me, and I whimpered at the friction. "What are you doing to me," he said, almost to himself. Then he glanced around him, seeming to remember where we were.

That was enough to snap me out of it.

Pushing him away, I staggered backwards until I was against the wall. I noticed his eyes go to the side of me.

"Little trickster," he murmured. "I should've known." My eyes followed his gaze to the painted mask, black with blue highlights. A permanent reminder of our night together. At least, until someone else graffitied over it, I guess.

A sigh escaped me, and I faltered for a moment, before pulling myself together. "We need to talk." I injected all the firmness into my voice as I could muster, and he took a step backwards, scrubbing his hand over his face.

"Talk." He threw up his hands. "Go ahead."

I steeled myself, then spoke, the words tumbling out of my mouth in a rush. "Why did you get me kicked out of drama club? I know you stole the money and framed me. If you could admit it and make it right, we could move past it and have a fresh start."

The change in him was instantaneous, like a switch being flicked. His jaw dropped and he stared at me, his eyes hardening, back to the Carter that I knew and disliked. "What the fuck, Raine?" In one movement he was in front of me, pinning me against the wall. "How fucking dare you accuse me of shit like that?" Anger vibrated through his whole body, and his hands came down either side of me. His fingers flexed next to my head like he wanted to grip my throat, but he was holding himself back.

"It's true, though. Isn't it?" My voice came out as a cracked whisper. "Please, Carter. Just put the money back, apologise, and we can move on. I...I like you."

"You like me?" His voice was low and dangerous. "You're accusing me of fucking stealing, and then you tell me you *like* me? Like you expect that anything could happen between us?"

My lip trembled, but I stayed strong, meeting his eyes defiantly. "I know you want me. You can lie to yourself all you want."

"I. Don't. Want. You." He snarled the words at me. "This?" His hips ground against me. "Nothing but a natural reaction. Fighting makes me horny. It's nothing to do with *you*. Why would I pick *you*, when I could have any girl I want?"

"That's a lie."

He stepped away from me, his jaw clenched. "Who the fuck do you think you are, Raine Laurent?"

I gathered the tiny piece of courage inside me. "I'm the best thing you'll never have." Then I moved around him and walked away, tears blurring my vision.

Behind me, I could've sworn I heard the urgent caw of a raven, but I didn't look back.

I was done.

EIGHTEEN

CARTER

Lunchtime in the cafeteria, sitting with the football team, I turned Raine's words over and over in my mind. I'd spent the night unable to sleep, constantly flipping between rage and confusion at her accusation. I needed to get to the bottom of what was going on.

As if the universe was taunting me, Chris spoke up. "Who's that?" He leered over my shoulder, and my stomach churned. Somehow, I knew who he was looking at.

"That's Raine, you dick." Xavier cuffed him around the head.

"Who's Raine?" Kian looked confused. Like he didn't know.

"She's literally been at school with us forever. She was in your maths class for three years."

"The one who gave half the football team a blowjob?" Chris spoke up again, and my jaw clenched. Counting to ten inside my head, I forced myself to remain calm, or at least give the appearance of being calm.

I caught Xavier's sidewards glance at me, which I ignored. "Yeah, that was her," I heard him mutter.

Tuning out their discussion, my head turned of its own volition, and a spark of pure lust raced through my body as I took her in. She was strolling over to the food counter, Lena right next to her. Her uniform was still the same—still ill-fitting, but it was the way she carried herself with confidence that made all the difference. Her chin was lifted, her shoulders set back, making her full tits look even bigger… My dick stirred, and I lowered my gaze to her feet instead. She was wearing low heels, instead of her normal flat shoes, making her legs look long and sexy. There was nothing else different, except her hair wasn't in its normal ponytail. Instead, it fell down her back in long, shiny waves that I itched to run my fingers through.

This girl was messing with my head, plain and simple.

Looking closely, I noticed the telltale signs of nerves beneath the confident veneer—the way she kept licking her lips, and the apprehension in her eyes. What was her game plan?

"Is she single? I wanna tap that. The geeky girls are always grateful for it. She's gotta be a sure thing, too, since she's been on her knees for half the team already." Chris was practically drooling. His words sent a shot of rage through me, and I had to grip the sides of my chair to stop myself from punching him in the face.

"Dunno, mate." Xavier shrugged. "Ask her."

"Yeah, think I will." Before I could even open my mouth, Chris was sliding out of his seat, and sauntering over to the counter where she was waiting to pay. I watched, unable to look away, as he waited while she paid for her food, then fucking carried her tray for her. All the way over to a table on the opposite side of the cafeteria. He said something to her, and she replied with a smile that didn't reach her eyes.

I held my breath until he returned to our table and flopped back down into his chair, all sulky. "Shot me down. She's seeing someone else."

My mind went straight to the event that had been stuck on repeat in my head ever since I'd found her crying on the school steps. The slap, the way she'd left me without a single backwards glance, jumping straight into Cassius Drummond's arms like she belonged there. She'd told me that she wasn't with him, but she'd lied to me before. I wouldn't put it past her.

"Did you know she was seeing someone?" Xavier caught my eye.

"Why would I?" I glared at him, and he held up his hands.

"No need to bite my head off. Just thought you might know, being her neighbour and all."

"You're her neighbour?" Chris stared at me.

Xavier huffed out an incredulous laugh. "How do you not know this?"

"Whatever," he muttered.

Across the table, Preston, who had been silent up until now, cleared his throat and spoke to me in a low voice while the conversation continued around us. "Can I have a quick word? In private?"

"Yeah, of course." Glad for an excuse to get away, I immediately stood, grabbing my bag. Preston threw me a small smile before he glanced over at Kian, who gave him a reassuring nod. My curiosity piqued, I followed him outside. It was a cold day, so there were only a few other people around. He led me to an empty table in the far corner of the courtyard. Taking a seat, he looked up at me.

"Can you sit down? You're making me nervous."

Sliding into the seat across from him, I eyed at him

expectantly. He stared everywhere but at me, his eyes bouncing around all over the place. I frowned. "Mate, spit it out. You're making *me* nervous, now."

His eyes finally met mine. "Sorry, man. I need to tell you something. I wanted to give you a heads-up, since you're the soccer team captain." Leaning his elbows on the table, he watched me intently. "A couple of people know already, but before rumours start spreading, I wanted to tell you myself. I'm...I'm gay. I want to tell the rest of the team. Get it out there, you know?"

I stared at him for a moment, processing his words in my brain. Preston was gay? Then I took in the way he was shifting restlessly, his eyes full of apprehension, and I realised I'd been silent for too long. I leaned forwards and placed my elbows on the table, mimicking his pose. Making sure I met his gaze so he could see that I was serious, I said, "I've got your back. You want me to tell the team?"

He shook his head. "I'll tell them. Do you..." His voice lowered, worry threading through his tone. "Do you think anyone will have a problem?"

My mouth twisted. "If they have a problem, they'll have to fucking go through me. If anyone gives you a hard time, *anyone*, you come straight to me, okay? And if you want me to be there when you tell them, I will."

He shot me a small, grateful smile. "Thanks, man. My ex...he, uh. His teammates didn't take it well when he came out to them. I'd appreciate it if you were there when I tell the others."

"Consider it done. Most of the boys are sound, but I won't lie and say it'll be an easy ride. I'll be around to deal with anyone who gives you problems, though. We're a team." Getting to my feet, I rounded the table and clapped him on the shoulder. "Whenever you want to tell them, I'll be there."

After giving me a quick nod, he climbed to his feet, and we headed back inside. "Thanks for being cool with it," he told me just before we reached the others, then immediately changed the subject. "Speaking of thanks, I never said thanks for organising the party."

Kian had come to me with this idea of a mass celebration to mark the eighteenth birthdays of three of the football team members—him, Preston, and Ben. Even though his and Preston's birthdays had already passed, all of us were up for an excuse to party. This one would be right after a football game, too, so either way, we'd have another excuse to celebrate or commiserate. With me and Kian organising, it was going to be the party of the year. "You're welcome." Before I could add anything else, the bell rang to indicate the end of our lunch hour.

Everyone split off to go to their respective classes, and I headed down the hallway to English Lit. I'd had to hand in my essay first thing in the morning, and now I'd see if I got to keep my spot as team captain. My stomach rolled. Fuck.

Instead of sliding into my usual seat at the back of the classroom, I found myself sitting next to the window, with an empty chair next to me.

"Um...excuse me. You're in my seat." I looked up to see Pete, the guy whose seat I'd taken. Not like we had assigned seats, but he'd been sitting in this exact spot every class so far.

"There's a free seat at the back." I lazily threw up my thumb in the direction of my usual table, and he scurried off to the back of the room.

I felt her enter the room before I saw her. I was aware of everything—her soft intake of breath as she saw who was in the seat next to her, the thump of her books as she slammed them down on the table, and the scent of caramel apples as she reluctantly sat next to me.

"Why are you here?" Her voice was annoyed, and it made me smile.

Turning my head, I finally met her eyes. "What's with the new look?"

"I don't...what? I don't have a new look."

My gaze raked over her, and her breathing quickened.

Reaching out, I threaded a strand of her silky hair through my fingers. "Okay, not a new look. But there's something different." I tugged gently at her hair before releasing it, not missing her shiver.

"Why are you here?" she hissed, all fired up despite her body's reaction to me. "Last night you told me you didn't want me, and you were—never mind."

"I was what?" I leaned closer to her. "Angry? Because you falsely accused me of stealing?"

She sucked in a harsh breath. Turning her head, I saw the anger disappear as her eyes met mine, wide and unsure. "If it wasn't you, then who was it?"

Before I could say anything else, Prof. Patel was in front of us, handing us our essays.

"Looks like I have Raine to thank for this." He looked between us, his eyes narrowed.

I glanced down at my paper. B. Fuck, yes!

"Nothing to do with me," Raine said softly. I glanced over at her paper—A, of course. I couldn't even be mad, though. With her help, I'd somehow managed to bullshit my way to a B. My sense of relief was immediate—my place on the football team was safe for now.

"Today, we're going to continue watching our recording of *Macbeth*," Prof. Patel announced, returning to the front of the room and flicking on the projector. "This will cover the entirety of Act 2, and we will follow up with a discussion." He dimmed the lights, and I settled back in my seat, my legs stretched out in front of me. Raine shuffled in her seat next to me, then did the same, kicking her legs out in front of her. My eyes were drawn to her smooth thighs, covered in sheer tights, and I had a sudden urge to touch her.

After looking around to check no one was paying attention, I lifted my arm and rested it casually along the back of her seat. I smiled at her sharp intake of breath as I leaned closer to her and spoke low in her ear. "Tell me what I'm supposed to have done to get you kicked out of drama club."

She sat in silence for a moment, then turned her head slightly, still facing the screen but angled towards me, her mouth close to my ear. "Someone took the money from the cash box that we use to buy stuff for the costume department, and I'm the only student who knows the combination." Her voice wobbled. "Mrs. Whittall blamed me, of course. I can't even blame her for that—it's the obvious conclusion."

My fingers curled around her shoulder. "Maybe she made a mistake?"

Raine shook her head almost violently. "No, there was four hundred and twenty pounds missing. And now—and now I've been kicked out of the drama club unless I pay the money back. Where am I going to get that kind of money from? You know the situation with my uncle." Her body was trembling, letting me know how much the news had affected her.

"Four hundred and—what the fuck, Raine?" My grip on her shoulder tightened, before I realised what I was doing. Moving my hand to her hair, I started sliding my fingers through it, soothing her. "It wasn't me. Fuck, Raine. You drive me insane, but I wouldn't do that."

She stiffened under my touch. "No, you'll just post photos everywhere to make people think I'm a slut. Do you know what people have been saying about me?"

My mind went to Chris, earlier, and unreasonable jealousy pulsed through my veins, followed by a surge of anger at the reminder that she'd tricked me.

Fuck, should I have posted the photos? It wasn't like I hadn't done worse than that to people before. I'd never felt any remorse in the past, though.

Her soft sigh hit my ears, distracting me from my thoughts, and I leaned closer to her. "I'm sorry about the photos, okay? But I didn't take the money."

"If it wasn't you, then who was it? No one else has access to that box."

I couldn't be sure, but I needed to pay a visit to a certain blonde ex-girlfriend of mine. In the meantime, I needed to distract Raine from questions I didn't have the answer to.

"Remember how you came all over my hand at Fright Night?" My voice was low and seductive as I leaned over to whisper in her ear.

She swallowed hard, her chest rising and falling as her breathing became shallow. I slid my hand onto her thigh, waiting to see what she would do.

Another hiss of breath, but she didn't say anything. I glanced around to make sure no one else was paying us any attention as I moved my hand a little higher. The guy in the same row was oblivious, glued to his phone, watching YouTube under the table.

"What would your boyfriend do if he knew I was touching you like this?" I murmured. I squeezed her skin lightly.

She turned her head to mine, our faces so close, I was almost tempted to kiss her. Fuck, I probably would have if we weren't in a classroom surrounded by people. Then she said five words that shouldn't have made me happy, but they did.

"I don't have a boyfriend."

NINETEEN

RAINE

As soon as the words fell from my lips, I clamped my mouth shut. Why did I say that? What was going on? Why was I sitting here, in the middle of my English class with Carter's hand inching up my thigh, and why did I like it so much?

As I turned to look into his eyes, I noticed the confusion in his gaze. He looked just about as lost as I was, so at least that made two of us. Maybe I was having a temporary lapse of insanity, because I decided to experiment. I liked him like this, wanting me, even though I knew he didn't want to want me. Even though everything between us was messed up. After a quick glance at Prof. Patel, who remained focused on the screen, I reached up and lightly gripped Carter's jaw, my fingers shaking slightly. Turning his head, I whispered in his ear. "What are you doing? You don't want me, remember?" Then, I flicked my tongue across his ear.

The low, masculine groan that fell from his lips made me instantly wet. The fact that I'd been the one to have that effect on him, despite my inexperience, satisfied me more than I would've imagined.

"Raine..." His fingers tightened on my thigh. I wanted him to mark me, to leave bruises so I had a visual reminder of what he'd done to me. Did that make me messed up?

Suddenly, he was rising out of his seat, and then he was gone. The guy sitting across from me glanced over, and I shrugged. He shrugged, too, returning his gaze to his phone. Somehow, Prof. Patel had remained completely oblivious, still staring intently at the screen.

The next moment, my phone vibrated with a text. Three words.

Carter: Room 103. Now

My feet had made the decision before my brain had even had a chance to catch up. With one last glance at Prof. Patel, I was rising out of my seat and slipping out of the door.

Carter's lips were on mine the second I'd stepped foot in the darkened science lab. He pushed me up against the door, grinding against me as he tangled his hands in my hair.

"Wait." I broke away from the kiss, panting. "Let me." My head may have been completely messed up with everything that was going on between us, but I needed to make him feel. Needed to see him fall apart. For *me*. I slipped my hand between us and ran my palm across the hardness in his trousers.

"Fuuuuck."

Emboldened by his reaction, I stroked over his length again, until he was groaning, thrusting his hips forwards. He reached down and undid his trousers, then pushed his boxers down and guided my hand to his cock. "Is this okay?"

The husky rasp in his voice made me shiver. "Yes," I whispered, letting him guide my movements as he wrapped both our hands around his cock. I wished I could see more than a shadowy outline, but I knew that I would have lost my nerve if we could see each other properly. Here, in this dark, empty classroom, it almost felt like we were in a dream.

I didn't let myself think about my inexperience, or the fact that there was a possibility that someone could walk in and find us. I concentrated on the slide of our hands over his cock, and the way he thrust into me, harder and faster as he chased his release. When he came, his hot cum soaking our hands, he slumped forwards, pressing his forehead to the door, breathing heavily.

"What are we doing?"

I had no answer.

Silently, we cleaned up, making the most of the lab sinks and paper towels, before he disappeared out of the door without another word to me. When I eventually made my way back to English class and slipped into my seat, there was no sign of him.

To say that Carter was messing with my head was an understatement. I couldn't think straight when I was around him, and the way he was acting around me, and what had happened earlier—it made my head spin. Not only that, but I didn't know if I believed him when he insisted he hadn't had anything to do with taking the money. I wanted to. The problem was, if it wasn't him, then who was it?

After gathering up my things, I made my way to my locker, my mood low. Normally on a Monday I'd be heading to drama club. But now that had been taken from me, my Mondays were depressingly Mondayish. As I neared my locker, I noticed Dylan waiting for me, a wide smile on his face. When I drew level with him, his smile widened further.

"Mrs. Whittall wants to speak to you. Come on."

At his words, hope flared inside me. Had the whole thing been a mistake? I hurriedly shoved my things into my locker, before following him through the school to the office belonging to the head of the drama department. "She's expecting you. Come and find me afterwards." Dylan beamed at me, and I couldn't help returning his smile.

I heard a "Come in," almost as soon as I'd knocked on the door. Entering the room, I found Mrs. Whittall sitting behind her desk, her fingers steepled, peering at me over the top of her glasses. "No need to take a seat. I'll keep this brief. As the money has been returned, you may resume your position as costume designer. However, should this happen again, you will be instantly barred, and I will have no choice but to mark it on your permanent record." She held up a hand when she saw me open my mouth to speak. "No arguments. The only reason I'm being so lenient with you is because of your prior track record and the situation with your uncle leaving. Now, you're dismissed. I believe that Xavier's jacket needs adjusting, so you may start with that." One brow raised expectantly when I remained in place.

"Oh...yes. Okay. Sorry. Thank you," I mumbled,

whirling around and leaving the office. Confusion warred with elation. The money had been returned. By who?

Collapsing into the chair in the costume storage room, I began pulling out supplies from the drawers, ready to get started. A throat cleared, and my head flew up to see Dylan in the doorway, grinning at me.

"Welcome back." He took a step into the room and perched on the edge of the sewing table.

"Do you know anything about this?" Grabbing a pot of pins from the back of the table, I unscrewed the lid, then turned to face him.

"Don't be mad." His smile suddenly dropped, and he was the same unsure, scared guy I'd always known. "I...I'm rich, Rainey. It was no problem to replace the money."

"Dylan!" I stared at him in shock. "Y-you can't do that!"

"It's already done." Crossing his arms, he gave me a stern look.

What was I supposed to do? "At least let me pay you back." Even as I said it, I had no idea how I would actually achieve that.

He picked up a spool of thread from the table, rolling it along his palm. "Seriously, don't worry about it. I don't want to hear any more talk of you paying me back, okay?"

"I can't let you do that." Looking up at him, I shook my head, and he shrugged.

"It's nothing. Can't friends do something nice for their other friends?"

"They can, but this is a lot of money. Please let me pay you back. It...it might take me a while, but I'll pay back every penny."

He sighed, looking resigned. "You're not going to give this up, are you? Fine, you can pay me back, if it makes you feel better. But you can take as long as you need, and you're under no obligation."

I sat back, reassured by his words. "I can't thank you enough, Dylan. This is so generous of you."

"What are friends for? I knew how upset you were, and how much this means to you." With one last smile, he left me to my sewing.

TWENTY

RAINE

Dylan was kind enough to drop me off at home, which I was grateful for, since I had no idea where I stood with Carter, especially with everything that had happened recently, and I didn't want to take the risk of being shot down by him again. My mind was racing, thinking of ways to pay back the money. Lying on my bed, I picked up my phone and sent Lena a text.

Me: Know any ways to make a bit of cash?
Lena: Drug dealer?
Me: *eye-roll emoji*
Lena: Serious?
Me: Yep.
Lena: How much are we talking, and how quickly?

The next moment my phone was vibrating, and she was calling me. "I'm just leaving a friend's house. Five minutes from you. Want me to come over?"

Fifteen minutes later I was seated on my bed, and Lena was seated at my desk, deep in thought, idly flipping through my costume design sketch pad. "I've got it." She tapped on an open page, where I'd sketched out a ballgown design, long and flowing with lace embellishments. "Can you make this?"

"Yes..." I nodded slowly. "Why?"

"You know there's a winter ball for the Alstone elite?" I vaguely knew of it, although I didn't have a chance to reply as she carried on speaking. "Some of the girls going would kill for a custom, one-off design, but they don't want to pay the huge price tags. And I know of someone going who would be really keen to support an up-and-coming designer." She grinned at me.

"Up-and-coming designer? And who?"

"I don't want to get your hopes up until I've spoken to her, but I'm talking about my cousin's girlfriend." She snapped a few pictures of my sketch, before scrolling through her phone. "Do you have any photos of the stuff you've made? Like the costumes?"

"I do, but what... Are you suggesting that I make a dress for someone? An actual dress that they're going to wear to an event?"

"Yep. Send me the pics and I'll see what I can do."

And that was apparently the end of the conversation, as Lena jumped up. "Next. I just had an idea. You're coming across as so much more confident than you were even a few weeks ago. We need to keep up the momentum. I checked your social media just now, and...you don't post a lot, do you?"

"Not really."

"It's fine. All I was going to say was, you should start adding pictures. Help to get you out there, less hiding away and more pushing yourself forward. It's a good idea, right? I'm not saying take loads of selfies, but maybe a few every now and then, and post some stuff showing what you're up to, or whatever."

Grabbing my phone from my nightstand, I started scrolling through my embarrassingly bare social media account. "I suppose it wouldn't hurt to post a few more pictures."

"No time like the present." She grinned at me encouragingly.

"Okay." A smile spread across my face. "I'll do it. Starting now. In fact, I'll start with a selfie." I stepped right next to Lena, flipping on the selfie camera. "What's the best angle? I never take these."

She tutted. "Sometimes I feel like you hide yourself away too much. You're gorgeous, Raine. You need to appreciate your own looks."

My cheeks heated at her words. "Ha. I know I should try to appreciate myself. It's just...I-I don't really know how to."

"Tell yourself every day. You already have so much more confidence in yourself than when I first met you. You just need to keep it up."

"I'll try."

"Good. Okay, selfie tips." She took the phone from my hand. "Ponytail out, flip your head, and get all that hair shaken out."

I followed her commands. "Now what?"

"Now, we take five million pictures and pick the best one to post." Turning the phone towards us again, she pressed her face up next to mine. "Silly poses. Tongue out. Fingers up." I ended up in fits of laughter as she made me do a series of increasingly ridiculous poses and facial expressions, until eventually she stopped. "Go through the pictures I just took, and pick the best." She handed the phone back to me, and I flipped through the images, smiling. I actually looked like I was having fun. There was a sparkle in my eyes and a genuine smile on my face. I selected an image of us mid-laugh, neither of us looking directly at the camera, and added a filter effect.

Looking at it objectively, I could admit to myself that it was actually a pretty good photo.

"Don't forget to tag me. I've got loads of followers."

"Of course you have."

She rolled her eyes. "Not because it's me, but because of my brother. Every time I post a photo with him in it, people go crazy. Look." Swiping through her photos, she paused on one of Cassius holding her in a headlock, both of them laughing. They were on a beach somewhere, both wearing sunglasses, and Cassius' ripped, tattooed body was prominent in the picture. I stared at the likes. "*How* many thousand?" I whispered, shocked.

"Yeah. That's the power of Cassius Drummond." Another eye-roll accompanied her words, and I laughed as I handed the phone back to her.

"I guess you must be used to it by now. Anyway, what caption should I put with our photo?"

She shrugged. "Whatever you want."

"Posting it now." I captioned the image with just one word—"friends"—and posted it, making sure I tagged Lena.

"Perfect." Lena viewed the picture on her own phone. "Maybe I should ask Cassius to take a photo with you—that'd get people talking."

"I don't want people talking. I just want it to look like I'm doing fine on my own."

"Comfort zone."

"Stop saying that to me."

"Remember, you can handle anything. You're strong."

"I don't feel very strong."

"Raine. You. Are. Strong."

She gave me a quick, unexpected hug. "I'm proud of you, you know? Now, send me those pics so I can forward them to my cousin's girlfriend."

"Okay. And thanks. For everything." Smiling, I navigated to my photo albums, bringing up the folder where I'd saved the images of the costumes I'd made. Selecting some of the best, I forwarded them to her.

Later, once she'd left, I decided to post another photo of the costume I was working on, arranging my sewing machine and supplies as artistically as possible. Once I'd done that, I flipped to the photo of me with Lena and was shocked to see that I already had some likes and comments, mostly from people I'd never spoken to in my life. People I went to school with. And the most shocking thing of all? They were all positive comments. I didn't kid myself that it would stay that way, but it was a nice surprise.

My phone buzzed, and I checked the notifications that had popped up. I had a few new followers, and the username of one was @kingblackthorne. Tiny butterflies fluttered to life inside my belly, and I clicked on his profile.

On the outside, looking in, his life looked amazing. Photos of him holding up football trophies, posing with Kian and Xavier, posing with girls (I scrolled past those as quickly as possible), on the beach, even a photo of him from Fright Night with a group of masked guys. I tapped the image, then realised I'd added a heart reaction. Oops. I quickly removed it, hoping he hadn't noticed.

He had.

The next minute, a message alert popped up, and I steeled myself as I hit the button to view it.

Carter: I saw that heart

I groaned.

Me: My finger slipped
Carter: Sure it did
Me: Scout's honour
Carter: You weren't a scout
Me: How do you know?

He didn't answer me, instead changing the subject.

Carter: Whose car were you getting out of earlier?
Me: Were you spying on me?
Carter: Answer the question, Raine
Me: Dylan Rossiter's
Carter: Who TF is that?
Me: He's in drama club with me. He works on set design. I think he's in your business studies class???
Carter: No idea who he is

The next moment, my phone lit up with an incoming video call. Shit. He was calling me on the app? I shrieked in fright and threw my phone. It hit the floor with a thud.

"Raine?"

I stared at the phone, lying face down on the floor. How had I managed to answer it when I was throwing it?

"Raine? Let me see your face."

His voice was slightly muffled. I groaned, prodding my phone with my toe. Maybe I could pretend I wasn't there.

Lena's voice appeared in my mind, shouting "comfort zone!" So annoying. I swiped my phone from the floor and glanced at the screen, my stomach giving an involuntary flip at the sight of Carter's face. From what I could see, he was lying on his bed, the navy fabric of his pillow behind his head. His hair was tousled, and his brows were pulled together in a frown.

"Tell me why you were in his car," he commanded in a low tone.

"Not that it's any of your business," I began in a haughty tone, and his frown deepened. "My *friend* Dylan got me reinstated in the drama club, and he gave me a lift home afterwards. Because he's nice, and that's what friends do."

His eyes darkened. "You don't want nice."

"We're just friends, Carter." I huffed in exasperation. Why was I even bothering to explain myself?

He ignored my comment. "You should've waited for me. I would have taken you home."

I gaped at him. "Would you, though?"

"Raine." His voice softened. "I thought we were—hold up. How exactly did he get you reinstated in the drama club?"

Those were details that Carter didn't need to know. "You're not the only one with influence at Alstone High," I said instead.

I could've sworn he growled as he stared menacingly at me through the screen. "You'd better be telling the truth about just being friends with him. He wants you, Raine."

Argh! He was so frustrating. "We are *just friends*. He doesn't want me. Some people are capable of being friends without wanting more, you know. And how do you know that he wants me, which he doesn't, by the way! You don't even know who he is!" My voice grew louder and higher in pitch, and I winced at the sound, but I made sure I glared at him through the screen. "And also, why do you even care?" I added in a quieter tone.

"I wish I fucking knew," he muttered, before the screen went blank, and he was gone.

TWENTY-ONE

RAINE

The sound of laughter and talking filtered through my open bathroom window as I stood at the sink washing my hands, not loud enough to be an issue, but the sound carried through the still night air. Although I couldn't see his house from the window, I knew the sound was coming from Carter's. My aunt was working, and Carter's parents were probably out, given the noise. While Carter had been adamant about not being behind the money theft, there were still doubts in my mind—after all, who else would have a reason to do that to me, or even have the means to? I stood at the window, hesitating for a long moment, before I made my mind up. I *had* to know.

Slipping out of the back of the house, I made my way down to the bottom of the garden, to the corner where it joined to Carter's. Unfortunately, there was no convenient broken fence panel or gap to slip through to get into his garden. Instead, I dragged the recycling bin from its position by the back gate that led out into an alleyway and placed it against Carter's fence. Then, I climbed up onto it, feeling it wobble beneath me, and gripped the edges of the fence and peered over.

It looked like I was in luck. The large panel of doors was wide open. Before I could think through what I was doing, or even how I was going to get back into my own garden, I was swinging my legs over the fence and dropping to the ground. I made my way up the garden as quickly as I could, thankful that the outside lights were on, meaning the security lights wouldn't be activated. As long as I kept to the side of the garden, no one should see me.

When I reached the house, I peered in through the open lounge windows, seeing several of Carter's friends sprawled out on the sofas, *Black Panther* playing on the giant TV screen. There was another cluster of people standing around and talking at the far side of the room, and I was totally unprepared for the jolt of pure jealousy when I realised that Carter was there, leaning against the wall with his arm loosely around Tina's waist. I gritted my teeth, tamping down the inexplicable urge to scratch out Tina's eyeballs, or maybe Carter's, or both, although Carter barely seemed to be paying her any attention. Instead, I turned my attention to the open doors that led into the huge kitchen.

The kitchen was empty, and I knew I had to take my chance before anyone came in. My heart pounding, I slipped through the doors and ran for the hallway that led to the stairs.

It seemed that luck was on my side for once. I made it to the stairs and raced upstairs as fast as I could. At the top, I took a moment to catch my breath before I crept along the landing towards Carter's bedroom. Turning the handle softly, I inched inside and closed the door behind me. The room was dark, but the blinds were open, and from the glow of the streetlights I could easily make out the features of the room. I had the torch on my phone that I could use, too, because there was no way I was going to risk turning on a light.

First up, I went for Carter's desk drawers, flipping on my phone torch after opening the top drawer. Reaching inside, I shuffled the items around—pens, an old camera—

"Carter!" My head snapped around at the giggling word coming from outside the room. Shit! Where could I hide? Slamming the drawer shut, I dived for the door next to me, shoving my way into piles of material. Oh, bloody hell, I was stuck inside his wardrobe. I left the door cracked open, because who knew if it could be opened from the inside? I wasn't about to be stuck in here all night.

"Mmmm. So this is what Carter Blackthorne's bedroom looks like." Tina strutted across the room as Carter flicked on a lamp, and I was suddenly unreasonably jealous. He pulled her to him, and my eyes closed. I couldn't watch. If only I could close my ears, too.

"What do you want, Tina?" His voice was bored, yet he was still holding her. "What was so important that you had to speak to me in private?"

"What do you think? I wanted to get you alone. Want me to give you a blowie?" Her voice grated on me, and I wanted to rake my nails down her face. Again. My eyes flew open, and I watched her caress the front of his jeans, unable to drag my gaze away even though I was only torturing myself. "Huh. Not feeling it today? Brewer's droop, maybe?" Her voice was disappointed, and I found myself smiling.

He scrubbed a hand over his face. "Not today, Tee. Why don't we go back down to the others? Shots?"

That seemed to appease her, and she nodded. "Yes! Got

any of those apple ones?" They moved towards the door, and Carter opened it, letting Tina walk through first.

"I'll see you down there. Just got to do something first."

Then he closed the door.

Oh, no.

I pressed further back, and held my breath, trying not to make a sound. Then the next thing I knew, the wardrobe doors were being flung open, and he was yanking me out.

"*Raine?* What the actual fuck?"

Our bodies were aligned, and every part of me was pressed up against him, tingling with awareness. Panic overcame my reaction to his nearness, and I pushed away from him and ran for the door. I only made it two steps before he was behind me with his hand gripping my throat.

For a second, time slowed, and I was aware of everything. My harsh, unsteady breaths, the electric current of lust that was sparking between us, the goosebumps that were breaking out all over my skin. Then, he was spinning me around to face him, and his mouth was on mine.

I couldn't resist him even if I'd wanted to. My lips parted, and I let him in, kissing him back, feeling his tongue slide against mine. He lifted me into his arms, and I wrapped my legs around him as he walked us backwards, our lips never leaving one another's.

Spinning us, he pushed me down onto the bed and climbed on top of me, kissing me again. As he settled his heavy body between my legs, I felt his cock, hard as steel between us. My legs wrapped around his waist. "No brewer's droop, hmm?" Tearing my mouth from his, I couldn't resist teasing him, and he laughed against my lips, grinding his hips into me.

Lifting himself onto his elbows, he slid my top up, over my stomach. Dropping his head, he pushed down my bra cup and took my nipple into his mouth. He bit down lightly, and I moaned.

"Fuck, Raine." His voice was a rough, tormented whisper. "*Fuck.*"

I slid my hands up his back to his broad shoulders. "Carter."

At the sound of his name, he stilled, then raised himself above me. He blinked a few times, the haze of lust disappearing, replaced with a dark expression. "Wait. Why are you in my bedroom? How did you get in here?"

Oh. He was asking the difficult questions now. I was pinned in place, unable to move, and as I stared up at him, his jaw clenched. "Answer the fucking question."

"I...um..." I licked my suddenly dry lips. "I..."

Turning his head, he scanned the room, and when he inhaled sharply, I followed his gaze to the desk. *No.* The top drawer wasn't closed all the way. "Have you been snooping in here?" His voice was hard.

"I just wanted to see—"

"Is this about the money?" he interrupted me, hissing the words through gritted teeth.

The silence between us stretched, until it was unbearable, and the word fell from my lips.

"Yes."

Hauling me off the bed, he shoved me in the direction of the door, sending me staggering into the wall. "Get. Out."

"Carter, I—"

"*Now.*"

For a moment, we stared at each other. The unmistakable anger and hurt in his eyes was too much, and I realised what a mistake I'd made in coming here.

"I'm sorry," I whispered, then turned on my heel and left. There was nothing more I could say.

TWENTY-TWO

RAINE

The car park in front of the large warehouse was completely full. After circling around fruitlessly, Lena spun the wheel and turned out of the car park, coming to a halt in front of a roll-up door with a "no parking" sign on it. "This'll do. No one will be around to check at this time of night." We piled out, and I stretched my arms up in the air, working out the kinks from being crammed in the back seat next to Lena's friends. My T-shirt rode up, exposing a sliver of skin, and I tugged it back down again. This outfit...it was most definitely out of my comfort zone. Not as skimpy as my Fright Night costume, but the difference was, I couldn't hide behind a mask this time. I wore a loose black T-shirt, strategically ripped, exposing my cleavage, and tiny black shorts that made me cringe when I'd put them on. Of course, this was Lena's doing. She wore similar, but with her tall, slim body she looked like a model.

At least I had on flat shoes. Old black Chucks, to be exact. I didn't know exactly what was going to be happening at this party, but we'd been told to wear clothes that we didn't mind being ruined.

There was a ball of nerves in my stomach, but overriding that, there was a sense of pure excitement. This party to celebrate the birthdays of three members of the AHS football team was open invite, so even though I knew that Carter would be there, I was hoping it would be busy enough that I wouldn't run into him. After everything that had happened, he had backed right off, and although I couldn't stop the way I felt about him, I was starting to realise that maybe things were better this way. We'd had our moments, when I thought we'd really connected, but I was starting to come around to his way of thinking—I was no good for him.

I pushed aside thoughts of Carter and turned to face the reason for my excitement. The party.

People milled around outside the large warehouse, set slightly apart from the others. Flashing lights and the thud of heavy bass spilled from the cracked panes of the small, high windows running down the side of the building.

"I can do this," I mumbled to myself, and then the old familiar panic rose in me as I took a step closer to Lena.

As if she was aware of my thoughts, she squeezed my arm. "I'm proud of you. All you need to do is fake it until it becomes real, yeah?"

"Okay." Pushing my misgivings way, way down, I allowed the excitement to bubble up as we entered the building, passing through an entrance foyer and into the main warehouse.

The dark, cavernous space was lit by pulsing neon lights in bright colours. Machines pumped out slow, lazy clouds of smoke, curling and drifting around people's feet and up into the air, making everything appear hazy. At the far end of the space a DJ was up on a platform, and at the near end, close to the entrance, was a bar area. Bodies filled the space, most covered in splashes of colourful neon paint, glowing under the black lights.

"Drinks first. Can you get them? I'm not legally old enough." Lena gave me her best innocent look, speaking loudly to be heard over the music.

Raising a brow, I stared at her. "You expect me to believe you don't own a fake ID?"

She smirked. "But yours is real. Get us both whatever you want to drink. I'll only have one since I'm driving."

"Fine." After pushing my way to the bar, I scanned through the limited options available and ordered us both bottles of some fruity alcoholic cider. Returning to Lena, I handed her one of the bottles.

After taking a sip, she turned to me with a grin. "Rule one. Finish this drink, but don't leave it unattended. Rule two. Dance for at least one song. Rule three. Find a boy, and practice flirting with him."

"I have to do all that?" Actually, it all sounded easy enough, except for the flirting part.

She nodded, still smiling at me.

I sighed. "Fine. Are you going to do the same?"

"Yep. Except the flirting."

"Why do I have to flirt and you don't?"

Her eyes shuttered. "Because there's no one here that I want."

I raised a brow at her firm tone but didn't push it. "Fine. Let's get this over with." Lifting the bottle to my lips, I let the ice-cold berry liquid slide down my throat. "Mmm. This is nice."

"You don't drink much, do you? Best not to have too much," she warned me.

We moved further into the warehouse, among the crowd of bodies, weaving in and out. I kept a tight grip on

Lena's hand, not wanting to lose her in the crowd. She followed her friends towards a doorway at the far side of the warehouse, and after pushing our way through a crowded corridor, we ended up back outside, this time around the back of the warehouse. There was a huge open space, all pitted, cracked concrete, and filling around two-thirds of it was what looked like a kind of obstacle course made of what I would class as junk—sheets of corrugated cardboard, crates, and tyres. People were running through it, being pelted with water balloons filled with bright neon paint, and colourful smoke bombs were being set off at regular intervals along the course, reducing the visibility. Over at the side, the large red shipping container with "Chillout Zone" sprayed on the side in huge letters caught my eye.

"The paint run," Lena's friend Jax announced. "Wanna go?"

I glanced back to the shipping container. "Lena? I'm going to check that out while I finish my drink. Meet you after?"

She smiled and nodded, handing me her drink, and then joined the others while I headed towards the shipping container.

As soon as I entered, I realised my mistake when I recognised the people inside. Kian leaned against the wall, facing away from me, talking to Chris, another guy from the football team. This was where the popular people were. I took a couple of steps backwards, ready to flee, when I was stopped by a hand on my arm.

"Leaving already?" Looking up, I was met by a pair of sapphire eyes, blond hair, and a chiselled jawline. Preston Montgomery III, one of the football team strikers, recently moved here from the USA.

"Yeah. Sorry, I…"

"You don't have to go." He took a step closer. "Raine, right?" A smile curved across his lips at the surprise on my face.

"I don't belong here," I said softly.

His eyes darkened. "You do. Come with me." He tugged my arm gently, and I let him lead me over to the side of the container. "First up, we need to give you your war paint."

"War paint?" What was going on? Placing the bottles down next to me, I let him seat me on a stool, where he spun me to face him. He gestured to the smears of paint decorating his face and body.

"Kian's idea." His smile grew soft, and he glanced across to where Kian was standing. As if they were connected by an invisible thread, Kian's gaze immediately went to Preston's, a completely unexpected, huge smile appearing on his face, and I *knew*. Preston's eyes flew to mine at my sharp intake of breath. He read my expression correctly and stiffened. "Please don't tell anyone. We're...I..."

"I would never. It's not my place," I assured him.

He relaxed at my words. "Thanks. I mean it. It's..."

"If only we didn't have to hide," I murmured, and I didn't know if I was referring to his situation or to mine. "If only we were free to be ourselves without judgement."

"Yeah." We both sighed, then laughed. I'd never spoken to Preston before, but there was something about him that made me feel comfortable around him. Dipping his fingers in the neon paint, he carefully smeared it across my cheeks, then took my hand and led me towards the back of the container. When we arrived, he directed me onto an inflatable sofa, handing me the bottle he'd been carrying for me, and sat down next to me, slinging his arm across the back of the sofa.

I finally gathered together the courage to look up and

immediately wished I hadn't. All eyes were on me, and most were hostile. Grouped on sofas, crates, and on the floor around a large, upturned crate that was serving as a table were half the football team plus Anastasia and her group of friends. I didn't dare to look over at the sofa where Carter sat, Xavier on one side and Anastasia on the other.

"Are you lost?" The girl sitting across from me gave me a pointed glare, looking between me and Preston.

He bent his head close to my ear and spoke so low that there was no way anyone else would hear him. "Don't let them scare you away. They just feel threatened by you."

"She can stay." Kian slumped down on the sofa perpendicular to mine, pulling his lip ring into his mouth. Wow, what was this? First Preston, now Kian? He stretched out his legs, his trainer nudging against Preston's, and I saw a small smile play across his lips. "Spin the bottle, anyone?"

His words stopped everyone staring at me, thankfully. But spin the bottle, really? I had no idea people even played it. Of course, this was technically my first party.

"I don't want her here." Anastasia spoke low, but I still heard her. Giving me a disdainful look, she snuggled up to Carter like she had every right to. He hadn't even acknowledged my presence yet, but he threw an arm around her neck and whispered something in her ear, making her laugh and glance over at me. This was so hard. If it wasn't for Lena shouting *"comfort zone"* in my head, and Preston's presence next to me, I would've bolted.

I watched, breathless, as the bottle was set on the coffee table, and Kian gave it an experimental spin. Looking around at the people playing, I knew that if I joined in, it was going to be awkward whoever I ended up kissing. Carter's presence, and the fact I was an outsider here and none of them liked me very much…it had the potential to mess up all my progress so far. I downed the rest of my bottle quickly, catching Imogen's eye in the process. She gave me a reassuring smile, which I returned shyly. Maybe not all of them were so bad.

"Chris. You wanna start?" Kian grinned. "Usual rules. Kiss whoever it lands on, or do a forfeit."

This didn't sound good. I had no desire to find out what the forfeits would consist of, and I didn't want to know. I was pretty sure kissing anyone here had to be better than one of Kian's forfeits.

Chris spun, landing on Carter. "Oh baby, pucker up."

"Fuck off." Carter's mouth set in a flat line. "Do the forfeit."

"Aren't you dying to taste these sweet lips?" He pouted, and I couldn't help the laugh that bubbled up.

"Who knows where that mouth has been." Carter stared at him.

"On your mum's pussy."

"You're fucking gross."

"Hate to interrupt the chat, but some of us want to get on with the game," Anastasia piped up. "Kiss or forfeit. It's not difficult." The boys glanced at each other, then both shrugged. Chris leaned forwards, placing a kiss on Carter's lips, and then they both started cracking up.

"Do that again." Anastasia's voice was all breathy. "That was hot."

"Ana, please." Carter gave her a kind of frustrated smile, and she smiled back up at him. Out of nowhere I was hit by an irrational surge of jealousy, as I watched Carter return her smile with a proper one.

"Ana, your turn, baby." I'd never been so happy for Kian interrupting, as they stared into each other's eyes.

She tore her gaze away from Carter, shrugging out from

under his arm to lean forwards and spin. The bottle seemed to spin forever, and we all watched in silence as it slowed. Most of the boys looked hopeful—and why wouldn't they? Anastasia was beautiful, and popular, and connected.

The bottle slowed to a stop, and my stomach sank. Her eyes flicked to mine, and the dread I felt was reflected in her eyes. "No. I pick a forfeit." Her voice was firm.

I stared down at the bottle, not really taking it in. It was pointing directly at me.

"What's the matter? Scared of kissing me?" *Who am I and what are these words coming out of my mouth?*

"I'm not scared. I just know where your mouth's been, and I don't want to catch anything." She grimaced, then added, "You shouldn't even be here. You don't belong with us."

The combination of the alcohol, the jealousy, and the pure frustration with my situation with Carter sent the words pouring from my lips before I could censor them. "Says who? What exactly is it about me that makes me so undesirable, huh?"

Stop talking! What am I saying?

Everyone stared at me in shock. Anastasia's mouth opened and closed a few times. "You don't fit in with us," she eventually said.

"Ana." At Imogen's soft reprimand, Anastasia sat back with a huff.

"I already know what your forfeit is gonna be."

Before Kian had even finished speaking, Anastasia flew to her feet, storming around the crate to me. "Fine. I'll kiss her." Then she grabbed my arm, pulling me to my feet. We both froze, our faces close together. Up close, I could see the jade green of her eyes, with silver flecks, and the light dusting of freckles across her tiny nose. She licked her lips, and I realised she was nervous.

Anastasia, nervous? The untouchable ice queen? Her pause gave me the confidence to do what I did next. I closed the gap between us and placed my lips on hers. She kissed me back hesitantly, then gaining confidence, followed my lead.

We must've only kissed for a few seconds before we both pulled away from each other, but everyone around us had gone completely silent. Anastasia's hand flew to her mouth, and then her expression turned hard. She tossed her glossy hair over her shoulder, back to her usual self.

"Not bad, Laurent. I guess you kiss alright, for a frigid virgin."

Fuck you.

"That was hot as fuck," Xavier murmured to sounds of agreement, and I suddenly became aware of everyone staring at us. My cheeks reddened at the attention. I couldn't help my gaze flicking over to Carter, and I was surprised to see anger there. I watched as Anastasia slid back into place next to him, and he threw his arm over her shoulder again, burying his face in her hair.

It was all too much. "I need some air," I said, and fled, making my way for the safety of the door.

TWENTY-THREE

RAINE

"You're so far out of your comfort zone, you're in another orbit." Lena's voice stopped me in my tracks. Making my way over to the dim corner of the container where she was standing, I sat on an upturned crate, my legs shaky.

"What does that even mean?" I turned to look at her paint-splattered face, which was beaming with pride.

"I never thought I'd see the day when you and Anastasia Egerton would kiss. I've been watching you, and honestly, I thought you would've tapped out before they even started playing, but you've surprised me. In a good way. You're a lot stronger than you realise, Raine. Look how you held your own over there." Her voice held a note of impressed disbelief, if that was even a thing, and warmth filled me.

"I did, didn't I? I managed to hold my own." My voice lowered. "I think I made Anastasia nervous."

Lena nodded. "Yeah, she's not as confident as she pretends to be. Most of those guys over there, they're all too afraid to be themselves. Too scared of losing their position at the top, too scared to be different." She smiled at me. "You? You're being yourself."

With those words, a series of mental images flashed through my mind—Carter, gripping my throat. Pressing his fingers into my thigh. Roughly kissing and touching me.

"What if there's another side to me I keep hidden?" I whispered the words, hardly daring to say them aloud.

"Like what?" Lena stared at me, intrigued. I glanced around us, but nobody was close enough to overhear or pay any attention.

"A side I only discovered recently. I..." I swallowed nervously. "I think I like...umm. Kind of rough stuff. With a guy."

Lena's brows flew up, her eyes almost popping out of her head. "Totally not what I expected you to say." She studied me. "Is this to do with Carter?"

I nodded slowly. "I know it doesn't make sense. I... before I got to know you, last summer I had a thing with this guy, Ralph. We mostly just fooled around, never went too far. Just you know, hands." I blushed, dropping my gaze to the floor. "I never got turned on. I was attracted to him, and he was good-looking, kind of Clark Kent vibes. I thought there was something wrong with me. Until Carter."

"What does that mean? How does it relate to being rough? Raine, did he hurt you?"

"The first time he...he had his hand around my throat, it was like someone flicked a switch in me." I clamped my mouth shut, unable to look at her, too afraid of what she would think.

"Flicked a switch how?"

My throat was so dry, and I could feel my cheeks burning. "I-I liked it. It turned me on. *He* turned me on. Please don't judge me."

"I would never judge you. So you like that kind of thing, so what?" My eyes met hers. Of course, she was so experienced that what was a big deal to me probably didn't even register with her.

"Is there something wrong with me?" My voice came out as a whisper.

"No! Raine. Not everyone likes the same thing. There's nothing wrong with you, so don't even think that for a second. But I need you to answer me something, and this is really fucking important, so be honest with me."

I nodded, taken aback by her deadly serious expression.

"Has Carter, or anyone for that matter, ever done anything to you against your will? Sexually, I mean."

I shook my head slowly. "N-no. Every time he's touched me, I've...liked it. Wanted more. Even when I didn't *want* to want more."

She breathed a sigh of relief. "Good. I want you to promise me that if you're ever in a situation that makes you feel uncomfortable, or anyone tries to get you to do something against your will, you tell me. Please, Raine. Don't let yourself become a victim." There was a kind of glazed, faraway expression on her face, and her eyes were looking a little glassy.

"Lena? Is there anything you want to talk about?"

A tear gathered at the corner of her lashes, and she angrily swiped it away. "No. I'm fine. I just...just stay safe, okay?"

"Okay." I reached out and squeezed her hand, and she gave me a small smile.

"I need to get out of here," she muttered.

"I'm going back to play."

"Are you sure?" She stared at me in surprise, and I nodded resolutely.

"I need to stop running away. Stop acting like they're better than me."

"That's the spirit. Promise me you'll leave if you need to, though, okay? I'll come back and find you a bit later, or you can text me."

"I will. Go. I'll be fine." And for the first time since this whole comfort zone experiment had begun, I meant it.

After she'd left, I took a breath, then jumped off the crate and headed back over to them with my head held high. Carter's gaze immediately went to mine, and he frowned, studying me intently. Could he see my newfound confidence? I couldn't believe I actually had Anastasia to thank for my little epiphany.

I leaned over the crate, tugging the bottle from Kian's grasp. "It must be my turn by now."

There was a shocked silence for a moment—story of the evening—and then he rocked back on his heels. "You missed your turn, so you have to do a forfeit as well as a kiss."

"Fine." I gave what I hoped was a casual shrug, battling between holding on to my courage and the nerves that were bubbling up inside me. Quickly, I placed the bottle on the table and sent it spinning wildly. I held my breath as it slowed, creeping around the circle, nudging past Carter, and coming to a stop in front of Xavier.

I heard Imogen's sharp intake of breath and felt the electric current of Carter's rage snap against my skin. I felt kind of bad about kissing Xavier when he and Imogen were still obviously hung up on each other, but it was the nature of the game, and I was now all in.

Rising from my seat, I met Xavier's dark eyes, and he gave me a small smile. I took a step towards him, when Carter's leg came out and knocked into the crate. The bottle moved incrementally to the left, and it was now sitting in between Xavier and Carter. People were exchanging glances, and my courage was quickly evaporating.

"Looks like it stopped between us both." No one missed the sarcasm in Xavier's tone. "Who's it gonna be, Raine? Or do you want to spin again?"

I kept my gaze on Xavier. "I pick y—"

"Me." Carter's voice sliced through the air, stopping me in my tracks. My eyes flew to his. He didn't look happy. "Look, we all know X-man and Immy have a thing for each other still. Let's not make this any more awkward. Raine, come here."

"Carter!" Imogen's tone, laced with hurt, came from behind my head, where she'd moved to stand, leaning against the wall.

"I have a better idea!" Kian shouted over everyone, dispelling the tension in the air. "Raine's forfeit is to kiss both of you, until I call time."

"At the same time?" I managed, blinking at this sudden turn of events.

"Y—" Preston kicked him. "Not unless you want to."

My shoulders sagged in relief. "One at a time, then. Fine. I accept." Ignoring the muttering and whispers around us, I stalked over to Xavier before I could talk myself out of it and leaned down, placing my lips on his. As he opened his mouth for me, his hand coming to the back of my neck to hold it in place, I felt like I was having an out-of-body experience or something. Was this really happening?

Xavier's lips were full and firm, and he kissed with utter confidence, owning my mouth like he knew exactly what to do to make me feel good.

His kiss did nothing for me, as I expected. I could feel Carter's presence next to us, and I kept my eyes closed.

"Time's up," Kian called, and Xavier released me, a slow smile spreading across his face.

"You got skills, baby."

"Carter, you're up."

Our eyes met, the gold flecks sparking as he took me in, a dark look on his face. This was the first time he'd properly looked at me since he'd thrown me out of his house, and the full force of his gaze was almost too much. I was barely aware of Anastasia abruptly shooting off the sofa and moving away as I came to stand in front of him. He lazily spread his legs so I could step between them, casually indifferent, but the electric connection between us snapped and pulsed, and a wave of desire shot through me, so strong that I had to clamp my teeth down on my bottom lip to stop a whimper from escaping.

"Raine." My name slipped from his lips, and as if it was the most natural thing in the world, he reached up at the same time I leaned down, and our mouths collided as he pulled me onto his lap so I was straddling him.

Xavier owned me with his kiss, but Carter obliterated me.

"Time!" Kian's voice penetrated the fog surrounding me and Carter, and we broke apart, both breathing heavily.

"Is something going on here? I called time five times."

Carter stiffened, glancing over at Kian, and the heat disappeared from his gaze. "Nah. Just an experiment to see if the geek can actually kiss." He didn't even look at me.

I closed my eyes, taking a deep breath, then opened them and climbed off him. "I think I'll leave now." My voice was quiet but steady, and I'd never been so grateful. Without another word, I pivoted on my heel and walked out without looking back.

Lena caught up with me outside. "What happened?" I

gave her a rundown, and her eyes darkened. "I will fuck him up. What the actual fuck is his problem?"

"I don't even want to know anymore. Can we just go—"

"I'm not letting him scare you away."

"I wasn't going to say that." A small smile curved over my lips. "I was going to say, can we just go and dance and forget about him?"

She returned my smile. "Yep. Let's go." We made our way back into the warehouse, and I pasted a bright smile on my face as we began to dance, ignoring the ache that was spreading deep in my chest.

TWENTY-FOUR

RAINE

I lost myself in the music. Gradually the pain in my chest receded, and one song merged into another until I was breathless and dying for a drink.

"Lena!" Shouting over the music to be heard, I waved my hand to get her attention. Her head swung around to face me. Lifting my hand, I mimed drinking a drink, then pointed to the bar with my eyebrows raised. She pulled her phone out of her pocket, glanced at it, then shook her head with a sigh. Stepping closer, she spoke loudly.

"I've got to go now really. I promised my mum I'd be back by 1:00 a.m. She's taking me into London tomorrow to go shopping for a dress for the winter ball." She pulled a face, letting me know what she thought of that idea, and I laughed.

"Do you mind if I stay? I could get an Uber back with Jax and the others?" I'd heard Lena's friends mention they were going to book an Uber home, and I knew at least one of them lived close to me.

"You don't need my permission to stay." Grinning at me,

she squeezed my arm. "Stay, have fun. You're doing great. I'm proud of you."

I smiled at her. As usual, my aunt was doing an overnight shift at the hospital, so I had nothing to rush home for.

Bounding over to Jax, she spoke into his ear, and he glanced over to me with a nod and a thumbs up, and I shot him a smile. After saying my goodbyes to Lena and promising to text her, I made my way over to the bar, where I ordered a bottle of water. Downing the water, I leaned against the wall, people-watching.

Through the smoky haze I noticed a large walkway above me that circled the warehouse. Heading over to the metal steps, I ducked under the barrier and made my way up to the top. After I'd placed my bottle of water down on the floor, I leaned on the railing that ran along the side of the walkway, my arms folded, just watching the people down below me. Everything was still hazy, but the crowds had thinned out a little, allowing me to focus more clearly on the individuals.

Something caught my eye, far down below. Darting between the dancing bodies were figures in LED masks, randomly pelting people with paint bombs. I laughed, but my laughter died away almost instantly as the sight of the masks brought back memories of Carter.

With a sigh, I leaned down to pick up my water bottle.

My spine prickled with awareness.

When I straightened up, I realised I was no longer alone on the walkway.

My head turned, slowly, almost against my will. I blinked, my focus fixed on the far end of the walkway where a swirl of thick red smoke was pumping from a metal cylinder, obscuring my vision. As the smoke grenade dropped to the walkway floor with a clatter, a figure dressed in black, with a smooth, black mask concealing their features emerged through the clearing smoke.

The fear was instantaneous. This wasn't even like when Carter had grabbed me. This was bone-deep, a chill that surged through my veins, urging me to get away *right now*. My water bottle fell from my fingers, forgotten, as I froze in place.

There was only one way off this walkway, and it was behind the figure.

They stepped closer. Despite being clad in an oversized hoodie, I could tell that they were shorter than Carter, with a slim build that was nothing like his bulk. "Wh-what do you want?" I breathed out, attempting to keep my voice even as my earlier confidence evaporated. At the same time, I reached into my shorts pocket, grasping my keys. Threading them between my fingers, I took a step towards the figure. The figure hesitated, and I took my chance, feinting to the left and then darting to the right. As I passed the figure, they reached out a gloved hand, gripping a handful of my hair and yanking my head back.

My heart hammered hard in my chest, and on instinct I threw my hands out, grabbing the round bar running along the top of the railing. Throwing my head forwards, I managed to tear my hair free, hearing a high-pitched grunt come from behind me. I didn't waste any more time, clattering down the stairs as fast as I could and leaping off the last few, smacking blindly into a large body.

All the air was knocked out of me. Arms came around me, encircling my waist. "Little trickster. Where are you going in such a hurry?"

I had never in my life been so glad for Carter's presence as I was right then. I shivered against him, and his voice changed, concern threading through his tone. "What's wrong?"

Raising my face, I stared up at him. He had on his mask, and I couldn't make out his eyes. I couldn't speak. He grasped my chin in his hand. "What is it?"

"Th-there's someone up there. On th-the walkway. They tried to grab me."

"*What?*" His entire body stiffened. Moving back, he scanned the walkway high above us, slowly and carefully, before he shook his head, looking back down at me. "Raine. There's no one there."

My whole body trembled in his grip, and he pulled me into him. I rested my head against his solid chest, my heart rate slowly returning to normal.

He lowered his head to my ear. "Do you want me to go up and check?"

Shaking my head, I threaded my arms around his waist, realising I was still clutching my keys in my hand. I felt him sigh against me, and then he let go of me, tugging on my arms so I released him. Reaching down, he took my hand in his and began weaving us through the crowds. I kept a tight grip on my keys, every masked figure suddenly seeming like a threat, as they ran in and out of the dancing bodies, throwing the paint bombs at unsuspecting partygoers. One hit me square in the chest, and I gasped with shock as the cold blue paint trickled down between my breasts. Carter never let up his stride, though, so I didn't even have a chance to stop and wipe off the paint. After what had just happened, I didn't want to leave him. As much as he'd upset me earlier, and despite the way he acted a lot of the time, he felt safe. I felt safe with him. I *knew* he wouldn't hurt me.

Leading me into the warehouse foyer, he stopped and tugged his mask off. "I'm taking you home."

"But I don't want to go." I folded my arms, tilting my chin up stubbornly and glaring at him. Somehow, I managed to block out what had happened up on the walkway and chose to focus on the here and now. It was actually easy to do when I was in Carter's presence. He commanded my full attention, and everything else faded into insignificance.

My reply just made him smile. "You've had enough fun for tonight, don't you think?" His gaze lowered, his eyes darkening as he took in my paint-covered cleavage. "You're all covered in paint." One finger came up, dipping into the still-wet paint and trailing it up, over my collarbone. "So fucking gorgeous," he said softly, his voice so low that I could barely hear him.

I barely repressed the delicious shiver that ran down my spine. Stepping closer, I ran my hand up his chest, feeling the alternating combination of his soft cotton T-shirt and dried paint under my palm. "I don't want to go," I said again.

He swept his fingers down into the wet paint again, sending goosebumps popping all over my body. Dragging his hand up until he was lightly gripping my throat, he leaned closer. "What do you want, then?"

"Hmm?" I was distracted by his touch and his mouth so close to mine. Just a few millimetres closer and our lips would be touching.

"I said, what do you want?" His breath was hot on my lips.

Before I could reply, someone bumped into us, with a muttered, "Sorry, mate," and Carter seemed to remember where we were. His head came up, and he glanced around us. I could see indecision playing across his face, and then he seemed to come to a decision. Letting go of me, he stalked over to a door off to the side of the foyer, throwing it open.

"Get out," he commanded to whoever was inside, and the next minute a couple walked out, the guy zipping up the fly of his jeans and the girl straightening her hair, her lipstick smudged around her mouth. The guy gave me a curious look, but the girl blushed, rushing out of the foyer to the outside.

Once they were gone, Carter crooked a finger at me, a smirk playing across his lips as I walked over to him on shaking legs. Closing the door behind me, he locked it. "Idiots didn't even bother locking the door," he muttered with an eye-roll, presumably talking about the couple who had just left. Once he returned to me, he lifted my hand and pried the keys from my grip, tossing them on the desk at the side of the room, along with his mask. "You don't need those anymore."

Okay, then. Pulling my phone from my pocket, I placed it on the desk with my keys, then looked at him, unsure. He grinned at me, a sudden change, pulling a few paint-filled water balloons from his pockets, adding them to the items already on the table. I took him in. Standing there in front of me, his hair all mussed up and his body decorated with splats of paint, he suddenly looked playful. And that smile... his *smile*. It gave me full-on butterflies.

I licked my lips nervously, backing up against the desk, and he prowled towards me. "Now, where were we? Oh, yeah, you were going to tell me what you wanted." Planting his hands either side of me, much like he'd done in his bedroom the evening I'd been coerced into helping him with his essay, he leaned down so our faces were level. "Are you gonna tell me what you want, Rai?"

My eyes flew to his in shock. "Y-you called me Rai."

He pressed closer. "I did."

"What was all that about, earlier?" I finally gathered the courage to ask the question that I really, really needed an answer for.

"Anastasia." His face hardened, and I stared at him.

"What?"

"I can't say for sure, but I have my suspicions that she might have been behind the money theft."

"What?" was all I could repeat.

"Yeah. She...she didn't take it well when I left her, and I think she sees you as a threat." His eyes met mine, the gold flecks sparking. He licked his lips. "She's tried to scare off other girls I'm interested in already."

"You're interested in me?" I whispered shakily.

His eyes darkened, and he reached up, cupping the back of my head. "What do you think?"

Before I could even formulate a response, he closed the final bit of distance between us, and his lips came down on mine.

The kiss went from zero to a hundred in the space of about two seconds. Eventually I tore myself away, breathing shakily, my lips swollen. He stared at me, his eyes black, then lunged forwards again.

"Wait." With an effort, I held a hand up, pushing at his chest. A frown appeared on his face, and I rushed to continue. "I haven't forgiven you for the way you treated me." He tried to shut me up with a kiss, but I ducked away, fumbling behind me. My hand closed over the water balloon. "Show me your body."

"That's supposed to be a punishment, is it?" Without any hesitation, he pulled off his T-shirt in one swift movement, and my breath caught in my throat as I raked my gaze over his hard lines. "Like what you see?" A smirk tugged at his lips.

Before I could second-guess myself, I slammed the paint-filled balloon onto his chest. It burst on impact, spraying us both with bright blue paint.

His mouth fell open in shock, and I couldn't help the laughter that poured out of me, even as I was wiping the paint splats from my face. "Oh, you're going to pay for that," he warned in a dark tone, lunging for the remaining balloons. I scrambled for them, but he managed to grab one. Taking my T-shirt in his hand, he ripped it down the middle at the point I'd placed my strategic rip earlier and retaliated by marking me in the same place. I gasped as deep purple paint ran down over my breasts, soaking into the black fabric of my bra. It took me a moment to register that he'd ripped my top in half.

He stilled, tracking the paint as it trickled downwards with his hot, hungry gaze. I took advantage of his momentary distraction to reach up and slam the remaining paint bomb on top of his head.

The rich brown of his hair disappeared under the burst of lime-green paint that ran down the sides of his face and dripped to the floor. I grimaced, looking at the mess I'd made, torn between laughter and fear of his reaction. He stared at me, and then a tiny smile appeared on his lips. In one swift move, he picked me up and pushed me backwards on the desk, dragging his paint-covered head across my stomach and making my cry out with laughter.

Then his head went lower, and all laughter stopped.

"I want you, Raine." He raised his head to meet my eyes. "Will you let me touch you?"

He must've read the hesitation in my eyes, because he straightened up, pulling me upright. "I'm sorry for..." His hand scrubbed across his face, smearing paint everywhere. "Fuck. Sorry for everything. Does that cover it?"

Our eyes met, and unexpectedly, I saw a tiny hint of vulnerability in his gaze that completely threw me. Instead of replying, I wound my arms around his neck and pressed my lips to his. He growled, biting at my bottom lip and tugging me closer. Our paint-slicked torsos slipped against each other, and I laughed as he pulled away. He looked at me from under his lashes. "Fuck. Do you want to get out of here? Clean up a bit?"

I stared at him for a moment, then made up my mind. "My aunt's working an overnight shift."

He reached down, swiping his T-shirt from the floor and tugging it over my head. After picking up my keys and phone, he grabbed my hand, pulling me towards the door. "My truck's outside."

TWENTY-FIVE

RAINE

Carter had given me space. We'd showered all the paint off separately, and he'd told me to wait for him on my bed. Naked. Apprehension flooded me as I heard the shower turn off, and I huddled under the covers. What was he going to think of me? He was so experienced, and I was... the opposite. Should I even be doing this after everything? I growled with frustration, burrowing into my pillows, trying to silence the voices inside my head. Of course, he had to walk out of my bathroom at that point, rubbing his damp hair with a towel, his paint-splattered T-shirt covering his torso and his jeans slung low on his hips. For a moment I forgot everything, just drinking the sight of Carter Blackthorne, the football god and king of Alstone High, in *my* bedroom, looking at me like he wanted me.

He stopped at the foot of my bed and gently tugged at the sheets covering my body. "You don't have to hide from me."

Swallowing nervously, my cheeks hot, I closed my eyes and let him pull the sheets away from my body. There was complete silence in the room, and my breathing sounded loud in my ears.

"Open your eyes, Raine."

With a groan, I cracked one eye open.

"Look at what you do to me." He palmed his erection through his jeans, and I whimpered.

"Wh-why are you wearing clothes?" My voice came out much shakier than I wanted, and he smiled.

"Because I want to focus on you first."

Oh.

He settled himself over my body, supporting himself on his elbows, and stared down at me. "So fucking beautiful." I could barely get my head around the fact that Carter was seeing me naked—as dimly lit as the room was, he could see me clearly—and he'd just said I was beautiful? The person he'd called Plain Raine?

As if he could hear my thoughts, he lowered himself, positioning his head above my breasts. "There's nothing plain about you, is there, Raine?" With those soft words, he took my nipple into his mouth, sucking and flicking his tongue over it while his hand went to my other breast, teasing and caressing. My body's reaction was instantaneous. My nipples hardened, and I could feel the wetness between my thigh as he moved over my body.

Letting go of everything else, I silenced my thoughts, concentrating on the feel of his mouth and hands on my skin, sending shock waves through my whole body as he moved lower. I stiffened as he dipped below my belly button, his mouth dangerously close to the apex of my thighs.

"Don't worry, baby. I'll make it feel good." He spoke against my skin, pressing soft kisses just below my belly button. "Has anyone else ever done this to you?"

I shook my head, and he smiled, wide and satisfied. "Good. I like knowing I'm your first." He moved so suddenly I wasn't prepared, sliding back up my body so that his face was in front of mine. Gripping my jaw, he tilted my head to the side, then ran his teeth over the shell of my ear. "I haven't been able to stop thinking about Fright Night. The way you responded to me, how your little pussy gripped my fingers so fucking tightly."

A shiver ran through my body at his low rasp.

He dipped a hand between my legs, and I immediately stiffened. "I'm not gonna be rough with you tonight." Placing a reassuring kiss to the side of my face, he ran his finger through my wetness, rubbing over my clit.

"I like your roughness," I admitted, my voice the quietest whisper.

"I know you do. You have a dark side, don't you, my little trickster?" He kissed down my jaw and pulled my bottom lip between his teeth before releasing it. "Tonight, though, this is me making up for all the times I fucked up and showing you how much I want you."

My legs fell open as he pushed one finger inside me, then another, slowly moving them in and out. A soft moan escaped my lips.

"There. Does that feel good, baby?"

"Yes." I wrapped my arms around his strong body, going for the bottom of his T-shirt to lift it so I could feel his skin next to me.

"Not now. I might lose control, and I don't want to hurt you."

What could I even say to that?

He made his way back down my body, all the while keeping up the slow, lazy movements of his fingers pumping in and out of me, until I was gasping for breath. Pausing between my legs, his breath hot on my clit, he slid his fingers out and sucked them into his mouth. "You taste so fucking sweet." Lowering his head, he licked along the length of my soaked slit, and...*fuck*.

"Don't stop, don't stop," I moaned, my hands going to his head as his tongue delved inside me, his thumb going to my clit. "Oh fuck."

He hooked my leg over his shoulder, opening me up to him more, and he stroked his tongue across me again, sliding his finger back inside. He took my clit into his mouth, flicking his tongue over it, and at the same time added another finger, curling them inside me.

The combined sensations built inside me, until I shattered with the most blinding, breathless, full-body orgasm I'd ever experienced in my life. I couldn't think, couldn't breathe, my whole body shaking with the intensity.

"Fuck, Rai. You're so sexy when you come for me." I blinked, becoming aware of where I was again, and looking down to see Carter looking up at me, his autumn eyes sparking, his pupils dilated more than I'd ever seen them before. My wetness was all over his mouth and chin, and I was suddenly embarrassed.

"I-I..."

He silenced me by crawling up my body, slanting his lips over mine. When our mouths met, I tasted myself on his lips, and I kissed him harder, my hands running all over the muscles of his back.

"Carter." I broke away from him with an effort, and he stared down at me. I could feel his hardness between my legs, and my eyes lowered. "Should I...?"

His heavy-lidded gaze met mine. "Fuck... Do you want to?"

I really did. "Yes."

"I might..." His voice came out low and hoarse. "I might get rough with you. I'll try not to, but I can't make any promises." He brushed my hair off my face, running his fingers through the length of the strands. "Can you handle it if I do?"

I nodded, although I honestly wasn't sure. Could I handle someone like Carter? Experienced and powerful, with this darker side that he kept hidden?

The thing was, though? I liked that side of him.

"I want to do this." Sliding my hand down between us, I moved it to the bulge in his jeans and squeezed lightly. He groaned and lifted himself off me, moving to the edge of the bed and standing.

"Tell me if you want me to stop at any time, okay?" His eyes searched mine, waiting.

I nodded my assent, and then I made my way to the edge of the bed.

A blackness had come into his gaze, and I could see the monster that he kept leashed, pacing behind his eyes, ready to come out and play. "On the floor."

I should've been scared. I *was* scared. The kind of thrill of fear when you get to the top of a roller coaster, just waiting for the drop. My hands went to the top button of his jeans, and he swallowed thickly. With shaking hands, I unbuttoned his jeans, and then his hard cock was right in front of my face, straining against his boxers. There was a darker patch where his precum had already soaked through, and I ran my finger lightly over it. My sexual experience was limited to hand jobs, but I was going to attempt to do whatever I could to make it feel good for him.

"Stop teasing." His hands came down to grip my hair. I eased down his boxers and stared at his cock. This time we weren't in a dark classroom, and I drank him in. I'd always thought penises were ugly, but his was beautiful. Steel, veined, precum glistening at the tip, and as I wrapped my hands around it, the skin was so soft underneath my fingers, a complete contrast to the hardness underneath.

Dipping my head, I tentatively ran my tongue across the tip, tasting his salty flavour, and he let out a long, low groan. "More, baby." He pushed my head forwards, and I opened my mouth as wide as I could, taking the entire tip into my mouth. How did people fit the whole thing in? I dipped my head at the same time he pushed me forwards, taking more of him into my mouth, until he hit the back of my throat and I had to fight the sudden urge to gag. He let me pull my head back slightly, and I ran my tongue over his shaft, hoping that he was enjoying it.

I was suddenly pulled backwards and fell to the floor in shock. Wide-eyed, I stared up at him, as he looked down at me, breathing heavily. What had I done wrong? My stomach churned, and I cringed away from him.

"Fuck, Rai. Your...*fuck*. I was about to blow my load after five seconds of being in your hot little mouth."

"Why did you stop?" I frowned, confused.

"Because I need to fuck you." He reached down to the bottom of his T-shirt, pulling it off in one smooth movement, and stepped out of his boxers. Swiping his jeans from the floor, he tugged out a foil packet, then stood, right there in front of me, his hard body on full display.

Carter Blackthorne was the hottest guy I'd ever seen. Carter Blackthorne, naked? He was a god.

"Raine?" he prompted, after my open-mouthed, blatant perusal stretched on far too long.

"Wait. You want us to have sex?" My voice was shaky as his words finally registered with me.

He leaned down, pulling me to my feet and lifting me onto the bed. "Yes."

"Will it hurt?" I whispered. It didn't even occur to me to say no. He turned me on like no one else, and I wanted this. Wanted it beyond words. Wanted *him* to take my virginity.

"Yes." He didn't try to sugar-coat it, and I was grateful for that.

"Okay."

"Okay?" He studied me, his gaze searching. "Sure?"

I nodded and wrapped my arms around him. There was no doubt in my mind. "I want it to be you. I want you to be the one to do it."

"Raine." He spoke my name reverently and kissed me, his touch softer than it had ever been before. His hand went between my legs, stroking across my wetness as he kissed down my neck. He positioned himself between my legs, replacing his fingers with his hard cock. I stiffened. "It's okay," he assured me. "Relax." He rolled his hips, sliding his cock up and down, along my pussy, melting me with another kiss. My body responded, the space between my thighs growing slick with my arousal as he moved against me. "That's it, baby. Fuck, you feel so good. I can't wait to be inside you."

After ripping open the foil packet and rolling the condom on, he guided the head of his cock so it was positioned at my entrance. "Stay relaxed." Then he pushed inside me, his movements slow and careful. Even so, it hurt as his thickness stretched me. He stopped suddenly. "This is going to hurt," he hissed, then pushed forwards with a sudden movement. A sharp pain tore through me, and I cried out, tears filling my eyes.

"It hurts so much," I whimpered.

"I know." He stilled his movements, kissing me again,

telling me how good I felt, how beautiful I was, how well I was doing. Then he moved again, slowly, and I gasped with the pain.

"Concentrate on the feeling, baby. Your little pussy gripping my cock. It feels so good. Use the pain." He moved again, starting an achingly slow pace, his hand going back down between us as he pressed his thumb to my clit.

An unexpected spark of arousal shot through me, and I moaned softly. "That—that feels good."

"Yeah, it does." He smiled against my jaw, nipping at it as he worked his thumb over my clit, keeping up the same pace. "How you doing?"

"Good." The pain was still there, and I knew I'd be sore tomorrow, but as he touched me, the pleasure was coursing through my body, setting every nerve ending alight. Every single inch of me became aware. Aware of his weight pressing into me, the light sheen of sweat between our bodies, his breaths in my ear, and his hard, hard cock, inside me, filling me completely.

I never knew it would feel so good. I hooked my legs around him. "More," I whispered, pulling him closer. "I want more. Don't hold back."

Our eyes met.

His were black.

He let himself go.

He slammed into me with such force that I bounced, my head knocking into the padded headboard. Pleasure danced with pain, setting me on fire as his head came down to my neck, and his teeth clamped down on my skin as he thrust in and out of me with hard, savage movements. His fingers bit into my skin as he gripped me tightly, and I knew without a shadow of a doubt he'd leave bruises wherever he touched me.

I wanted to be marked by him.

"More." I moaned against him, digging my nails into him, touching him everywhere I could, the fast pace sending me spiralling closer to the edge.

Suddenly, he was pulling out of me and spinning me over. "Up," he commanded roughly, tugging at my hips. When I raised my hips in the air, he slid a pile of pillows beneath me, then lowered me back down. "This will feel good, and it'll be more comfortable for your first time." He placed a kiss to my shoulder, and unexpected butterflies fluttered in my stomach. Even though he'd said he would probably get rough with me, he was looking out for me.

The gentleness didn't last for long. He thrust back inside me, pounding into me, one arm on the bed and the other gripping my throat. As his fingers tightened, I gasped for breath, and he released his grip, bringing his hand round to tug on my hair and pulling my head backwards as he kept up his relentless pace. My hips were being pounded into the pillows, the friction against my clit so good, yet not quite enough, keeping me teetering on a knife edge.

"Fuckfuckfuck," he groaned, his movements becoming less controlled. Releasing his tight grip on my hair, he slid his hand under me, his fingers against my clit. It only took him a few, short movements, and then I was coming, pulsing around his hardness, gripping onto the sheets as I fell over the edge. My orgasm triggered his, and I felt his cock jerking inside me, spilling his release into the condom.

He collapsed on top of me, his bulk crushing me, our bodies sticking together. I couldn't catch my breath. Thankfully, he rolled off me almost straight away, making me wince as he pulled out of me.

"Are you okay?" He turned me to face him, brushing my

hair out of my eyes. The concern I saw in his eyes was unexpected, but it warmed me from the inside.

A huge smile spread across my face as I nodded. "I...I'm sore, but I feel good. Really good."

"You don't regret it, do you?" His hand continued to stroke through my hair.

"No. I'm glad it was you," I told him honestly. Throwing my arm over my face, I added, "I didn't think I would come, since it was my first time."

He let out a soft laugh at my mumbled confession, before he leaned over and kissed my forehead. "I knew you would."

Now it was my turn to laugh at his confident statement. Lowering my arm, I watched as he left the bed to dispose of the condom in the bathroom. When he returned, he had a damp washcloth that he used to carefully clean me up. "There's a bit of blood on your sheet."

"I'll change the sheets in a minute." As I stretched out, I sighed before smiling up at him. I was sore and tired, but happy. So happy.

He stood at the side of the bed, an unreadable expression on his face. "Okay. I guess I'll see you at school, then?"

My face fell. He was just going to leave? After he'd slept with me for the first time? Was I just a conquest to him?

"Stop overthinking." A frown appeared on his face, and he bit his lip. "I'll stay for a bit, if you want me to."

"Only if you want to." I stared at him from under my lashes, pathetically hoping he'd say yes.

He looked torn for a moment, warring with himself, before his eyes cleared. "Yeah. I want to." His voice was quiet but firm, as he repeated his words. "I want to. Come on, I'll help you change these sheets first."

Once we'd done that, we climbed back into my bed. He

didn't attempt to hold me or anything, but he lay on his side facing me, every now and then running his hand through my hair or down my arm as we talked. We were exchanging inconsequential information, but the fact he was staying and talking to me filled me with hope. Hope that maybe there could be something more between us, something real.

When I could no longer keep my eyes open, I felt a soft kiss on my head, and then he slipped away.

Hope was a dangerous thing, as I soon found out.

Everything had changed, but nothing had changed.

TWENTY-SIX

RAINE

Monday morning, I woke at 5:30 a.m., after a restless sleep plagued by nightmares where I was being chased through the halls of Alstone High by a masked figure, who turned into a clown when it caught me. Eventually I gave up on sleep and made my way downstairs, where I downed a huge mug of coffee, hoping it would at least wake me enough to allow my brain to function properly. By the time Lena picked me up, my caffeine high had faded and I was yawning again.

At school we split up so she could head to her locker, and I made my way to mine in a daze, not realising that the hall had gone silent until I was standing in front of my locker.

I suddenly became aware of people's stares prickling the back of my neck. Reaching up to the fingerprint sensor on my locker, I paused, my eyes flying upwards. I sucked in a shocked breath, staggering back against the wall, trying to take in the scene in front of me. Painted in savage black slashes, the word "slut" had been sprayed in capitals across my locker door. And taped right at the bottom was a printout of a photo. Slightly grainy, but clear.

Me, reclining backwards on the desk at the warehouse, covered in paint with my top ripped in half, exposing my bra, and Carter, with his head between my legs. Above the image someone had written in black marker pen "Football team slut scores again."

No.

My hands shaking, I ripped the photo down from my locker, crumpling it in my hand, and made a run for it. Straight into the library, where I hid myself in the furthest alcove and finally let my tears free.

I didn't know how much time passed, but eventually my tears stopped. Wiping under my swollen eyes, I breathed deeply in and out, trying to regain a semblance of calm. Then, I did probably the worst thing I could do. I opened my phone to the AHS gossip account.

My fears were proven correct. The image was there, too, plus another of me kissing Carter. The accompanying caption said:

> RAINE LAURENT HAS BEEN A BUSY GIRL. LOOKS LIKE THE FOOTBALL TEAM SLUT SCORED THE ULTIMATE PRIZE - THE TEAM CAPTAIN. SHE'S BEEN HARD UP FOR CASH SINCE HER UNCLE LEFT, SO THE QUESTION IS, HOW MUCH DID HE PAY HER?

I couldn't even bring myself to look at the comments. My stomach rolled with nausea, followed by outrage. As if Carter would ever need to pay anyone for anything sexual. Why was that my first thought? The second thing that crossed my mind was the fact that the room we were in had been locked. Which meant that someone had planned this. Had Carter planned it? But why would he implicate himself? He was always careful never to be seen with me around school. But who else would have a reason to do this? One thing I was sure about though—whoever was targeting me, and whatever reason they had, I knew it had to have something to do with Carter.

There was only one thing I could do. I needed to confront him.

I made my way through the silent hallways, back to my locker. Staring at the huge word "SLUT," I steeled myself, and then I opened the door. Inside, everything was untouched, which I was beyond grateful for. Now I just had to make it through the rest of the day, and I could escape. This was going to be painful, though.

The sound of heels on the floor alerted me that I wasn't alone. "Ah, Raine, there you are." I turned around to see Mrs. Rushton, school secretary, standing behind me with a folder clasped in her hands. "The headmaster would like to see you in his office, please."

My stomach sank. This had to be about my locker.

As I followed her in the direction of the office, I felt a prickling sensation down my spine. *Someone was watching me.*

When I turned around, there was no one there. The hallway was completely silent and empty.

Hurrying to catch up with Mrs. Rushton, I brushed it off as my wild imagination. After everything that had happened at the party, and my subsequent nightmares, it wasn't really a surprise that I was so jumpy.

Seated in a buttery-soft leather chair, I looked across the large mahogany desk at Professor Sharpe, attempting not to let my nerves show. The one and only time I'd been in the headmaster's office was after my uncle had divorced my aunt, and there was a question of how my remaining school fees would be paid. Thankfully my uncle had come through in the end, although he was going to be washing his hands of me once the school year ended, which meant relying on student loans for my university education. I still felt the sting of the betrayal, that he'd thrown a twenty-year marriage with my aunt away for an affair with his work colleague, and had moved in with her at the first possible opportunity. His new family was his priority now, and he'd essentially lost all sense of responsibility towards me. My aunt had been devastated, but lately, she seemed herself again. And I actually had Carter's parents to thank for that in part, because they'd been there for her while she picked up the pieces.

My thoughts returned to the present as Professor Sharpe cleared his throat, eyeing me carefully from behind his glasses. He was a tall, imposing figure, with grey, swept-back hair and a permanently severe expression on his face. Today, though, his eyes were full of sympathy as he looked at me. He cleared his throat. "Miss Laurent. I have been made aware of your...situation. Here at Alstone High, we have a zero-tolerance policy regarding bullying. Can you give me the name, or names, of anyone you believe may be behind this?"

I couldn't. Because I didn't know. And even if I did, giving him names would only make me more of a target.

There was no winning in this situation. "I-I'm sorry. I don't know."

A huff of disapproval came from his mouth before he cleared his throat again. "I see. Rest assured, your locker will be back to normal by lunchtime today. If you have any inkling of who may be involved, or if you have any other concerns, my door is always open. I will not allow my students to be harassed within these walls."

"Thank you, sir." I gave him a small smile, which I hoped was believable, although I had the feeling that it was more of a grimace.

He nodded, dismissing me. "That'll be all. See my secretary on the way out, and she will give you a slip to excuse you from your missed class."

As I made my way to my class, my stomach churned. Everything was spiralling out of control in my life, and it all led back to one person. Carter Blackthorne.

TWENTY-SEVEN

CARTER

Everything in my head was so fucked up. What I'd done with Raine, both at the party and afterwards, had been completely unplanned. That wasn't what was fucking with my head, though. Sex had always been about mutual pleasure, but there had *never* been a connection like the one I'd felt between me and Raine. And afterwards I'd had a sudden, instinctive need to take care of her. I wanted to stay with her, to make sure she was okay. That wasn't something I'd ever experienced before. If I was honest, the whole thing had left me shaken.

Fuck. Between my dad banging on about her all the time and making me resent her, all the shit that had happened so far today, and my now almost uncontrollable want for her, I was beyond confused.

"Carter?" I looked up from my tray of food, and there she was, clutching her books to her chest, biting her lip as she looked down at me. I felt everyone's stares flying between us both. The increasingly hostile looks Ana and her bitch posse were throwing at her, the football team's curious glances, Xavier's knowing expression, and the weight of the stares of the students at the surrounding tables. All of this registered in an instant.

The gossip about her was already rampant. She didn't deserve any of this. Who knew what other shit people would make up about her next, if I gave her my attention?

"What makes you think you have the right to talk to me?" I spoke without meeting her gaze, unable to look at her.

A pained hiss escaped her lips. "I-I just..."

"Whatever it is, I'm not interested." I affected a bored tone, rocking back in my seat and stretching my legs out in front of me.

"You think because you whored yourself out to him, you have the right to be here, at our table?" My fists clenched at the sneering question from Tina, one of Ana's friends. Fuck, I needed to punch something. "Listen up, hun. People like us don't mix with people like you. Now, why don't you run along to your little chess club, or wherever your people hang out?"

Raine's soft gasp fucking pierced straight through me, and I physically winced.

"Drama club," Anastasia muttered from next to me.

"Okay, fuck off to your little drama club." Tina tossed her hair over her shoulder and made a dismissive motion with her hand.

"Hey, I'm in the drama club," Xavier pointed out. He glanced in my direction, and I could feel the "what the fuck" look he was boring into the side of my head.

Tina huffed. "Whatever." She turned back to Raine. "Since you seem to like being on your knees... If you're still hard up for cash, I heard the school is looking for a new cleaner."

Everyone else remained silent, waiting to see what I was

going to do, ready to follow my lead. Raine remained frozen in place in front of me, and I raised my gaze to hers, finally. The pain and sadness in her hazel eyes almost caused me to falter. Almost. I couldn't let people know how much she meant to me. Fuck, *no*. She didn't mean anything to me. She couldn't.

I was only fooling myself.

The connection between us sparked to life, as she begged me with her eyes to acknowledge it, to tell her she wasn't alone in this, to back her up. I took a deep breath and made myself hold her gaze as I forced the words from my lips. "Go, Laurent. Whatever you have to say, I'm not interested."

She stared at me in shock for a moment, before I tore my gaze away, unable to look at her any longer. "You really are a heartless bastard, aren't you? Fuck you, Carter. And your friends." Her words were spoken with anger, but her voice trembled. *Fuck*. I didn't look as she spun on her heel and walked away.

"Harsh, mate," Xavier commented in a low voice, and I sighed. Yeah, it was really bloody harsh, but I'd been there this morning when she'd found her locker. She hadn't seen me, probably too in shock to be aware of anything much around her. But I'd seen that look of total devastation on her face, how she'd crumbled and fled. I'd been listening to the whispers about her all morning. I hoped she understood that I'd pushed her away to protect her. Despite my fucking confusion about my feelings towards her, I didn't want her to be hurt anymore because of me.

It was better this way.

What I needed to do was to get Anastasia to admit what she'd done and make her pay. I knew she was the one behind it, but I also knew her well. And she wouldn't admit it unless she stopped seeing Raine as a threat.

On that note, I stretched my arm out along her chair, and she leaned back with a smile. I suppressed the urge to remove my arm and instead pretended I was interested in her superficial chat, while my thoughts were miles away, with a hazel-eyed girl who'd rocked me to my fucking core.

TWENTY-EIGHT

CARTER

Kian's wide grin distracted me from my thoughts at football practice. Today was the first day he'd been allowed to start training with the team again, although he was still suspended from the matches for now.

"Want to come over to mine for the soccer game on Sunday?" Preston asked as we stretched out our hamstrings, warming up for training drills. "My parents are out of town."

Kian shot him a dirty look. "It's not fucking soccer, it's football!"

Preston grinned at him unrepentantly, and after a moment, Kian cracked a smile, too. "What am I going to do with you?" he muttered, shaking his head.

"Enough talking! Three laps around the field, then cone drills. Go!" Mr. Anders, our football coach, shouted before blowing his whistle, and we took off running.

"What's going on with you and Raine?" Kian was jogging next to me, front of the pack, setting the pace as we rounded the first corner of the field, the grass spongy and damp under our feet.

"Nothing," I barked out.

"Didn't look like nothing. You want her?"

I stumbled, then regained my footing. "Fuck, no."

"It didn't seem that way at the party. I could tell you were really into her. What was with you icing her out earlier?"

My stomach flipped. My feet kept moving on autopilot, but my whole body was tense. "What? It meant nothing. I'm not interested in her."

"Chill, mate. It's no big deal if you are." He increased his pace, and I matched him. "But if you're not...you don't mind if I ask her out, then?"

The memory of him chasing her at Fright Night flashed through my mind, and I saw red. "She's not yours!" I shouted, my words torn away in the wind, and then I leapt on him, my fist flying at his body. He reacted straight away, punching me in the ribs. We skidded across the wet grass, falling to the floor, pummelling each other. Arms pulled us apart, and I heard the sound of the coach's whistle.

"Kian! Carter! See me in my office right now! The rest of you, carry on doing drills!"

He stormed off to his office, and we followed him in. We both stood there, letting him rant and rave, his face red with fury. Eventually, he calmed down.

"Kian, you're already on thin ice as it is. I agreed to let you start training again, and this is what happens your first day back?"

"Sorry, Coach." He tried his best to sound contrite, but the thing about Kian? He really didn't care.

"Carter, I expect better from you. You're the team captain. You're supposed to be setting an example for the others."

"Sorry."

"Both of you, get out of my sight, and sort out whatever shit it is you're fighting about."

I headed back outside, dropping onto the bench next to the field, putting my head in my hands. Everything was unravelling. Between all the shit with Raine and my parents constantly on my case, my head was a fucking mess. The pressure was getting to me, and now I'd taken it out on one of my best mates.

"Here." I looked up to see Kian holding out a bottle of water.

"Thanks." I took it, and he dropped onto the bench next to me.

"Sorry, mate. I was just trying to wind you up. I didn't realise you liked her that much."

I looked over at him in shock. "I don't like her."

He snorted. "Yeah, sure, if you say so."

"I don't."

"Uh-huh."

"Fuck you."

He laughed. "Whatever. No hard feelings, yeah?" He held out his hand and stood.

"Yeah. Sorry. I didn't mean to jump on you like that. Today has been fucked up." I shook his hand, then unscrewed my water bottle. My head was so messed up. Fighting with Kian over Raine? *Fuck*.

Kian stared down at me, serious for a moment. "She seemed really upset earlier at lunch."

She was. I needed to make things right with her. Now. While she was in drama club and Ana wouldn't be around to see. The last thing I wanted was for her to have another reason to target Raine.

Before I knew it, I'd downed my water, and I was

jumping to my feet and striding towards the school building.

"Say hi to Raine for me!" Kian's mocking laugh came from behind me, and I threw up my middle finger as I walked. *Bastard.*

Back in the school building, I eased open the auditorium door, sliding inside the darkened room. Up on the stage, Xavier was somehow managing to make an ugly as fuck costume look like custom tailoring, owning the stage, as Imogen watched him longingly. They seriously needed to stop fucking around and sort their shit out.

Where was Raine? I scanned the room, but I couldn't see her.

Then, there she was. I spotted her over in the wings, peering out. Moving closer, I kept my gaze on her.

She disappeared off the side of the stage, and I turned, opening the side door that led to the fire exit and side entrance to the backstage area. Backstage, a few people were sitting around in costume, and they gave me curious looks as I stalked past them. I ignored them and entered the room where the props and costumes were kept. I found her hanging a costume on a rack. Her eyes were rimmed with red, and her mouth was downturned. *I'd* done that to her. How many times had she cried after I'd taunted her?

I was a fucking asshole.

"Raine," I breathed, and her head shot up, her eyes widening as she saw me standing there.

"No," she whispered, her lip trembling. "No."

Then she darted away, through the costumes. I almost laughed. Did she think she actually had any chance of getting away from me?

"You can run, but you can't hide," I called, following her into the racks. I heard footsteps over to my left and spun, striking as she attempted to run past me. Gripping her small body tightly, I wrapped my arms around her, holding her back to my front and moving her over to the table that stood at the end of the rack. She fought against me, but I held her easily. I wrapped my hand around her throat, squeezing lightly.

"Caught you."

"Fuck. You," she cried, still struggling, even though her eyes had darkened. As much as she didn't want to admit it to herself right now, she loved it when I had my hands on her like this.

"Raine. Stop fighting me." I stroked my fingers across her throat, and she whimpered, before clamping her mouth shut. "I want to say something important." Biting her earlobe gently, I felt her growl against me, her nails raking over my football shirt. I waited a minute, letting her take out her frustrations, because, fuck, it was the least I deserved, before turning her around and lifting her onto the table. "This is important," I reiterated when her eyes finally met mine.

"What is it?" Her voice was flat.

"I'm sorry." I kept my eyes on her.

"Sorry for what? You'll have to be more specific than that. There's a lot you have to be sorry for, Carter."

"I know." I brushed her hair away from her face, and she shivered, then frowned as if she was annoyed with her body's reaction to me. "I'm sorry for the way I've treated you since the beginning of the year. I know I already apologised for that, but I want to make sure you know that I mean it. But most of all, I'm sorry for earlier today."

"Oh." She stared at me, the crease still there between her brows. I reached out and smoothed it out.

"Don't ruin that beautiful face with a frown."

"You think I'm beautiful? You have a funny way of showing it."

"You know I do. I told you that when I was in your bed." My cock stirred as images of fucking her flashed through my brain. Her cheeks flushed, and I knew she was thinking the same thoughts as me.

"What was today all about, then? The way you treated me—there's no excuse for that. I've still got the bruises from where you marked me. A reminder of something that was special to me. You took my virginity, Carter, and today you humiliated me and acted like it meant nothing to you." The devastation in her eyes was unmistakable, and I stepped closer, leaning down slightly and kissing her soft lips. I couldn't help it any longer. It was like a compulsion. She put her hand to my chest, and I thought she was going to push me away, but instead, she pulled me closer. "Why are you so sexy when you're all hot and sweaty from football training?" she mumbled to herself. "It shouldn't be allowed."

I didn't reply, just kissed her harder, wrapping my arms around her body.

The sound of a door slamming somewhere outside the room had her pulling back suddenly and shoving at my chest. "No. This isn't happening. You can't distract me with your kisses." Her mouth set in a flat line, and she leaned backwards, further away from me, her eyes turning hard. "You didn't answer my question. What was today all about? In the cafeteria?"

"Rai..." I stepped back, running a hand through my hair, and decided on full honesty. "We can't be together. Not in public. Not yet. Maybe not even at all. I can't allow you to get caught up in these rumours." And I wasn't sure I could handle my parents' reaction to us being together. I didn't voice that part aloud, though. My jaw clenched, and then I made a tentative suggestion. "Maybe we could see each other in private, for now? No one has to know."

"Are you actually serious?" She gaped at me. "First of all, you were the one who started everything. If it hadn't been for you spreading the rumour in the first place, none of this would have happened. And second, I'm not going to be your dirty little secret. Either you're with me, properly, like a boyfriend, or you're not with me at all."

"That's—" I started, but she held up her hand.

"I'm not finished. This is long overdue. Do you know how you dismissing me earlier made me feel? How you hurt me every time you pretend like you don't have feelings for me in front of your friends? For so long, I felt unworthy. Less. But you know what?" Her voice grew louder as she jabbed her finger into my chest. "I'm. Not. Less. I'm just as fucking worthy as you. And I'm done placing my hopes on a boy who cares more about untrue rumours and reputations than the girl who's falling in—" She cut herself off, absolute fury and pain darkening her face, and she shoved me backwards with all her strength, jumping off the table and flying from the room, slamming the door behind her.

I was fucking stunned. Her words burned through me, shocking me to my core.

"You can be a real dick, sometimes." The soft voice came from the open doorway. I hadn't even noticed the door opening.

"You heard that?" I looked at Imogen's disapproving face, and she nodded. "I heard enough." She stepped closer. "Why would you care what people think?"

"It's not that," I insisted, shaking my head. "She's got it wrong. I'm trying to protect her." *And my head is so fucked up...* I shook my head again, trying to dislodge my thoughts.

She raised a brow, leaning against the wall with her arms folded. "Do you like her?"

I shrugged, and she glanced over at the open door, then moved away from me and pulled the door closed. "Do you want her?"

I shrugged again.

"How would you feel if she was with someone else?"

Jealousy lashed through me, and I gritted my teeth, my fists clenched.

"It's clear to me, and probably everyone else that saw you two kiss, that there's something more between you. You're Carter Blackthorne. King of the school. If you want her, then there's no one to stop you."

"What if I make everything worse or completely fuck things up? What if she becomes even more of a target? What if I lose everything?" The words spilled out of me before I could censor them.

"Forget those what-ifs for a minute. What if you gain something worth losing everything else for?" Her voice softened, and she reached out to touch my arm. "Is Raine worth the risk? Only you can decide that."

Raine had disappeared by the time I got outside. I guess it shouldn't have been surprising. I bet she'd got a lift home from that drama club kid. The thought filled me with unreasonable jealousy, and I gritted my teeth as I made my way to my truck.

When I was home, I reclined on my bed, staring at the

ceiling, trying to make sense of my thoughts, before I gave up and reached for my phone.

Me: Talk to me. PLEASE.

The indicator to say she'd read my message popped up almost straight away, but after ten minutes with no reply, I sent her another text.

Me: I'm sorry
Raine: You say you're sorry, but nothing changes. I've had enough. As far as I'm concerned, whatever this was between us is over. DONE.
Me: Can we talk about this?

She never replied. And later that evening, when I couldn't stand it any longer and sneaked over to her house to climb through her window, it was locked, and despite my knocks to the glass, her bedroom remained dark.

TWENTY-NINE

RAINE

The shame that burned through me every time I thought of how Carter had completely humiliated me in front of everyone in the cafeteria eventually began to lessen, replaced by anger at the way I'd been treated, and finally settled into a kind of numbness. Every day, it became a little easier to breathe as the gossip died away and Carter avoided me. The Christmas break had given me some clarity and some space to step back and reflect. When I looked back on everything, it had been naive of me to expect that just because I'd given him my virginity and we'd spent the night talking about anything and everything, things would change. I wouldn't give him the chance to hurt me again. Now, I was staying as far away from Carter Blackthorne as I could. I couldn't fool my heart into believing that he didn't mean anything to me, though. That was impossible.

Walking into school on the first day back after the Christmas break, my eyes went straight to Carter. He was at the top of the steps, flanked by Kian and Xavier, scanning the school grounds with an air of superiority. His eyes met mine, sadness flickering in them before he masked his expression, and I took a deep breath, dragging my gaze away from his. Holding my head high, I walked past as if he wasn't even there. He didn't say a word to me, and why would he? The one boy I wanted, and he didn't think I was good enough for him.

Lena squeezed my arm reassuringly as we headed inside. "I'm proud of you. You're doing great."

I returned her smile. I was doing great because I'd managed to perfect my mask and hide how broken I was inside. She'd told me to fake it until it became real, but I was starting to wonder if that would ever happen while I was a student at AHS. I just had to get through the rest of the school year, and then I could get out of here. Out of Alstone and make a fresh start in a new place where no one knew me or had any preconceived ideas about me.

At lunchtime, I went to find Dylan, holding the envelope I'd been carrying around all morning. Eventually I found him in the computer lab, headphones on, engrossed in whatever he was doing on the keyboard. I debated whether to disturb him, but as I drew closer, his head shot up and a smile crossed his face.

Tugging off his headphones, he indicated towards the free seat next to him, and I sank into it, handing him the envelope.

"What's this?" He eyed it curiously, sliding his finger under the seal to open it. "Money?"

I nodded, smiling. "All four hundred and twenty pounds. I told you I'd pay you back."

"You didn't do anything illegal to get this, did you?"

We both laughed, and I explained. "It was actually Lena who came up with the idea. I designed and created an outfit for her cousin to wear at a winter ball, and she paid me for it. I couldn't believe it." She'd actually paid me four hundred and seventy-five pounds, and once I'd managed to get over the shock that someone was willing to pay that much for something I'd made, I felt a real sense of pride. That someone actually thought that an outfit I'd created was worth something. It had opened up new possibilities that I'd never dared to hope for before. I'd been a little out of pocket once I'd set aside the money for Dylan and factored in the cost of materials, but the promise of more dress design opportunities coming my way had more than made up for that.

"I'm not surprised. You're talented, Raine." Dylan grinned. "Now, since we're celebrating..." He trailed off and paused, swallowing hard. "Are-are you free after school? Or another day?"

"Why?" I asked warily, noting the nervous, hopeful look on his face.

"I thought we could maybe go bowling. At the pier. Or something else, if you don't like that?"

I noted the way he was chewing his lip. "Do you mean like a date?" He nodded, and my mouth twisted. I hesitated for a moment. Why couldn't I be attracted to someone like him? Uncomplicated, sweet, and unassuming, and even better, not part of the popular crowd. But I couldn't lead him on like that. It wasn't fair to him. "Uh...I like you, Dylan. *As a friend*," I emphasised.

"The words that no guy wants to hear when he asks a girl out. Is this to do with Carter?" He couldn't disguise the mixture of disappointment and bitterness in his tone.

I sighed. "No, it's nothing to do with Carter." That was a lie. It was, partly. But there was also the fact that I wasn't attracted to Dylan, not even a tiny bit. "It's just me. I..." I threw up my hands awkwardly. How was I supposed to let him down gently? I'd never been in this situation before.

His face dropped, and he turned back to his computer screen. "Say no more. I get it."

"I'm really sorry. Please don't be mad at me."

"I'm not mad. I'm...disappointed, I guess." Turning to meet my eyes, his voice softened. "It's not your fault. I'm not mad at you, I promise."

"Good." My body relaxed as the tension drained from me. "You're going to make an amazing boyfriend for some lucky girl, one day."

He gave me a wry smile. "I know. Maybe you'll stop being immune to my charms one day, too." We both laughed, although I couldn't tell if he was joking or not. I knew I'd hurt him by turning him down, no matter how unintentionally.

"Well...uh...I haven't eaten yet, so I'm going to go." I slipped out of the seat. "We're still okay, right?" I needed to make sure.

"We're still okay. And I'm still giving you a lift home after drama club." He tapped at his keyboard, and I took that as my cue to leave, after a whispered, "thanks" that he didn't acknowledge.

If only we could choose who we fell for. Life would be so much easier.

After school I'd ridden my bike down to the pier. There was a restlessness within me that I couldn't escape, no matter how hard I tried. I was hoping that the peacefulness of the beach would sort me out. Stretching out on one of the large flat rocks, my back against the sea wall, I watched the gulls circling overhead. Snapping a quick photo of the birds silhouetted against the darkening sky, I uploaded it to my social media account before sitting back again, breathing in the salty, fresh tang of the sea air. My eyes closed.

"Hi!" The loud croak had my eyes flying open, to see a large bird with shiny black feathers regarding me with one beady eye.

"Did-did you just talk?"

The bird hopped closer. "Hi!" This time there was no mistaking it. A smile spread across my face as I studied the raven. At least, I thought it was a raven. My bird knowledge was pretty much non-existent.

"You can talk. That's amazing," I breathed. *Why am I talking to a bird?*

A clicking noise came from close to me, and I spun my head to see a woman in a long black coat picking her way across the mixture of sand and pebbles towards me. Her dark curls tumbled wildly around her face, and she eyed me with a serene expression, as if she'd expected to find me right here on this quiet stretch of beach in the middle of winter. She clicked her tongue again, and the raven flew from the rock, landing on her shoulder where it cocked its head, still looking at me.

"It's you." My words came out softly, and the fortune teller nodded as she lowered herself to sit on the rock next to mine. "Aunt Marie? Marie?"

She nodded again. "Either."

Suddenly, I wanted to know all the answers. "That riddle...was that real? Or was it just a made-up thing?"

Her stare...it was like she could see right through me again. She remained silent, and the words just kept coming out. "I messed up." I sighed, kicking at a pebble. "Well, it wasn't just me. Everything went wrong."

"The gain will not come without a cost. Can you hold on when hope is lost?" She repeated part of the original riddle that she'd given me back on Fright Night.

"What is that supposed to mean? Help me out, here. Please."

The raven croaked. "Help!"

I glared at it, and it raised its head in a way that managed to be both disdainful and judgy at the same time.

Marie's eyes glazed over, and she touched a hand to my arm. "Both light and darkness lie ahead. Your path is shrouded with hidden dread. The question that you need to ask... What is hidden beneath his mask?"

She broke out of her trance, adding with a whisper, "Find out...before it is too late."

A shiver ran through me as the sun dropped below the horizon.

With her words echoing in my ears, she rose to her feet and disappeared into the distance, leaving me trembling, and not from the cold.

I rubbed my hand across my face, bringing my knees up and hugging them to my chest. Had that actually happened? The entire thing had felt like a dream. A creepy dream, if I thought about it.

Anyone who lives by the coast, or in the UK for that matter, knows just how quickly the weather can change. Lost in my own thoughts, I didn't notice the storm clouds rolling in. One minute I was surrounded by clear dark skies, the next, angry clouds were growling at me, and then the heavens opened.

Heavy drops hit my face as I struggled to do up my raincoat and get the hood over my head. My hands and nose were already turning numb as I made a run for my bike and unlocked it. I was resigned to getting soaked, but at least I could have a bath and hot chocolate when I was home.

Peddling as quickly as I could, I wobbled slightly on the bike, my lights weak in the driving rain, as I turned onto the large road that would lead towards the area I lived in. The one bonus was that the streets were quiet, since it was a weeknight.

I'd just swerved around a puddle when I heard the sound of a car coming up fast behind me, and I instinctively wrenched my handlebars towards the side of the road, hugging the grass verge. The car flew past me in a spray of dirty water, soaking me from head to toe.

I gasped at the shock as the first spray of water hit me, sending rainwater into my mouth. Wobbling off the road, I came to a stop on the grass verge, spitting the liquid out and recoiling at the taste on my tongue.

As I was about to start pedalling again, I heard the sound of another car coming from the opposite direction and steeled myself for another shock of icy water, hunching my body over instinctively. How much bad luck could I have this evening?

The car slowed, and headlights swung across my body, illuminating me in all my dripping glory.

"Are you okay?" a voice called over the driving rain.

My streak of bad luck wasn't over, then. Was I about to be kidnapped and taken away? Various scenarios ran through my mind, each sending me more and more hysterical. My imagination was running wild at this point, no thanks to Aunt Marie's mysterious riddle, and being out here, soaked through and helpless, had me almost paralysed with fear.

"Hey!" the voice called again, and I slowly turned,

wiping the rain from my eyes. Something even worse than kidnappers or killer clowns faced me.

Xavier Wright and Carter Blackthorne.

Kill me now.

"*Raine?*" Xavier's voice was shocked. "Shit, didn't realise it was you we sprayed water all over."

I couldn't find my voice.

"Raine. Get in the car." Carter's low, commanding tone easily reached my ears.

"No." I shook my head, sending raindrops flying everywhere.

"We can't leave her. She's soaked and shivering." Carter was speaking to Xavier.

"I know, mate, but what do you want me to do? Force her to get inside?"

While they were debating, I decided to get out of there. It wasn't like I could get any more soaked, and I couldn't bring myself to be near Carter. Not now. Not when my head was spinning still from Aunt Marie's riddle. And of course, there was my whole plan to avoid him. With that thought in mind, I steered my bike back onto the road and pedalled as hard as I could.

I'd just reached the cut through to my house, where there was a footpath and cycle path running alongside a small stream, when I heard a car again. I pedalled harder, hoping with everything I had it wasn't Carter and Xavier.

"Raine!" I heard my name called with a shout, and that spurred me on even faster. My muscles were burning and I couldn't catch my breath, but I had to make it to the cut through, where the car wouldn't be able to follow me.

"Stop!" I was suddenly in the grip of a large body, flailing around, fighting to get away. I screamed, and a hand immediately clamped over my mouth.

"Your girl's got some fight in her." I heard Xavier's chuckle next to my ear.

"She's not mine," came the reply. Carter's voice held a note of sadness, or maybe I'd just imagined it.

"You gonna stop struggling, Raine?" Xavier's attention returned to me.

"No," I hissed, and he sighed.

"Raine. I'm not leaving you here, so you may as well get in the car instead of wasting both of our time."

"Fine." A frustrated huff escaped me.

"Good girl," he praised. "Wait there a minute. I'm gonna grab a blanket from the boot. Can't have you dripping all over my seats."

Of course not. "I'm fine. Home isn't far from here."

He looked down at me, his face shadowed by his hood.

"It's my fault you got soaked." He shrugged, opening the boot and grabbing a blanket, which he laid over the back seat. "Just get in the car, would you, before we're both drenched?"

Deciding to cut my losses, I slid into the car without another word. The sudden warmth hit me, and I realised how cold I was, shivering, my teeth chattering.

"Fucking hell, Raine." Carter's voice sounded again. "Why do you have to be so stubborn?"

"I-I d-didn't ask for you to give me a lift," I managed to get out through my chattering teeth, then turned my gaze away from him, staring at the rain driving against the window. Shrugging off my wet coat, I leaned back against the seat.

"Stubborn," he said again. As I closed my eyes with a sigh, I heard the car doors slamming, and then the space next to me was filled with Carter's larger-than-life presence.

I inched further away from him, right up against the car door.

Xavier slid into the driver's seat and started the engine. "Your bike's on the back."

"Thanks," I whispered tiredly as another cold shiver racked my body. Suddenly, I was being grabbed and tugged against a warm, strong chest, arms holding me tightly.

"Raine." Carter's voice was a soft caress. He stroked down my back, then brushed my wet hair out of my face, uncaring that I was dripping rainwater everywhere. "I've got you." Placing a kiss on my head, he continued his soothing movements until I stopped shivering and gave in to the inevitable, letting my body relax against his, soaking up his warmth. Even though I knew I shouldn't.

I kept my eyes closed for the entire duration of the car journey, taking this tiny, stolen moment where I could pretend that Carter was mine.

THIRTY

CARTER

Everywhere I looked, she was there. No one else held my interest. In the halls at school, in my classes, every-fucking-where. She starred in my dreams, taunting me with thoughts of something I couldn't have. I couldn't concentrate on anything but her. Everything I did to push her out of my mind was a complete and utter failure. After I'd held Raine in my arms in Xavier's car, I thought that maybe things would change, but I was wrong. True to her word, she'd stayed far away from me, acting like I didn't exist. It was clear to me that she'd given up on any idea of us, and I knew it was my own fucking fault. Anastasia wouldn't admit to anything, so the whole point of me staying away had been a failure, and I'd had to deal with Ana getting her hopes up again and then me letting her down. She could join the queue. I was letting everyone down. My head was fucked. My grades were slipping again, and the disappointment of my parents weighed heavily on me.

Everything fucking sucked. Kian and Xavier wouldn't

get off my back, telling me I was moping around like a fucking girl.

The truth? I missed Raine.

"You look like shit." Kian threw his bag into the seat next to me.

"Thanks."

He shrugged. "Just telling it like it is."

We fell silent as our Business Studies class began, but I couldn't help my mind wandering to Raine. As the teacher started up a PowerPoint presentation, I pulled out my phone, half hiding it under my textbook. Before I knew it, I'd navigated to my message thread with her, and I typed three words that I'd never written before. Not to anyone, not even my ex-girlfriend.

Me: I miss you

Five minutes later, I got a reply. Not the reply I was hoping for.

Raine: I'm not sneaking around with you
Me: Can't we just keep it quiet for now? The pressure will be insane
Raine: No

I growled under my breath. Why did everything have to be so fucking complicated?

Me: Let me explain
Raine: You don't have to explain anything. I know you think I'm not good enough for your group of friends and your precious image

Me: It's not like that. I was talking about my parents and the fact you might become a target again. I saw how upset you were, baby

Raine: First. What do your parents have to do with it? Second. It's MY decision about whether I become a target. Third. DON'T CALL ME BABY. YOU DON'T HAVE THE RIGHT

Kian glanced over at me, and I shielded my phone with my hand. "Do you mind, mate? I'm trying to have a private conversation."

He smirked at me, then shrugged before pulling out his own phone. "If you can't beat 'em, join 'em."

I returned my attention to Raine. Fuck, what was I supposed to say?

Me: Parents. I'm under a lot of pressure. They constantly compare me to you. ALL the fucking time

Raine: That makes no sense

Me: You have to be aware of this. I've told you before and I know you've seen it for yourself. In their eyes you're perfect. Perfect grades. Can do nothing wrong. It's all Raine this, Raine that, why can't you be more like Rainey? E.g. Last night my dad was telling me how proud he was that you were up for a model student award yet when I get awards for football he dismisses them as frivolous. You should be fucking proud BTW. That's just an example

Raine: I didn't know the extent of it. I'm sorry.

That's not right. They're your parents, they should support you

Me: Now you know. Another reason why you and me would never work

Raine: That makes no sense. And if we would never work why are you texting me now?

I put everything I was feeling into my reply.

Me: Don't you see? If you were my girlfriend they'd have even more interest in you and your life. I'd be constantly compared to you, even more than I am now. At least now you're just my neighbour and I know this shit has an expiry date because you're not sticking around once school finishes and you leave for uni

Me: You want to run away. I get it. I'd run away too if I had a choice. If I hadn't worked so fucking hard to get to where I was. If I wasn't going on to Alstone College next year

Me: And the reason I'm texting you is because I fucking miss you

Raine: Would you run away with me?

Would I? For a minute, I allowed myself to think of a different future, where Raine and I were together. A future that wasn't a possibility.

And that was the final nail in the coffin, right there. I could only offer her something temporary, where we'd sneak around and only have stolen moments. She deserved better than that. Better than me.

Raine: Since you're taking forever to reply I'll take that as a no. I'm moving away once the school year is up and you have all these issues surrounding me, so I think it's best if we stay out of each other's way. I'll try to avoid coming over to your house with my aunt. There's plenty of excuses I could come up with.

Me: Fine. You're right. I shouldn't have texted you. I'm sorry. For how everything turned out

Raine: Me too. Goodbye Carter. Please don't contact me again

Covered by my waterproof jacket, I jogged around the school building to head for the car park, when I stopped in my tracks. Raine was huddled on the steps, a bag clutched in her arms, sheltering from the rain and watching the road with anxiety all over her face.

I stood, not even noticing the rain as I watched her try calling someone, then hanging up with a resigned look on her face. She started down the steps, flinching as the rain hit her, then darted backwards under cover again. She was pulling off her coat. What the fuck? I watched as she covered the bag with her coat and hoisted her backpack onto her shoulders, then stepped out into the rain.

Fucking hell, Raine. Her school blazer wasn't even waterproof. Did she want to catch hypothermia?

"Raine!" I shouted. She didn't turn around.

I ran towards her, skidding across the wet tarmac as I reached her. Throwing my body in front of hers, I forced her to a stop.

"Go away." Her voice was expressionless, and she didn't

even look at me, shivering in the rain, the water plastering her hair to her head.

"Raine. It's fucking raining. Let me take you home."

"No." Her little chin set stubbornly. "We agreed we'd stay away from each other, remember?"

"Fuck, Raine." I scrubbed my hand across my face. "What will it take for you to get in the car with me?"

"A personality transplant," she muttered, then stepped around me, splashing through the puddles as she stormed off down the road.

I don't think so.

I easily caught up with her, tugging on her backpack and spinning her around to face me. "Hold on." That was the only warning I gave her before I scooped her up, bag and all, and began carrying her towards my truck.

"Stop manhandling me!" She couldn't fight back since her arms were full with her huge backpack and her coat, so I ignored her ranting until we reached my truck. Putting her down, I held her in place with one hand while I juggled with my car keys, finally managing to press the button to unlock the boot.

"Why are you doing this? You're just making things harder for us both." She raised her eyes to mine, the rainwater glistening on her lashes. No make-up, she was fucking beautiful.

I didn't have an answer, so I kissed her instead.

She shoved at my chest with her bag, refusing to kiss me back. I teased at her lips with soft licks and caresses, and *finally*, she gave in with a sigh. The feel of her lips against mine—*fuck.*

Raine was made for me.

The sound of a car horn, blasting long and loud, had her tearing her mouth away and ducking around my body. I could only watch as she made a run for a huge matte-black SUV, disappearing inside before I could even catch my breath.

I didn't go straight home. I drove around aimlessly for a while, barely paying attention as the rain slowed and eventually stopped, the sun coming out from behind the clouds.

As I neared my house, I slowed my truck to a crawl and sucked in a breath as I rounded the corner onto Raine's road. *What the fuck?* Cassius Drummond's car was parked outside Raine's house. Something that felt a lot like jealousy stabbed at my gut as I passed his SUV at a snail's pace. There was no one inside, which meant Cassius was inside her house. Where he must've been since he picked her up from school.

How the fuck could I compete with Cassius Drummond?

Wait, why was I even thinking this? I didn't want or need to compete with him. A relationship between me and Raine wasn't going to happen. It didn't matter who she was spending her time with.

Even as I told myself this, I knew it was a lie.

The notification lit up my screen, and I swiped so fast that my finger was a blur. Raine had posted a new picture. And yeah, I'd changed my settings so it would notify me whenever she posted.

The image loaded, and I gritted my teeth, rage boiling through me.

Now. Now I was *really* fucking jealous.

I swiped my car keys from my desk and ran for the garage.

THIRTY-ONE

RAINE

"It's surprisingly easy to talk to you." I smiled up at Cassius as we walked along the seafront pier, gulls circling overhead, and he returned my smile with a wink. I wasn't used to feeling so comfortable around people, yet with him, I did. I'd unloaded all my confused feelings on him, and he'd listened without judgement. I was still confused, but I felt lighter. And the one thing I knew for sure was that my feelings for Carter hadn't gone away. Not even slightly. After he'd kissed me, I knew I'd just been lying to myself. The question was, what was I going to do about it? Should I even do anything about it?

Being around the Drummond siblings had made me realise that I didn't want to live my life with regrets, so I was going to give Carter one last push. Hence the reason for me arranging to meet up with Cassius today. Not just to get a guy's point of view on the whole situation, but to get his advice on what to do.

Cassius threw one of his chips in the air, out towards the sea, and laughed as gulls swooped for it, fighting for a piece. The winner made a break for it, hotly pursued by three others. I pointed out the large sign attached to the pier railings. "Did you notice the 'do not feed the seagulls' sign over there?"

He laughed again as he threw another chip. "I choose to interpret the sign as a guideline rather than a rule."

Rolling my eyes, I punched him playfully, and he grinned. I watched as the gulls circled closer, eyeing his almost empty bag of chips. "It would serve you right if they took that bag out of your hand."

"They wouldn't dare." He shoved the last couple of chips into his mouth, then wadded up the bag and threw it in one of the bins that were spaced out at regular intervals along the pier.

Tucking a strand of my windswept hair behind my ear, I turned to him. "Being serious for a minute, thanks for the advice."

"Anytime, babe. I don't know much about relationships, but I do know a lot about how men think. Since I am one and all." We stopped at the end of the pier and stood at the railing, and he sighed. "Men are stubborn bastards. One of my best mates, Cade—he was really into a girl, but he couldn't admit it to anyone. Not even to himself. Even though it was really fucking obvious. To me, at least."

"What happened? I stared out to sea, towards Chaceley Rock and the old, abandoned lighthouse there. I could just about make out the small patches of snow that hadn't been washed away by the earlier rain.

"I came up with a plan that involved making him jealous enough to snap. Two plans, actually. I kissed the girl he was into...twice. First time was at a party at our house, and he was being a complete dick and was all over another girl, even though it was clear he wanted Winter. That's the name of the girl he liked. Second time, because he was still being a stubborn dickhead, I roped in our two other best mates, and two of us took turns kissing her, knowing he'd react."

"*That* was the idea you came up with?" I eyed him sceptically. Suddenly I wasn't so sure about taking his advice. "And that worked? It doesn't really seem like a great plan to me. I don't want to kiss anyone else."

"I wasn't suggesting you should do it. I was just making a point." He gave me a grin that looked kind of devious, and I was suddenly nervous. "This situation was different. And okay, maybe I had my own reasons for doing what I did. But it wouldn't hurt to show Carter what he's missing, would it?"

"What are you suggesting?" I asked slowly.

"Give me your phone." Hesitating for a moment, I stood there, just looking at him, and his gaze softened. "Trust me." Releasing a heavy breath, I handed it to him. "Okay, turn around and lean back against the railings." He put his arm around me, dipping down so his face was close to mine.

"You're not going to kiss me, are you?"

He laughed loudly. "Don't sound so horrified. Do you know how many girls want to kiss me? Men, too, for that matter."

"Oh, I've heard all about your popularity from Lena. Sounds like nothing's changed since you were at school." Finally relaxing, I laughed, too, and he gave me a huge grin as he snapped a photo.

"There. Post that. Natural smiles look better. I can always tell when people are faking, and we want him to think you're moving on without him. Make him wonder if there's anything going on between you and me."

I stared at the photo. It did look pretty good. Our heads were close together, and Cassius had his arms slung casually around me as we looked at each other with huge smiles. The winter sun was setting behind us, giving the photo a soft orange glow, and our faces were shadowed, but you could easily see we were both smiling. Chaceley Rock was silhouetted on the horizon, just visible behind Cassius' shoulder, and the sea sparkled where the rays touched it. The photo could mean everything or nothing—it was completely open to interpretation.

"This is a really nice photo."

"I know. Post it, then I'll post this at the same time, to prove I was there." He snapped a selfie of his face with his own phone, an easy grin on his lips. I envied his casual, carefree attitude. Both he and Lena were so assured, so confident.

I posted the photo with the caption "sunset" and tagged Cassius, then turned my phone off so I wasn't tempted to look at the notifications.

"Thanks for helping out." We started walking back down the pier.

"That's what friends are for. Anytime you need a favour, tell me."

We reached the end of the pier, where Lena was waiting for us. Cassius gave her a quick hug, and she smiled at him. Even though she'd recently dyed her hair a pastel pink, there was no mistaking the fact that they were siblings. Both tall and gorgeous, with almost identical smiles, it was easy to see why they attracted attention whenever they were together. Lena turned to me, surprising me with a quick hug, too. "Everything okay, now?"

Smiling, I nodded. "I think so, yeah. Or at least, everything feels less confused in my head. Your brother's a good listener. Both of you are, in fact." Turning to Cassius, I met his eyes. "Thanks for taking the time to do this."

"I did have an ulterior motive. It was the excuse I needed to get everyone here so I could kick their asses at bowling." He waved his hand towards the bowling alley that stood at the end of the pier, on the seafront. "You wanna join us?"

Hanging out with Cassius and Lena was one thing, but with their friends there as well? I shook my head. "Thanks, but no thanks. I need to get back and make a start on my homework, plus I have to send some design sketches to a client." *Client.* I actually had people who were willing to pay for my designs—it hadn't been a one-off. Of course, it was all very sporadic at the moment, with my schoolwork taking priority, but it gave me hope for the future.

"Okay. Lemme get your bike from my car." Cassius jogged away before I could reply, and I sat next to Lena on one of the wooden benches at the bottom of the pier.

"How can I repay you for all this? You've made my life so much better since you came into it." I glanced over at her, and she grinned.

"You have nothing to repay me for. That's what friends are for." She pushed a strand of hair behind her ear. "Are you sure you don't want to join us?"

"I'm sure." It wasn't that I didn't want to, but meeting Cassius' college friends? All of whom were part of the most powerful families in Alstone? I wasn't quite ready for that. That was so far out of my comfort zone.

Cassius returned with my bike, and I took it from him, swinging my leg over the saddle.

As I waved goodbye and started pedalling away, I heard someone shouting Cassius' name in a commanding tone. Curious, I stopped pedalling and turned to see a guy in a leather jacket with messy black hair and a brooding look on his face stalking in the direction of the bowling alley.

Caiden Cavendish. My heart rate kicked up a notch—no doubt about it, he was absolutely gorgeous, even more so than when he'd attended AHS, but to me, he came across as completely intimidating. As I watched him, I saw him suddenly stop dead as another shout came from behind him. His face completely transformed with a huge grin, as a beautiful dark-haired girl ducked under his arm and he pulled her into him. She stared up at him with an adoring smile, and he leaned down to kiss the top of her head before they both made their way over to Cassius and Lena with matching smiles on their faces.

As I pedalled away, it suddenly clicked with me. The girl with him was Winter—the one Cassius had kissed. Well, I guess it had worked. They looked as if they were both completely smitten with each other. A sudden pang of longing hit me. I wanted this. Wanted to be with someone who wasn't afraid to be seen with me. Someone that was as interested in me as I was in them.

The hard, desperate way Carter had kissed me showed me he still had feelings for me, but would that be enough? Was I enough for him? Would the photo push him to take action? Would he still find reasons to push me away? I had so many questions, but what I did know was that if he wanted something, I wasn't going to settle. If he wanted me, he was the one that needed to make the decision to be with me properly.

The ball was in his court, now.

THIRTY-TWO

CARTER

What the fuck was I doing here? Pulling up at the pier car park, which was quiet thanks to the time of year and the fact it was a weeknight, I easily spotted Cassius Drummond's huge SUV next to a matte-black Audi R8. Parking at the opposite end of the car park, I slid from my truck, palming my keys. My head was fucked. Raine's words kept echoing through my mind, and that picture of her with Cassius that she'd posted... *Fuck.*

Because I was quite clearly a sadist, I opened up the social media again, staring at the photo. She looked so happy. Anyone could see how genuine her smile was. They looked like a proper couple, staring into each other's eyes with the sunset behind them. I sucked in a harsh breath. It hurt to see her happiness and know that it was caused by another man.

She had hundreds of likes. And the comments... I wish I'd never looked. Both at the comments that congratulated her, saying what a great couple they made, and even worse, the comments that implied Cassius was too good for her. He'd be fucking lucky to have her.

I'd be fucking lucky to have her.

What was I doing?

I wanted Raine Laurent.

I wanted her to be mine.

The revelation seared straight through me, and I knew I had to get out of there. I couldn't stomach seeing her with him in person. Not now. Not ever.

The next morning, the revelation still burned through me. Confusion, anger, and jealousy had warred within me all night, leaving me unable to sleep. I'd driven around aimlessly for hours when it was clear my head was too fucked up to think straight. Then as soon as I was home, the same thoughts were still running rampant in my head. Hence the lack of sleep.

The school day passed in a blur. To make things worse, Raine's name was on everyone's lips again, after someone had posted the picture of her and Cassius on the AHS gossip account. This time, though, it was more...envious. Envy that someone like her had managed to attract the attention of Cassius Drummond. Every time I heard someone make a malicious comment, I had to bite my tongue, and by the end of the day, I was wound up so tightly, I needed to work out my frustrations or I was going to snap.

Instead of going to my final class, I headed to the gym so I could lose myself in the mindless routine of weight training, before I met up with the rest of the football team for our additional training session.

The gym didn't help. All it did was give me a pounding

headache. We had a massive game the following week against Highnam Academy, and I had to use every opportunity to practice, but I couldn't seem to focus during training.

"What the fuck is wrong with you?" Kian hissed, after I'd let myself get taken down by a slide tackle I should've seen coming a mile off. "This game is gonna be our make-or-break game, not to mention it's the first one I'm allowed to play in since my suspension. You're the captain—get your shit together."

"I know." I scrubbed a hand down my face, defeated.

The coach blew his whistle for a break, and we jogged over to the side of the pitch, grabbing our bottles of water.

"Do you want me to set up a fight?" Kian asked in a low tone, after looking around him to make sure no one was paying us any attention.

"Yeah. Or...fuck, I don't know. My head's fucked up right now," I muttered.

He studied me closely, pulling his lip ring between his teeth. "You know what...you haven't been the same since Halloween. Did something happen then?" His voice lowered further, and he shuffled his feet. "Is there anything you want to talk about?"

I was taken aback. Conversations like this between me and Kian didn't happen. Ever. We didn't get deep. From his worried expression, though, I knew he wouldn't let it drop, and it was killing me to keep all this inside. I made a snap decision to confide in him. "That girl I was with at Fright Night? It was Raine."

His head whipped up to mine, his eyes wide. "What the fuck? No way! But she was like, hot as fuck."

"Yeah, she was," I agreed. *Is*, I added in my head.

His gaze sharpened. "I see. It's obvious now."

"What's obvious?" I tried to tamp down the rising panic that was threatening to engulf me.

"You want her."

I stared at him. "How..." I trailed off.

"Come on, I'm not blind. I see the way you look at her. I've seen the two of you together, at the party and, y'know, the photos and stuff. And let's not forget our fight over her. Remember? My first practice after my suspension?"

"I remember," I gritted out, but he hadn't finished speaking.

"I just hadn't realised you'd had a thing for her for so long." He grinned. "You know she's with Cassius Drummond now, right?"

"She is not." My voice came out as a low, challenging growl, and Kian laughed.

"You've got it bad. What's stopping you? Think it would be weird with Ana—wait, do you still want Ana?"

"What? *Ana?* I already told you I was never going back there again."

"Just checking. Okay, so what's the problem, then?"

"She's...she's been targeted because of me. All the fucking rumours."

"Rumours which you started," he commented dryly. "So what about the rumours? People will get over it."

My mouth twisted, and my shoulders slumped. "I just don't want her to be hurt because of me."

"That's all very noble of you, but shouldn't that be her decision as well?" He swigged from his water bottle, running his hand over his mouth, before returning his attention to me.

I sighed and filled in the rest of the gaps. "It's not only that. There's the fact that my parents are always on my case comparing me to her."

His eyes darkened, and I held my breath, knowing that parents were a touchy subject for him. His parents...they were selfish assholes, to put it bluntly. "Who gives a fuck what your parents think? Seriously, mate? That's just..." He shook his head, his frustration and disappointment clear.

A grimace crossed my face. "You know how they are. Fuck. It sounds really stupid when I say it out loud, doesn't it?"

"Yeah, it really does. Sort your shit out, Carter. If you actually want to be with her, and she wants to be with you, man the fuck up and do it. Stop making bullshit excuses."

I gaped at him. "Harsh, mate."

"It's true, and you know it." He gave me a pointed look.

"Yeah," I said quietly. "A while ago, I asked her if she wanted to be with me, in secret, and she said no. At the time I didn't get it, but now..." I trailed off, realising how it must've looked to her. "Now I get why she was so upset. Who wants to hide their relationship? I wasn't ashamed to be seen with her. It wasn't fair of me to ask her to keep it a secret. She didn't deserve that."

Next to me, Kian went very still.

"Kian? You okay?"

"No. No, I'm not," he mumbled. His eyes closed briefly, and then an apprehensive expression came over his face. "I need to tell you something. I...uh...I've been. I've been having a secret relationship of my own. And I think it's beyond time it was out in the open. Time *I* was out." He swallowed hard, dropping his gaze from mine. "I'm with Preston."

"You what? Like—"

"As in, Preston is my boyfriend."

I didn't even know what to say. "I didn't know you were into men," I said eventually, shrugging.

He smiled then, glancing over at Preston, who was doing hamstring stretches at the side of the pitch. "I'm into him." A sigh escaped him. "Really, really fucking into him. I asked him to keep it quiet. It was all new to me, you know? But—" He broke off and waved Preston over. When Preston reached us, Kian stepped forwards and put his arm around Preston's waist, then planted a hard, possessive kiss on his lips. Preston stumbled in shock, but then a huge smile spread across his face. A couple of the guys on the team wolf-whistled in the background.

"I take it the secret's out?" Preston looked between me and Kian, and I couldn't help grinning. The news had shocked me, mainly because I'd never had any inkling of Kian being into guys, let alone being in an actual relationship. A relationship with anyone, for that matter. But looking at them right now, anyone could see how happy they were together, and that was enough for me. Kian was one of my best mates, and he deserved happiness, and Preston was a good guy.

"I'm happy for you both," I told them, and I meant it. "How long has this been going on?"

It was Kian who answered me. "Since Fright Night."

Now it was my turn to smirk. "I wasn't the only one to have a secret hook-up over Halloween, then." Kian grinned at me, and I returned it, suddenly feeling lighter.

We continued the second half of training, and somehow my unexpectedly serious conversation with Kian had helped more than anything else had so far. My concentration was back, and the team gelled, working together instinctively. We didn't always manage it, but when we did, it was pure magic. We were untouchable, unstoppable.

I kept an eye on Kian and Preston until practice was over and we'd showered and headed to our cars, needing to make sure there'd be no trouble from any of our teammates after their announcement. After seeing how no one on the team seemed to have a problem with Kian coming out as openly being with Preston, or at least, not to his face, I realised something. We were the kings of the school. We had power. People wouldn't dare to go up against us—they didn't want to risk a drop to the bottom of the food chain. If Raine wanted to be with me, I'd protect her. Shield her from any hurt. Try my fucking hardest to make it better.

My head was clear for the first time in weeks, and I knew what I had to do. First, I needed to have a talk with my dad. Next, I needed to check out what exactly was going on with Raine and Cassius Drummond. And then...then, I needed to come up with a plan to make Raine Laurent realise that she was mine.

THIRTY-THREE

RAINE

"I really don't want to do this," I muttered under my breath as I reluctantly opened the door of Imogen's car. To say I'd been completely shocked when she'd invited me to go with her to watch the football match was an understatement. Aside for the fact that we'd never actively hung out before outside of school, she was most definitely part of Carter's group of friends, and therefore not someone who would ever choose to hang out with me. Carter and I... I closed my eyes briefly. The photo hadn't worked. He'd kept his distance from me all week, not even sparing me a look despite my constant glances in his direction.

Imogen had cornered me after drama club on Monday and asked me how I was doing, with all the gossip that had been flying around the school about Cassius Drummond, and I'd told her nothing was going on and Cassius and I were just friends. She'd made it a point to come over and talk to me all through the school week, just little moments here and there, but I really appreciated the gesture.

Anyway, all this had ended up with me agreeing to go to the football game with her. Lena had flat-out refused to come, but she'd encouraged me to go. Maybe I was being a masochist, but the thought of seeing Carter in his element, running all over the field, was a mental image that I definitely wanted to replace with the real thing.

Unfortunately, what I hadn't realised was that I was being taken to the game with Anastasia.

"Hi." Imogen beamed at me as I slid into the back seat, placing my jacket down next to me, and I returned her smile. "This is Emmeline, Ana's sister." She indicated to the pretty girl in the front seat, who gave me a brief smile. I recognised her from school—she was a couple of years below us, so I'd never spoken to her, but I'd seen her around. "And you know Ana."

We eyed each other warily across the back seat; then Ana gave a small huff and an eye-roll. "No need to look at me like that. I won't bite."

"No, but you might try and kiss me again." I laughed, then suddenly stopped dead. Why had I said that? And to Anastasia, of all people?

She stared at me for a moment, and then a laugh burst out of her. "I think you're safe. My tastes extend to men, and men only." Then she gave me an actual smile that reached her eyes, which I returned. What was happening? I thought back to Carter's suspicions that Anastasia had been the person behind the money theft and the vandalising of my locker. Was this sudden change prompted by guilt?

"Am I being set up? Why are you guys being nice to me?"

Anastasia's gaze flicked to Imogen's in the rear-view mirror, and Imogen frowned at her. She pursed her lips, then turned back to me. "Believe me, you weren't my first choice of people to be around. But you're not so bad." She waved a casual hand in my direction, her manicured nails glinting with some kind of subtle, shimmery polish. "You scrub up well. If I didn't know you, I might be interested in being friends."

"Um. Thanks? I think?" I sat back in my seat, clipping my seat belt into place as Imogen pulled away from my house. I stared down at myself. I wasn't even wearing anything special.

Okay, that was a lie. I'd made way, way more effort than I would normally. Not even because the thought of seeing Carter sent alternate shivers of excitement and dread racing through me. I had to remind myself that he wasn't interested anymore. I wanted to do it for myself. For me. I was done hiding. Yeah, I didn't have to wear make-up and get all dressed up. No one should have to, if they didn't want to. But I wanted to. I liked wearing make-up. I liked experimenting with clothes. My desire to remain in the shadows… I hadn't realised until recently just how stifling that had been. I was trying to suppress that side of me that wanted to get creative and try new things, and I was ready to let it free.

There hadn't been that much of a change, in reality. I had on light make-up, and I'd curled my hair so it hung in waves down my back. I'd paired tight jeans with my tan leather boots and a black V-necked jumper that clung to my curves.

We parked at the school, and I followed the girls to the stands. Of course, we had to sit right by the football pitch, in the prime seating area.

"I'm not sure if it's a good idea to be this close to the players." I hesitated in front of the seats.

"All the players, or one in particular?" Imogen gave me a knowing look, and I sighed.

"I might just go and sit up there." I pointed to the empty seats on the end of the row, right near the top of the stands.

"No, you're sitting here." Imogen dragged me down the row and pointed to a seat. "There." She sat on one side of me, and Anastasia sat on the other side, with her sister next to her. "Okay, now you're here. Do you know anything about football? Anything at all?"

I rolled my eyes. "Just because I haven't been to any games before, doesn't mean I don't like football. It's more... not wanting to be around people, I suppose."

"Get ready to be taken out of your comfort zone, then." She said the words that Lena had repeated to me over and over, and it made me smile.

"I'm ready. That's why I'm here." I undid my jacket, because it was actually not so cold under the floodlights, sandwiched between the girls. "Actually, I lied when I said I know about football. I mean, I watch the international games, but I have no clue about the rules. Especially the offside rule. No idea how that works."

"No one has any idea how that works," Anastasia muttered next to me, then laughed.

"As long as you cheer when our team scores a goal, you'll be fine." Imogen gave me a reassuring smile. I relaxed into my seat as the girls conversed quietly, actually making an effort to include me, and I was surprised to realise that I was actually having a good time.

"Selfie," Anastasia suddenly announced, and I automatically shrank back in my seat. "Stop hiding. You're in this." She gave me a severe look, then a tiny smile. "We do it before every game. It's tradition. If we stopped now and the team lost, it would be our fault."

"Superstitious, much?" Emmeline piped up, vocalising my exact thoughts.

"We can't take that risk," Anastasia said. "Anyway,

smile!" She held her phone out, and we all leaned in together as she snapped a photo. "Mind if I tag you?"

"N-no," I managed to say. Anastasia Egerton taking selfies with me? Had I been dropped into some parallel universe?

"Done," she said a couple of minutes later. "While I'm on here..." Her fingers flew over her phone screen, swiping across to my profile. "I see you've been hanging out with Cassius Drummond. If you ever feel like introducing us, I'd owe you one." She gave me a bright smile, flashing her teeth.

"Is this why you invited me? Because of Cassius?" I stared at her suspiciously.

"No. No it wasn't." Her immediate, emphatic denial made me feel a little better, although I still couldn't quite suppress the twinge of uncertainty. "He's just..."

"Insanely hot? The sexiest man to ever roam the streets of Alstone?" Imogen supplied.

"Exactly." Anastasia nodded in agreement. "Have you *seen* him?"

"He's gorgeous," Emmeline added.

"Okay, okay, I get it." I laughed.

Whatever anyone else was about to say was forgotten as the stands started filling up around us. Music blared through the speakers around the stadium, and the atmosphere became electric, buzzing with anticipation. I realised I was actually excited about this. Why had I avoided coming for so long?

"I didn't realise so many people would be here." I stared around me, at the almost full stands. Even the stands across the other side of the football pitch, where the away team fans sat, was full.

"It's not always this busy. But this is the championship quarter-finals, and Highnam Academy are kind of our biggest rivals, I guess, so everyone wants to be here." Imogen flashed me a grin, then turned to greet another girl who had sat down behind us.

"I see that." Pulling out my phone, I took a couple of photos to send to Lena, then sat back, waiting for the players to make an appearance. My nerves returned, as thoughts of Carter invaded my mind.

Someone dropped into the seat next to Imogen, and I turned when I felt, rather than heard, her small gasp of surprise. Xavier had taken the empty seat, and he sprawled out in it, his long legs taking up all the space in the aisle. He and Imogen stared at one another in silence for a moment, and although I couldn't see her face, I could see his gaze grow softer as he looked at her.

Breaking their connection, he looked around her to me. "You made it. Now for the finishing touches..." He reached down to the bag at his feet that I hadn't noticed until that point, and pulled out a bundle of fabric which he handed to me. "Put this on."

I stared at him, confused. "Huh?"

"You want to match the rest of us or not?" He gave me a huge grin, and I unfolded the fabric to find a football shirt in the team colours.

"I have to wear this?"

"You don't have to, but we're all in the team colours. See?" Imogen pointed to herself, then to Anastasia, and I realised they were wearing black and green, the school team colours.

"But you're not wearing an actual football shirt, though," I pointed out.

"That doesn't matter. Just put it on over your jumper. It'll probably be really big on you," Xavier told me. As they looked at me expectantly, I sighed.

"Okay, I'll put—" Lifting the shirt, I noticed the huge number 7 on the back. "Hang on, this is Carter's number, isn't it?"

Xavier gave me a suspiciously innocent look, then shrugged. "That was all I could get hold of on short notice, sorry."

I wasn't sure whether to believe him or not, but I pulled the shirt over my head, knowing that they wouldn't let me get away with not wearing it, and there was no way I was going to cause a scene. Xavier was right, it was huge on me. It was the team's winter shirt as well, meaning it had long sleeves, which I could at least pull down over my cold hands. Even though I shouldn't allow myself to hope for anything after Carter's silence all week, I couldn't help the nervous, excited feeling fluttering in my belly at the thought of me wearing a shirt with his number on.

And then, there he was. The music cut out and a voice was announcing the teams, and they filed onto the pitch, Carter leading the way for Alstone High, the captain's armband on his bicep. My stomach flipped, and I couldn't look away. He didn't look at me, not once, and I couldn't help my disappointment, but I reminded myself that it was only to be expected.

The pre-game stuff passed in a blur, as my whole focus shrank to Carter. I watched as the teams shook hands, and my eyes stayed on Carter, watching as he made his way down the line of players with practiced efficiency. The coin toss came next, and then suddenly, the whistle was being blown and the game was starting.

Cheers, whistles, boos, shouts—the whole stadium was a cacophony of noise. I found myself actually getting into the game, my eyes glued to the action. When Carter passed the ball to Kian, who sent it flying to Preston in a perfect arc, I held my breath. The ball seemed to hang in mid-air for a moment, before Preston booted it straight into the goal. I flew out of my seat with a scream, along with the other Alstone High students and supporters in the stands, jumping and cheering. Anastasia turned to me and actually pulled me into a hug, all breathless excitement, and I froze for a minute, then hugged her back, shocked.

At half-time, both teams disappeared, and I sat back in my seat.

"How are you enjoying your first school football game?" Imogen smiled at me as she opened a bottle of Coke.

"I'm... It's fun. I want to do it again." I was surprised to find that I meant it. Even though everything had gone wrong with Carter, I still wanted to come back. The atmosphere, the feel of being part of something—everyone around me all on the same side, willing our team to score a goal, all of us experiencing the highs and lows together—it was like nothing I'd ever experienced before.

"The players are good to look at, too. Aren't they?" She smirked at me. "Got your eye on any one in particular?"

"No." Both she and Anastasia laughed at my emphatic denial, clearly not believing me. Thankfully they decided to stop tormenting me, and the conversation turned to Anastasia's upcoming birthday.

The second half was tense as Highnam Academy scored a goal almost as soon as the whistle blew, making the score 1-1. We *had* to win this. When did I start thinking of the team as a "we"? Guess I'd found my school spirit.

The clock seemed to count down so slowly as the game neared the end. Time slowed to a crawl. The referee blew the whistle, and the voice over the speakers announced there would be two minutes of added time. This was it. The whole ground was silent as Carter took up position on the side of the pitch for a free kick. I held my breath as he stepped back, then ran and sent the ball flying in a perfect arc, straight towards Kian. Kian seemed to leap into the air and headed it straight into the goal.

The stadium erupted in cheers and whistles, and as the team celebrated, I found myself cheering along with them, standing, clapping until my hands hurt. We just had to get through another forty seconds, and then we would have the win.

Three blasts of the whistle sounded, signalling the end of the game. Alstone High had done it.

I couldn't stop smiling. Then Imogen elbowed me, hard, and my head shot around to her in surprise.

Carter, she mouthed.

I turned back to the pitch, and there he was. *Now* he was looking at me.

Only me.

THIRTY-FOUR

RAINE

I watched, trapped by his gaze as he left his teammates celebrating on the pitch and jogged towards me, right to the edge of the stands. Imogen gave me a small push forwards, until I was right in front of him, just the low barrier separating us. He was all sweaty, breathing hard, his dark hair wet and tousled, his eyes sparking with triumph at the team's win.

"Nice shirt." His eyes raked over me, heating my body. "Enjoy the match?" His voice was raspy, probably from shouting instructions to his teammates all game.

I nodded, momentarily unable to speak.

"Good."

We stood, staring at one another, and I started to feel uncomfortable, aware of people's attention turning towards us as their team captain stood in front of me. What was this?

"Fuck it," he muttered, then reached out and lifted me up, over the barrier, and into his arms. My arms and legs automatically went around him, but he held me effortlessly.

"Carter? What—"

His lips were suddenly on mine, and I was gone. I

wound my arms more tightly around his neck, kissing him back with everything I had.

"I'm sorry. So sorry. I want you. I want to be with you. Only you." His words were quiet but spoken with so much intensity that I had no doubt he meant them.

"You want me?"

"So fucking much. If you can forgive me. I know I don't deserve your forgiveness, but I'm shamelessly hoping you feel the same way about me and want to give me another chance."

"You're not ashamed to be seen with me?" I probed, just to make sure.

"I've never been ashamed of you. I want you to get any of those thoughts out of your head." He looked at me intently, the kaleidoscope of browns and golds in his eyes holding me captive. "My... Fuck, Rai. My head was a mess. It took a while for us to be on the same page. That's if we are still on the same page?"

I let out a shaky breath. "Is this real? Are-are you serious?"

"Baby, look at where we are right now. I just claimed you in the most public way I could think of. If that doesn't tell you that I'm serious about this, I don't know what will."

Good point. "Oh no. Everyone's watching us, aren't they?" I buried my face in his shoulder.

He laughed. "Yeah. Watching their team captain kiss the fuck out of his girlfriend."

Girlfriend? I raised my head, and his expression turned hesitant. He bit his lip. "That's if you want to be?"

There was no hesitation on my part. Not anymore. "Yes. Yes, I want to be. So much." Glancing behind me... yep, everyone was staring, I huffed in mock-annoyance. "I guess I'd better get used to the attention, huh? Since my boyfriend is kind of an attention whore."

"Attention whore?" He lowered me to my feet, grinning. "I can't even deny it." Leaning down, his lips skimmed over my ear. "I'm your boyfriend. You're mine now, little trickster." Drawing back slightly, he smiled, then slayed me with another kiss.

"I need to get back to the team. Wait for me?" He suddenly looked unsure again, and something about his open vulnerability made my stomach flip.

"I'll wait." This time I kissed him.

He gave me another blinding grin, then placed a kiss on the top of my head, before jogging back to his teammates.

I stumbled back across the barrier, almost going flying, but was steadied by Imogen at the last minute. "When Carter wants something, he goes all out." She grinned at me as I collapsed back into my seat.

"I wish everyone would stop looking at me." I slumped downwards, but I couldn't stop my smile. Happiness filled me, as my mind replayed what had just happened between me and Carter.

"Stop hiding. You have to get used to it, now. Don't worry, everyone will get used to it, and soon enough, something else will become the new gossip," Anastasia told me.

"Did you know about this? Is this why you brought me here?" I looked between her and Imogen, and Imogen nodded.

"Yes. I knew...not the details, but he asked me to make sure you made it to this game and stayed until the end."

"Our boy's got it bad." Xavier leaned around Imogen with a grin, and my cheeks heated even as my smile widened. I didn't miss the way his arm was casually leaning on the back of Imogen's seat, and I made a note to ask her about it at some point. If we were going to be friends, I had to know these things.

Anastasia leaned over to me, catching my attention. "So... Now you and Carter are together, you're officially invited to my birthday party. If you want to come, that is."

The words were falling out of my mouth before I had a chance to censor them. "Are you really okay with all of this?"

Her brows pulled together, but then her expression smoothed out. "I was a bitch. I know. I just, well, I am a bitch. Apparently." She laughed humourlessly. "I will admit that I felt...possessive of Carter, I guess, at the beginning. But it's become clear to me that you both have feelings for each other. I'm not hung up on him or anything. I promise you that."

My mind raced, going back over what she'd said. "Wait. Those pictures that appeared. Did you have anything to do with those?"

She recoiled as if I'd slapped her. "What?" Her shocked whisper was louder than a shout. "Are you serious? Did someone say it was me?"

"If it wasn't you, then who?" Icy tendrils of dread prickled my spine. "What about the masked figure? And the money?"

"What are you talking about?" Confusion was followed by worry. "Raine, are you in trouble?"

"Tell us what's going on." Xavier's tone was commanding. He reached over and scooped Imogen into his lap, then sidled across to her empty seat. She leaned back on him, but her gaze was focused on me. Anastasia moved closer, Emmeline occupied talking to one of her friends on the other side of us.

In halting tones, I told them everything. How the

money had been stolen and made to look like I'd taken it, and Ana had been the only person other than Carter and the teaching staff who had known about my financial situation at that point; how the masked figure had appeared at the party and tried to grab me; and how someone had managed to take photos of me and Carter through a locked door and post them and deface my locker. By the time I'd finished speaking, my voice was wobbly from trying to hold in the tears.

"Raine." Ana swallowed hard and placed a tentative hand on my arm. "I'm sorry. I had...I had no idea how bad things were. I know that's not an excuse. When you came to the table at lunchtime and Carter shot you down, I...I felt really bad. You didn't deserve to be spoken to that way. I should have said something to Tina. The stuff she said to you...that wasn't right."

Imogen interrupted her. "It couldn't have been Anastasia at the party, anyway. Straight after the spin the bottle game, we were both doing shots with some of our friends, and Ana ended up drinking too much, and I had to take her drunk ass home."

A cold trickle of fear made its way down my spine.

Xavier pursed his lips, deep in thought. "Okay. I think there's an explanation for the party photos. Earlier that night, before the spin the bottle game we, I mean, I was in the office briefly." I noticed Imogen's cheeks flush as he spoke. "There's a window. It's quite high up, so you might not have noticed it, but anyone could take a photo through there if they climbed up on something. Wouldn't need to even be anything that big. A crate or something would probably be enough."

I thought back to the angle of the photos. "You're right. I don't know why I never thought of that before. But I don't know who it could be. Who else would hate me that much?"

Nobody had any answers. Eventually Xavier sighed. "Let's talk about it more later. You need to go and meet Carter. He'll kill us if we don't get you there. He's got plans for the two of you."

Suddenly, the fear was replaced with warmth. Excitement coursed through me, and my smile reappeared. "I'd better go and meet him, then."

THIRTY-FIVE

CARTER

A combination of relief and exhilaration was filling me, leaving me with a permanent grin. So much of tonight had relied on outside factors—Imogen keeping her word to bring Raine with her, everyone else going along with my plan, and more importantly, Raine actually forgiving me after all the shit I'd put her through.

After I'd seen the picture of Raine with Cassius and pretty much lost it, I'd got to work. My mind flashed back to the most awkward part of the week.

"Dad? I need to speak to you. Both of you, I guess." My parents stared at me across the table, seemingly taken aback by the serious tone of my voice.

"Speak up, then. What is it? Is this about your grades?" My dad placed the fork on his plate with a clatter.

I shook my head, gritting my teeth and balling my fists, forcing myself not to react. "No. It's about Raine."

He raised a brow, leaning forwards slightly as he studied me. My mum dabbed at her mouth with her napkin, glancing between me and my dad, before she gave a short laugh. "I think I see what's going on here."

"Really?" My dad turned to her. "Because I don't."

Instead of replying to him, she turned back to me. "Speak, Carter."

"Okay." I swallowed, then went for it. "I like Raine. What I don't like is your constant comparisons between me and her."

My dad frowned. "What do you mean?"

"You're always comparing me to her. Everything she does is perfect, in your eyes, and nothing I do is ever good enough. You're always asking me why I can't be more like her." My fucking voice cracked, and I cleared my throat, clenching my jaw so tightly I knew I was going to give myself a headache.

"Oh, Carter." My mum's eyes filled with tears. "Is that what you really think?" At my nod, she sniffed a little, before she gathered herself. "I'm so sorry that you thought that we were comparing the two of you. That was certainly never my intention. We, well, I praise her because she doesn't have anyone else to do so. You know what Pam can be like. She takes Raine's intelligence for granted. And I'm not blind, Carter. I know that she doesn't seem to have much of a social life, and I know that you're the...the opposite, I suppose. Popularity has always been a part of your life. You're used to the adoration of your friends, and Raine...I get the impression that she doesn't really have the same support network you do."

My dad nodded. "I concur. And Carter, the reason I ride you so hard about your schoolwork is because I know how intelligent you are, and I know that if you apply yourself, you can reach the same high standard in all your classes." He sighed heavily. "I hadn't realised that you felt that way. You never said anything before."

"I shouldn't have had to. It would be nice to have some support from my own parents," I said bitterly.

"You like her as more than a friend, don't you?" My mum had been studying me silently, her eyes still a little watery, but a gleam came into them as she spoke.

I nodded. No point denying it.

A smile flitted across her face, before she turned to my dad. "I think I speak for both of us when I say that we'll make an effort here. But I want you to try, too."

"Don't think I'm going to stop giving you a hard time about your schoolwork," my dad added gruffly. "But I want you to know that we're proud of all you've achieved."

"Okay. Good. Thanks." Suddenly I wasn't sure what to say, and I shuffled in my seat, suddenly needing to get away. My dad cleared his throat.

"Was that everything you wanted to discuss?"

"Yeah. That was it."

"Alright. Then if you'll excuse me, I need to make a couple of phone calls." He stood, placing a quick kiss on the top of my mum's head, before leaving the dining room.

My mum also stood. "Be careful with Rainey, Carter. She needs to be taken care of. But for what it's worth, I think the two of you could have something special." She smiled at me, before leaving me alone with my thoughts.

Since that conversation, my parents had backed right off. Still riding me about my schoolwork, but no more comparisons. I'd roped Imogen into the rest of my plan. She made me fucking grovel when I told her what a dick I'd been, and to start with I wasn't even sure she'd help me. When I flat-out begged, I think she finally realised I was serious, and she'd agreed to help.

All through the game, my focus had been on football. I owed it to my team to play my best game and not allow any distractions. As soon as the final whistle had blown, though, the euphoria from our win was drowned out by the pressing need to get to Raine and put in place the final part of my plan.

I hadn't even allowed myself to look for her in the stands, but I saw her straight away, watching me with the same intensity I was watching her. As I ran towards her, I could see the apprehension in her expressive hazel eyes, and all I could do was hope that the statement I was about to make was enough for her.

When I lifted her over the barrier and into my arms, the win suddenly became completely insignificant, and I knew that this was the most important moment of my life so far. As I staked my very public claim on her, everything inside me settled. Nothing and no one was more important than her, and I intended to show her just how much she meant to me.

"Mate. That header was fucking epic," I called to Kian across the changing room as I finished pulling my clothes on after the showers. "Nice work."

"I know." He gave me a smug smile as he grabbed his jacket from the peg next to him. "Give yourself some credit, though."

"Oh, I have," I assured him, making him laugh and roll his eyes.

"Great teamwork," I added. "All of us. I'm really fucking proud of us."

He grinned, picking up his kit bag before moving over to Preston. "Yep. Although, with me back on the team, a win was inevitable, really."

Preston gave him a pointed look and he grinned. "I

suppose our golden boy had something to do with it, too. I'll share the praise with Preston, since we both scored a goal."

"How generous," Preston muttered, but he was smiling as he grabbed Kian's hand.

I laughed. "Look at you. You finally learned to share, and it only took you eighteen years."

"Fuck off." Kian threw up his middle finger at me, and I returned the gesture, before I pulled on my hoodie.

"As much as I'd love to hang around and insult you all night, I've got my girlfriend waiting for me." Grabbing my bag, I hauled it over my shoulder and pushed past Kian in my rush to get outside, leaving him laughing behind me. The friends and families of the players were clustered around waiting for us, but I couldn't see Raine anywhere. Frowning, I leaned against the wall, pulling out my phone to check if she'd sent me a text. Nothing.

The crowds thinned out, and soon there were only a few people left. Glancing at my phone again, I saw almost fifteen minutes had passed. Where was she? I hit Xavier's number and waited.

"Carter! What's up?"

"Is Raine with you?" My eyes kept scanning the area around me, in case she appeared.

"No, I thought she was with you?" His tone instantly put me on alert. "When we left her, she was walking to meet you. We didn't hang around because I knew you had plans with her on your own, and we didn't wanna be in the way."

"She's not here." I swallowed hard. "She's not...I haven't seen her. How long ago did you see her?"

There was a pause. "Uh...I think about forty-five minutes ago?"

Fuck. Fuck, fuck, fuck.

"I'm gonna try her phone." I hung up on him without saying goodbye and immediately dialled her. The phone rang and rang and eventually went to her voicemail. Frustrated, I navigated to her social media to see when she was last online. As I did, my phone sounded with a new message alert. I hit it instantly, and the relief at seeing her name was instantaneous.

Raine: Went home. Feeling sick. Sorry. No drama, I promise. I'll feel better after a good sleep. See u Monday. BTW don't forget your business studies homework!

My stomach churned. Something wasn't right. And what the fuck was she talking about my Business Studies homework for? She wasn't even in that class with me.

The unease grew and grew, until it was suffocating me.

"Raine! Raine!" My head flew around just in time to see the large black shadow take flight against the darkening sky, the urgent caw echoing around me.

That was the only sign I needed.

I ran for my car.

THIRTY-SIX

CARTER

As I drove, speeding through the streets of Alstone, I called Xavier back. "She sent me a text saying she'd gone home ill. Something isn't right; something seems off about the whole thing, and I can't put my finger on it." Even I could hear the anxiety threading through my tone. I willed my car to go faster, while at the same time praying there were no police around to pull me over.

"What's the plan? What can I do?" Xavier was instantly on alert.

"I'm on my way to her house. Can you...I don't know. *Fuck.* Can you be on standby in case I need you?"

"On it." His words were simple and firm. "I'm calling reinforcements, if we need them."

Ending the call, I sped up, shooting through a set of traffic lights as they changed to red, and threw my truck into a sharp turn, spinning the wheel and sending me skidding onto Raine's road. I screeched to a halt outside her house and threw open my door, barely allowing the engine to stop before I jumped out, keys in hand.

I ran up to the front gates, wrenching them open, and

up to the front door. The house was dark and silent, and no one answered my increasingly frantic pounding. Fuck. What was I supposed to do? Ducking around the side of the house, I made my way to the tree I used to climb up to her room and scaled it as quickly as possible.

As soon as I drew level with her window, I sucked in a harsh breath. Her curtains were wide open, and the moonlight allowed me to see clearly into her darkened room. The bedcovers were undisturbed, and there was no sign of her. No sign of life anywhere in the house that I could see.

She wasn't home.

Where the fuck was she?

"Mate. She's not at home." As I called Xavier back, I realised that my hands were shaking. "I need help. Please."

"On my way," he said, and then he was gone.

Think. What else could I do?

Scrolling through my contacts, I hit the button of someone I hadn't spoken to in a long time.

"Weston? It's Carter Blackthorne."

Weston Cavendish's voice came over the line, sounding confused. "Alright, mate? What's up? I heard about your win earlier. Good job."

"Yeah, yeah, never mind that," I rushed to interrupt him, not wanting to waste any more time. "Not wanting to seem rude, mate, but I really need to get hold of Lena. Have you got her number?" I crossed my fingers, hoping he'd come through for me. He was Cassius Drummond's best mate, so he was my best bet at getting hold of Lena since I didn't have Cassius' number.

"Lena?"

"Yeah. Look, I know you probably don't want to give her number out, but my girlfriend's missing, and Lena's her closest friend at school. Please, West. This is really fucking important."

I heard him mutter "shit," and then he was speaking again. "Forwarding it now. If there's anything I can help with, call me, alright?"

Thanking him, I ended the call and immediately dialled Lena. She answered after a couple of rings. "Carter. Please don't tell me you fucked up already." Her tone was accusing.

"How did you know it was me? Never mind, I don't care. Have you seen or spoken to Raine?"

I heard her sharp intake of breath. "No. I haven't spoken to her since before the football match. Hours ago. Why?"

"She's missing." Panic was starting to set in now. "She's missing and all I have is one fucking text that said she was going home because she was ill, but she's not here."

"Where are you?"

"I'm at Raine's house."

I heard footsteps running and the sound of a door slamming. "I'm coming now. Be there in ten."

Fifteen minutes later, after I'd paced up and down Raine's driveway so many times that I was starting to wear a groove in the gravel, my friends arrived. Xavier and Imogen, followed closely by Kian and Preston, and finally, Lena. I gave them a rundown of the situation, showing them Raine's ambiguous text.

> **Raine:** Went home. Feeling sick. Sorry. No drama, I promise. I'll feel better after a good sleep. See u

Monday. BTW don't forget your business studies homework!

"There's something not right about this, and I can't put my finger on it." I kept pacing, unable to stand still.

"Yeah. I know Raine, and she wouldn't say 'no drama,' or use a '*u*' instead of writing out 'you' as a proper word," Lena muttered.

"And what's the Business Studies bit all about? She isn't in our class," Kian added. He pulled his lip ring between his teeth, thinking hard. "Is there something in our homework that could be relevant?"

I shook my head. "I already thought of that. We didn't even have any homework."

"What if it's like a coded message?" Preston's voice sounded loud in the night air. "What if she's trying to tell you something without saying it, if that makes sense? Maybe she's with someone and doesn't want to alert them?"

Fuck.

I stopped dead.

My blood ran cold.

Swiping up through the message thread, I paused, my finger hovering over the message she'd sent me so long ago.

Raine: He's in drama club with me. He works on set design. I think he's in your business studies class???

"Oh, fuck." My grip tightened on my phone, as the memories assaulted my mind. Raine, running to me in the warehouse, terror all over her face, insisting a masked figure had tried to grab her. Raine, getting into *his* car after drama club. The way he looked at her, the same way *I* looked at her.

I licked my lips, my throat suddenly dry. My heart was pounding as I forced the words from my lips. "Does anyone know anything about Dylan Rossiter?"

THIRTY-SEVEN

RAINE

I awoke, disoriented and confused. Where was I? The last thing I remembered was Dylan waving me over on my way to meet Carter, asking if I could spare a minute to check something with him. Then...nothing.

As I became aware of my surroundings, I realised I was in a moving car. A car I recognised. A car that I'd ridden in every Monday afternoon for a while now. Remaining perfectly still, I tried to make sense of what was going on. Why was I in Dylan's car? I was supposed to be meeting Carter, wasn't I? Or had that been a dream? My head was so fuzzy; I couldn't make sense of anything.

I trusted my instincts, though, and all my senses were on red alert. Something was wrong, and I didn't know what.

"Dylan?" It was an effort to form the words. My tongue felt thick, like it was too big for my mouth, and my voice came out as an unsure mumble. "Where are we going?" Turning to look at his profile, I watched a smile appear on his face.

"I wondered when you'd wake up. How are you feeling?" His tone was light and conversational, but there was something so off about him. He was all jittery, clasping and unclasping the steering wheel, his breaths coming in shallow pants.

"My head feels funny."

He chuckled. "That's an unfortunate side effect of the sedative. Don't worry, it won't last. I only gave you a small dose."

He *sedated* me? My brain tried to make sense of his words. It was such an effort to think.

I suddenly realised that he'd brought the car to a stop by the side of the road. "We're not getting out, but I need you to do something for me. I need you to send a text to Carter to tell him you've gone home, okay? Tell him you're not feeling well." He reached his hand out towards my face, and I jerked away on instinct. His eyes narrowed, and he shook his head. "No funny business, Raine. No trying anything stupid like attempting to run away. I don't want to hurt you, so please don't make me."

Make him? I could only watch as he placed my phone into my hands and waited, expectantly. Everything seemed so sluggish, like I was underwater or something.

"Send the text," he prompted, when I remained still.

Right. The text. *Think.*

I typed slowly while he watched my every movement, reading the words as I wrote them. "I'm making it sound more personal." I coughed, then licked my lips. "So...so he won't get suspicious." As soon as I hit Send, Dylan took the phone from my hands and turned it off, then threw it into the back of the car. All I could do was hope that Carter would understand my coded message. If he didn't...I couldn't let myself think about it. I had no idea what was happening, but the fact that Dylan had not only sedated me but had basically kidnapped me...my odds weren't looking great.

I felt a sudden, sharp sting in my neck, and everything faded to black.

CARTER

"Dylan Rossiter? Mr. Jackson's nephew?" Preston gave me a questioning look, his brow raised.

"How do you know he's his nephew?"

"Who's Dylan Rossiter?"

"What's all this about?"

Everyone was suddenly speaking at once, and I held up my hand. "Stop. Preston, what was that about Mr. Jackson? Are you talking about the school caretaker?"

Preston nodded. "Yes. I got talking to Mr. Jackson one afternoon—his cousin lives in Connecticut, close to where I'm from, and anyway, he mentioned his nephew attended AHS and told me his name. I'm not sure if it's common knowledge."

I doubted it was. Dylan was one of those people who, like Raine, flew under the radar. I barely knew who he was —it was only through his connection to Raine that I'd had any idea. But being related to the caretaker—that could explain how he had access to the office of the head of the drama department. That was if he was behind the other things that had happened to Raine.

The more I thought about it, the more the idea solidified. I didn't have any proof, yet every instinct was telling me that this was our guy. And if he was behind it all, and if Raine was worried enough to send me a coded message, then she could be in real danger.

Passing my phone to Xavier, I showed him Raine's earlier text, and he immediately came to the same conclusion. "You know, she was telling us about all this stuff that had happened to her, earlier. She thought Ana might have been behind it. Do you think this Dylan guy could be the culprit?"

I shrugged. "I have no proof, but...yeah. Yeah, I do."

He nodded. "Then we need to act. And fast."

"Where has he taken her? We don't even know his address." The panic was rising again. "Fuck. What do we do? Do any of you know where he lives? Can we...wait. Can we get into the school records?"

Across from me, Lena cleared her throat. "Maybe I can help with that."

We all stared at her. A small smile flickered across her face, before she turned her attention to her phone, her fingers flying across the screen. Eventually, she raised her head. "We just need to wait for a few minutes."

Standing in the cold night, we fell silent. Every one of my senses was on high alert. After the longest few minutes of my life, Lena's phone beeped, and she smiled triumphantly. "Got it. Full name, address, date of birth. I'll forward you the info now."

Less than thirty seconds later, I was staring at the information on my screen, memorising the address, committing all the details to memory, before I forwarded the information to Kian and Xavier.

Already moving towards my car, I spun to face the others. "Ready?"

Dylan Rossiter was going down.

THIRTY-EIGHT

RAINE

When I awoke again, I was lying on a soft surface. Blinking my eyes open, I attempted to focus. My vision was blurry, and my head was swimming.

The room eventually came into focus, although it appeared fuzzy around the edges, giving everything a dreamlike quality. I was in my bedroom. Relief flooded through me. It had been a nightmare. A very realistic nightmare, but at least it wasn't real.

Something was nagging at the back of my mind, though. I squinted at my bedside table. Where was my lamp? As I looked around, everything became clearer, and I let out a deep, shuddering breath.

This room...it looked so much like my bedroom.

Except. This wasn't my bedroom.

"Hello, Sleeping Beauty."

I jumped at the voice coming from a dark corner and spun to see a shadowy figure rise up and come to stand in front of me. He watched me carefully for a moment, before he sank down onto the bed next to me. "How are you doing? Is your head okay?" Dylan's concern was at absolute odds with how he'd treated me so far. As the slightly hazy memories came back, it sank in that he'd drugged me not once, but twice, he'd kidnapped me, and now he was holding me somewhere that bore such a close resemblance to my own bedroom, it couldn't be a coincidence.

I tamped down the fear, locking it up tight. I had to be cautious and look for an opening. The courage I'd been working so hard on gaining was there inside me, I just had to do what I always did—fake it until it became real. Fear was not allowed any place here. Not now. Closing my eyes, I visualised myself putting on a mask, a mask that would hide my true face and protect me.

I opened my eyes.

"My head is a little fuzzy, but I'm okay." Thankfully, my tongue didn't feel swollen like it had done the first time, and other than my incredibly dry throat, I was able to speak almost normally, although my voice sounded hoarse and scratchy to my own ears.

"Good." Dylan smiled at me. "How do you like my room?"

I stared around me, pretending to appreciate it, rather than show just how much it creeped me out. "It feels very familiar."

His smile widened. "I decorated it as closely to your bedroom as possible. I wanted you to feel comfortable here."

Smiling was an effort, yet somehow, I managed to make the corners of my lips turn up. "You did a good job." I took a breath, my next words cautious, although I tried to keep a light tone. "How did you know what my bedroom looked like?"

"I can't reveal all my secrets now, can I?" He laughed, and the sound chilled me.

"Talk to me, Dyl. I can call you Dyl, right?" My breaths

were becoming shallower, and a wave of dizziness overtook me. Taking a deep breath, I counted to five in my head. I had to keep it together, to not allow my mask to slip.

"Dyl. I like that." He shuffled a bit closer to me on the bed and reached out, clasping my clammy palm in his cold hand. "I'm sorry I had to sedate you." His thumb stroked across my skin, and I barely suppressed my shudder of revulsion. "I don't want you to be afraid, Raine. I'll never hurt you. Not unless you give me reason to."

"I believe you, Dyl," I managed. "What was this big gesture all about?" I waved my hand around to encompass the room.

"Everything I've been working towards is for you and me." He shuffled back on the bed until he was resting on the headboard. "You've always been so sweet, so kind to me." His grip on my hand tightened. "We're perfect for each other. I just needed you to see it. I suppose things changed at Fright Night. You looked so beautiful, almost irresistible. From the moment I saw you there, like some kind of goddess, everything changed for me. I couldn't get you out of my head."

Nausea churned in my stomach. "You were there?" I hadn't remembered seeing him.

He nodded. "I was in the haunted house. Did you like my clown makeup? That took me hours."

"C-clown?" This time, there was no suppressing the shudder that ran through me. The one thing I hated, above anything else, was clowns.

Laughing, he patted my hand. "Don't worry, I won't dress like that again. Not now I know you don't like it." He sighed, the smile slipping from his face. "Anyway, I wanted to talk to you, to ask you out at school on Monday, but then everything changed. Carter"—he spat the word—"Carter ruined it. I saw the picture, you see. The one from Fright Night of you and him holding hands. Yes, you had a mask on, but I'd seen you earlier, and I knew it was you." Another heavy sigh escaped him. "I almost thought Carter had managed to ruin things for himself, when the rumours started spreading about you with the football team, but it soon became clear to me that the two of you held some kind of infatuation with each other. That's when I knew I had to take precautions, to show you how valuable I could be."

"And..." I licked my dry lips, already knowing the answer to my question before I'd even asked it. "What did you do?"

"Nothing much. Just lifted the keys from my uncle, found the combination that Mrs. Whittall keeps locked in her desk drawer, and took the money from the cash box. There was no harm done—I replaced it afterwards, didn't I?" A pleased expression stole across his face. "That was the first time you really confided in me, and it solidified my belief that we were perfect for each other."

"But you—I. I paid you the money back."

"It's all here. I haven't touched a penny of it." He shifted on the bed, angling himself to face me. "I wouldn't do that to you."

How was he even justifying his behaviour? My head was spinning.

"The money thing worked for a while, then at the party, I saw Carter kiss you. It was only a game, yet it was clear that there were still residual feelings. I couldn't understand it. This was Carter Blackthorne. He belongs with silly, airhead girls, not with someone as special as you, Raine." His grip on my hand tightened to the point of pain, and I hissed through my teeth. He either didn't notice or didn't care, because he continued talking. "I tried to get you alone at the party. I wanted to kiss you, so you could feel our connection. So you could replace his memory with mine. But you slipped away."

There was no disguising my shocked gasp. "That was you in the mask? Up on the walkway?"

"Yes. All I wanted was to kiss you, and I knew that if I wore the mask I'd have more of a chance of getting close to you, knowing the way you reacted to Carter's mask." A disapproving note entered his voice as he continued. "You disappeared with Carter, *again*. So I did what I could. I managed to sneak a couple of photos, and I posted them to the gossip account, in the hope that it would make you realise that you didn't want or need that kind of attention." His mouth turned down. "It wasn't me that sprayed that awful word on your locker, though, or put the picture on there. I'd never hurt you like that."

I almost laughed. As if that made it any better.

He still wasn't finished. Now he'd started telling the story, it seemed like he couldn't get the words out fast enough. "It was Tina. Tina was the one who sprayed your locker and stuck the printout on there. Don't worry, though, she got her punishment."

"Punishment?" I echoed, bile rising in my throat.

"Don't look so worried." He gave a light laugh. "I simply slashed all the tyres on her car. Oh, and I sneaked into the headmaster's office after hours and altered a couple of her grades. Nothing major."

"Oh." It was the only reply I could give him, when he was looking at me so expectantly.

He didn't seem to notice my lack of response, or if he did, he didn't comment on it. "I must admit, when I saw the photograph of you with Cassius Drummond, I was concerned, but I concluded that he wouldn't be interested in someone like us. We...we're not supposed to be with the popular people, the bland, good-looking ones with their empty lives, who live to crush people like us underfoot. That's why I was so surprised by Carter's actions today at the football match." Finally, he released my grip, and he slid off the bed, pacing up and down. "I...I've had the sedatives for a little while now. They were only supposed to be a precaution. I'm so sorry I used them on you, Raine. Do you forgive me? Do you understand that I had no choice? I had to get you away from Carter."

"Y-yes," I managed to choke out.

His expression smoothed, and then he pounced, dragging me down the bed and throwing his weight across my body. Although he was much smaller than Carter, he managed to pin me, despite me trying to buck him off. My muscles felt so heavy. It was like they were refusing to work properly. Maybe it was the after-effects of the sedative, I didn't know. I froze as he lowered his head to mine. It didn't escape me that Carter had pinned me so many times, and yet, I'd always responded in pleasure, even when I hadn't wanted to. Now, all I felt was fear and revulsion.

"I'd planned to wait, to let you come to me, to choose *me*, but Carter gave me no choice." Dylan's mouth hovered over my cheek, and bile rose in my throat as he brushed his lips over my skin.

His hand went to the button of my jeans, and that was it. I would *not* let him do this. My mind raced. Maybe there was a way I could reason with him. "Dyl?" My voice was a soft whisper. I let my hand run up his arm, hoping he couldn't feel me shake. "Not like this. We need to wipe away all the memories of Carter."

He stiffened above me, and then he spoke. "What do you mean?" There was a note of intrigue in his voice, and I blew out a heavy breath, psyching myself up for the performance of my life.

"Well, what if we replace all of his memories with memories of our own? Carter loved chasing me…would you like that, too? Would you like to catch me all for yourself?"

His breath hitched, and he pressed into me. I bit down on my lip so hard that I tasted blood, lying completely still. After the longest moment of my life, he replied with one word that sparked a tiny ember of hope inside me. "Yes."

THIRTY-NINE

CARTER

We parked a little way away from Dylan's house, not wanting to alert him to our presence. "Masks." I hissed the word, grabbing a handful of our LED masks from the boot. "If there are cameras around, we don't want to be recognised." My voice lowered. "Take precautions and stay safe." Everyone put on a mask without protest, keeping the lights switched off this time, and we headed towards Dylan's house, keeping to the shadows as much as we could. Attempting to keep my mind clear was a losing battle, but I focused on the task at hand. The only task—getting Raine out of there as quickly and safely as I could.

The house was just as it had looked on Google Street View—a sprawling bungalow, with unnecessary ornate pillars and faux-Grecian sculptures draped over the outside. According to Dylan's records, he lived with his grandmother. There seemed to be a distinct lack of security around the property, other than a couple of outdoor lights with motion sensors. Peering in the front window, I could see an elderly woman, who must be the grandmother, sitting in a rocking chair, the TV cranked so high that I was able to make out all the dialogue from the show she was watching. We moved down the side of the house in a line, slipping through the night like shadows, avoiding the range of the motion-sensor lights which seemed to only be focused on the doors.

Reaching the back of the house, I stopped dead, a combination of rage and fear so all-encompassing filling me that everything else faded into nothingness, and I saw red.

"Carter!" Kian's sharp hiss sounded in my ear, his arms grabbing mine and lowering them—what the fuck? When had I raised my fists? "Carter!" His voice was more insistent, as he struggled to hold me in place. "Wait. We can't. Raine." The words penetrated the fog surrounding me, and I stopped struggling against him.

"Look, though." My voice was hoarse and desperate. "*Look.*"

Through the tiny gap in the curtains we took in the scene playing out in front of us. Dylan had Raine pinned on the bed. From where I stood, I could see her face, turned slightly to the side. She was barely fucking keeping herself together.

Raine.

I knew she was important to me, but until that moment, I didn't realise how much.

I'd burn the world down for her.

Why the fuck had I pushed her away? Let my own issues fuck everything up? If I'd got my shit together sooner, maybe we wouldn't be here right now.

Dylan's hand moved between them, and I tensed, every single part of me on edge, needing to get her out of danger, when I saw her lips move, and after a few moments, Dylan moved off her.

My relief was instantaneous.

"What's going on?" Kian murmured, although I knew he wasn't really asking me a question. They both disappeared from the room, and then a minute later, the back door was sliding open, and the security light came on. We barely jumped back in time, escaping to the shadows where the others waited.

"You've got ten seconds." Dylan's nasally voice sounded loud in the quiet night. "Ten..."

Before the word had even left his lips, Raine was running, her movements almost sluggish, slower than usual. What had that fucker done to her?

My eyes returned to Dylan. At this moment in time, it was more important that I keep an eye on him. He stepped out of the house, closing the door behind him, still counting. I watched him move further away from the house, my whole body vibrating with the need to run at him.

"What do you say?" Kian's low voice sounded close to my ear. "Shall we give him a show?"

I smiled at the dark intent in his tone. "Fuck, yes. One he'll never forget." Turning, I spun my finger in a circle, seeing Xavier's nod, and we began to move towards Dylan, keeping to the shadows. Reaching up, I set the switch for my mask to the flashing position as Kian did the same, knowing the others would follow our cue.

"Oh, Dylan?" I called out. "I think you have something that belongs to me."

He spun in a circle, all the colour draining from his face, and then he swayed on his feet. He knew he was trapped, surrounded by us, and he had nowhere to go.

"Get Raine," I said softly, trusting that the girls would help her out. She needed her friends right now, and I needed to teach Dylan Rossiter a lesson he'd never forget.

Stepping forwards, I got right in Dylan's face. I watched

as the light from my mask flashed across his terrified features. My rage was boiling out of control as I looked down at him, and I raised my arm.

A small body came barrelling into me from the side, and suddenly everything else was forgotten as I swept a shuddering Raine into my arms, breathing in her caramel apple scent. "You came," she choked out. "You came for me."

"Always." That was the only word I could get out, because the lump in my throat was too fucking big. Taking a huge step back from Dylan, I held on to her, trusting the others to keep Dylan cornered. Eventually, I lowered her to the ground. "Did he hurt you?" I asked in a low voice.

She hesitated, and dread crawled through me. "Not physically. He-he drugged me. Twice. And it was him. Be-behind all the other stuff." Her voice trembled.

I spoke very calmly. "Listen to me. I want you to go and wait for me in my car. Can you do that?" She nodded, and I ran a reassuring hand down her back before I released her. "You're safe now," I murmured, before glancing over at Preston. He nodded, coming forwards and taking hold of her arm gently, and I handed him my keys before I returned my attention to a struggling Dylan, who was being restrained by a masked Kian.

"Everyone else can leave us." I raised my voice. "This is between me and Rossiter."

"I'm staying." Kian's voice was threaded with excitement, and it almost brought a smile to my face. Almost.

"I'll keep an eye on the grandma," Lena muttered, before following the others down the side of the house. Once they were gone, I stretched out my arms, cracking my knuckles, enjoying the anticipation, before I nodded at Kian to release Dylan.

"I'll give you a ten-second head start. Just like you did for Raine. Ten..."

As Dylan stumbled away from us, I laughed, letting him run down the garden, losing himself in the shadows. "Make sure he doesn't escape down the side of the house," I told Kian, then flicked the switch on my mask to turn it off.

"On it, but I'm playing, too."

Instead of answering, I started stalking down the garden, Kian moving down the opposite side, ready to block Dylan if he made a run for it. Both of us moved silently, listening out for the telltale sound of Dylan's breathing.

There.

The panicked sound carried across the night air, and I struck at the dark shadow crouched beside the hedge, grabbing him easily. "You picked the wrong girl for your sick obsession," I gritted out, as I dragged him back up towards the house, throwing him down on the grass. He collapsed in a heap like the coward he was, whimpering and covering his face.

"Don't hurt me." His pathetic, shaky voice grated on me, and it was all I could do to restrain myself from—

He lunged for me, something sharp and metallic gleaming in his hand. I twisted away at the last moment, my reflexes honed from countless fights at the bowl, and snapped his arm back.

The howl he let out was almost inhumane.

"You might wanna get that arm looked at," I suggested, swiping his knees from under him so he fell to the ground. His arm dangled uselessly, a weird lump protruding from under the sleeve of his jumper, but I couldn't bring myself to care. Instead, I continued. "You *ever* come near Raine again and it won't just be your arm that's broken. Every. Fucking. Bone. In your body will be broken. Not only that, but do you know who Raine's closest friend is?" I paused for a moment. "Lena Drummond. I don't think I need to remind you just how powerful the Drummond family are."

Kicking at the ground, I saw the needle glinting in the weak glow of the security light. "You tried to *tranq* me? Why? Why did you fucking target Raine?"

Dylan groaned, his eyes unfocused.

"You fucking—" Before I could stop myself, I brought my Nike-clad foot down, booting him in the ribs. Dimly, I became aware of Kian pulling me backwards. Only after he'd booted Dylan, too.

"Carter. Stop," he said urgently. "Raine."

My vision cleared, and I straightened up. Crushing the needle underfoot, I spun on my heel and jogged away from Dylan, towards my truck. Towards Raine.

She was all that mattered, now.

FORTY

CARTER

Standing with Kian and Xavier at the top of the steps at the entrance to Alstone High on Monday, everything was the same, yet different. I accepted the praise from students as they passed us, congratulating us on our win, but the football game seemed like it had happened so long ago. I'd driven Raine to school this morning, as I would every morning, and I could tell the trauma of the last couple of days was still getting to her. She'd spent the last two nights in my bed, not wanting to be alone while her aunt was working overnight, plagued by nightmares that I did my hardest to soothe away. It was no surprise—Dylan Rossiter had completely blindsided all of us. The one good thing about it all, though? There was a connection between me and Raine that hadn't been there before. When I realised just how fucking much this girl meant to me, and she'd not only chosen me for comfort, but trusted me to take care of her... I guess it was true when people claimed traumatic experiences were bonding.

The urge to go to her was stronger than I'd expected, but she'd told me that she wanted to carry on as normally as possible. I got it, but I couldn't deny that it had been beyond difficult to let her go when we'd arrived at school.

Pulling my phone out from my pocket, I sent her a simple text.

Me: You OK?

I didn't have to wait long for a reply.

Raine: All good.
Raine: Thanks for checking up on me.

I smiled.

Me: See you at lunch. Text if you need anything

She responded with a string of emojis that alternated between a kissing face and a grinning face, and my smile widened as I pocketed my phone.

"You're looking suspiciously happy there, mate." Xavier eyed me with a teasing grin on his face. "You too." He swung his gaze to Kian, who was smiling as Preston jogged up the steps towards us.

Kian shrugged, then gave him a sly look. "Sorted things out with Immy, yet? Huh?"

"Working on it," Xavier muttered, the smile slipping off his face. The bell rang before I had a chance to get in a dig, and we headed to our classes.

All morning I was on edge, waiting to see Raine. It was a weird feeling—I'd never been that invested in someone else before. But I needed to see for myself if she was doing okay after all the shit that had happened.

Finally. There she was, standing alone in the doorway of the cafeteria. I couldn't stop the grin from appearing when I took her in. She stood, taking in the table where I sat with my friends, her gaze unsure, like she didn't know if she should join us.

Fuck that.

Pushing away from the table, I stood. *Come here*, I mouthed, holding out my hand to her.

A huge smile spread across her beautiful face, and she took a step towards me. Not quick enough, as far as I was concerned. I stalked towards her, and we clashed together in the middle of the crowded cafeteria. I lifted her into my arms, sliding my mouth against hers. Because I could. Because she was mine.

"You're going to give me a reputation," she murmured when I released her. Her cheeks were flushed, but she was smiling.

"I know you don't like the attention. I'm just...fuck, I don't know. Happy to see you."

"Yeah. I know." Understanding crossed her features, and she took my hand in hers. "I'm okay. I promise I'll tell you if I'm not."

"Good." Keeping a hold of her hand, I led her to our table, but I paused before we got there. "Are you okay sitting here, or would you prefer us to sit alone?"

She stared up at me, an unreadable expression on her face, before she shook her head with a small laugh. "I'm not used to this sweet and considerate side of you, yet. But I have to say, I really like it."

Laughing, I tugged her over to the table and pulled out a chair for her. I watched a shy smile curve over her lips as our friends greeted her. It was surprising how easily she'd been accepted into our group, but then, all our closest friends were aware of what had happened to her, and I doubted there was anyone that didn't feel horror and even guilt for the part we'd all played in driving Raine away.

It went without saying that Tina was no longer a part of our group, after the news that she'd been the one behind defacing Raine's locker.

"I guess I'll sit here." Lena threw herself into the seat next to Raine. Everyone stared at her, and finally she let out the world's most long-suffering sigh. "Raine's my friend. I'm eating with her." She turned her attention to her food, and that was the end of the discussion.

"Is this real?" Raine's voice was soft and only for me.

Shifting in my seat, I turned to face her. "It's real. I can't promise I'll get it right all the time—in fact, it's guaranteed I'll fuck up more than once—but you're worth it. I'm... changing for you. You know, working on being the man you deserve. For you."

She smiled. "Okay." Her voice lowered, and she slid her hand into mine. "I don't want you to change, though. I mean, yeah, I guess there are one or two parts of you I'm not totally in love with..." She shot me a teasing grin, before continuing. "But everyone has their flaws. I do, I know. We're all works in progress."

"Wait, so there are parts of me you're in love with?" I smirked at her, and she groaned, dropping her head to my shoulder.

"Why did you focus on that bit?" she mumbled against my blazer.

I laughed and kissed the top of her head. "You want to come over for dinner later? Mum's making shepherd's pie. You know how she always makes way too much."

My distraction technique worked, because she lifted her

head to mine, her hazel eyes sparkling, and nodded. "I'd like that."

"Can we drive around a bit before we go home? I...we need to talk."

Raine's words sent a spike of unease through me, and I swallowed hard before answering. "Yeah, whatever you need."

She gave me a tiny smile that didn't reach her eyes, and my stomach dropped.

After I'd been driving around aimlessly for twenty minutes, getting more and more worked up, Raine finally spoke, her voice quiet. "Dylan's officially left the school."

Taking my eyes away from the road briefly, I glanced over to her to see the combination of relief and distress written all over her face. "How do you know?" Shifting the car into fourth gear, I eased the wheel to the right as we headed along the clifftop road, the ruins of Alstone Castle up ahead, silhouetted against the sky.

"Joey told me. He's in the drama club with me. He's, uh...a friend of Dylan's." A sigh escaped her lips. "He knows what happened, and he seemed pretty shaken by the whole thing."

This wasn't a conversation I wanted to have when I was driving. Indicating, I pulled off the road onto the grass verge and turned the engine off. "Climb in the back with me." There was more room, and I needed to hold her. She nodded, and after we'd moved into the back seat, I tugged her into my lap, putting my arms around her. Curling into me, she was silent for a moment before she continued.

"Long story short. From the sound of it, Dylan called Joey when you...you know. Broke his arm."

"That was the least he deserved," I muttered, and I felt her nod against me.

"I know. Surprisingly, Joey agreed. From the sound of it, the whole story came out when he took Dylan to the hospital to get his arm sorted out. To say he was disturbed is probably putting it mildly. He seemed to get the impression that Dylan had kind of obsessive tendencies." She took a shaky breath. "Ones relating to me. He hated the popular kids, and for whatever reasons he justified in his head, your interest in me triggered him." Her voice dropped to a whisper. "Joey said he told him that he had a folder of photos of me on his computer." I felt her body begin to tremble, and I tightened my arms around her, kissing her head. "The fact he'd decorated his bedroom to look like mine creeped me out enough, but to know that he had a whole folder of photos of me which must've been taken without my knowledge...I mean, who does that?"

Her gaze met mine, her expression so anguished that it almost hurt to look at her. "I just kept thinking, why didn't I see it? He's never been anything more than friendly to me. I've been going through everything in my head, and I just...I don't understand it, Carter."

"That kid is seriously fucked up, Rai. Listen to me. There's nothing that you could have done any differently. His actions aren't normal. Why would your mind even go there? As far as you knew, he was your friend and you'd have no reason to think otherwise."

"Maybe." She sighed. "I don't know. Anyway, Joey basically told him that if he dared to show his face in Alstone again, he was going to press charges. Or that I was. Whatever. Joey wanted to press charges now, anyway, but he was worried that you'd be in trouble too, for breaking his arm."

"Fuck. Even with the pictures?"

She nodded, and I smiled grimly. "In that case, I need to make a couple of calls. I don't think he'd risk going up against the Drummond family, but I'm not leaving anything to chance. Kian and I...we know a guy, Mack, who has friends that could be useful in these situations. Or so I've heard. Let me investigate." At her dubious look, I lowered my head to kiss her softly. "Trust me. He's never going to hurt you again."

"I trust you." A real smile finally appeared on her lips, and I kissed her again.

"I'd do anything to keep you safe."

FORTY-ONE

CARTER

A few weeks on, and things were finally getting back to normal, or a new version of normal, now Raine was mine. I couldn't get enough of her, and I'd never had that with a girl before. And on a night like tonight, when she was dressed up for Anastasia's party and looking really fucking hot in a tight black top and tiny shorts, I couldn't stop touching her every chance I could. I drove with one hand on the wheel, the other on her thigh. At every red light, my lips were on hers. "I can't get enough of you," I told her while throwing up my middle finger at the driver behind us. He actually had the audacity to beep his horn at me, just because I was too busy kissing my girlfriend to notice the lights had changed from red to green.

"Watch the road." Her words came out on a breathless laugh. Out of the corner of my eye, I saw her bite down on her lip, and then she spoke quietly. "Maybe after the party we could go to Parton Park and re-enact Fright Night? I mean...you could chase me?"

I nearly swerved the car off the road, and she shrieked in fright. My grip on her thigh tightened, and I swallowed thickly. "Fucking hell, Rai. Why are we going to this party?" My cock hardened at the thought of catching her in the dark, wrapping my hand around her pretty little throat, and fucking her senseless. "I'm serious. Let's skip the party."

She laughed again. "No. You need to be there. You're the football captain and the king of the school." She accompanied her words with an eye-roll, but she gave me a grin to let me know she was just winding me up. "Besides, it'll make it even better. The wait, knowing that later you'll be getting to do all the dirty, depraved things to me that you want to do."

"How will that make it better? It's torture."

"Delayed gratification." She shrugged.

"And you say I'm the sadistic one in this relationship." I squeezed her thigh one last time before releasing it so I could change gear.

"I never said that." Glancing over at her, I saw her batting her lashes innocently, and I raised a brow.

"Bet you were thinking it, though."

"Maybe. You know I like your sadistic tendencies."

This girl. I was gone for her. Why had I ignored how perfect she was for me? Yeah, she did like my sadistic side. I knew how me restraining her when we fucked turned her on, and just how hard she came when I was gripping her throat. After everything that had happened with Dylan, I'd been hesitant to do anything that might trigger her, but she...I wasn't really sure I understood, but she said that she felt safe with me and trusted me. And I'd never do anything to break that trust.

We pulled up outside Anastasia's mansion, joining the crowd of cars that lined the gravel driveway, and I unclipped my seat belt. Glancing over at Raine, I saw her hesitant expression. "What's wrong?" I clasped her jaw, gently turning her face to mine.

"Nothing, really. I'm just nervous. Silly, right?" She laughed humourlessly. "I've just never fitted in at these places. Not that I've been to any of these parties as an invited guest, but you know what I mean."

Guilt, hot and suffocating, rushed through me. That was my fault. I'd beaten her down, made her feel like she didn't belong. "Raine. I'm—"

She lifted her hand, placing it to my lips. "I know what you're thinking. Don't blame yourself, Carter. I've forgiven you for your part. I wouldn't be here with you if I hadn't. A lot of this is in my own head, anyway. I just have to keep pushing myself out of my comfort zone, and I'll get there. Eventually."

"I won't leave you," I promised her. We exited my truck, and I pulled her close to me, tucking her under my arm. We'd left our coats in the truck, and I had a great view down her top to her full breasts. "Did you wear that purposely to tempt me?" I skimmed my hand up over her ribs, stopping just below her tits.

"I might've had you in mind when I chose the outfit." She gave me a coy smile from under her lashes.

"If you were trying to drive me crazy, you succeeded. All I can think about is uncovering your gorgeous body and filling you with my dick."

"Carter!" She gave a shocked laugh, before it turned into a smirk. "You want to see what's underneath?" As we entered the open door of the mansion, she ducked out from under my arm, peeling her top off and turning to face me.

I stopped dead, staring at her. I was actually speechless for the first time in my life. She'd worn the Poison Ivy costume she'd worn on Fright Night, or a modified version, at least. The skintight outfit clung to her breasts, and I could clearly see the outline of her nipples. I pushed her against the wall, grinding my hard dick against her, lowering my head to her ear.

"Are you trying to kill me here?" I asked her hoarsely. "How can I walk around here with you dressed like that? I'm about two seconds away from ripping your shorts off and fucking you right now."

"You'll have to wait." She pushed me away, then strolled past me without a care in the world. "Come on."

"Rai..." There was an actual whine in my voice.

"I'm putting the top back on, don't worry." She pulled it back over her head and turned back to me.

"Not doing anything to help."

She took a few steps back in front of me and smiled as she reached her hand out to grip my dick through my jeans. I groaned at her touch.

"I can't help it. Now I'm allowed to, I just want to torture you like you tortured me for months." She released her grip, and I tugged her into my arms, palming her ass.

"I've created a monster."

"Yeah, you have."

Not that I was complaining.

The party was...good. I was used to the constant attention, and yeah, I loved it, but having Raine there as my girlfriend made everything so much sweeter. Raine seemed comfortable now, taking it in her stride, other than the times people mentioned my PDAs with her. Something which caused Raine to blush, without fail. Every single time.

I fucking loved it. Loved having her there with me.

"You want to get out of here?" Raine was sitting in my lap on an ornate seventeenth-century sofa, sipping from her drink. At my words, she shuffled around so she was sitting sideways and could look at me. I kept one arm around her as I lifted my other hand to brush the hair away from her face.

"Have you had enough?" She leaned over and kissed my jaw, before drawing back with a hesitant expression. "Am I being too pushy? We can stay as long as you like."

"Hmmm." I pretended to think it over. "Stay here, watching everyone getting drunker and louder, or go somewhere I can have you all to myself. What do you think?" I smiled at her, stroking my thumb across her soft cheek.

Instead of replying, she slid her hand up my chest, over my shoulder, and around the back of my neck, and then her lips were on mine.

"Get a room!"

We broke apart, and I saw Xavier grinning at me. "Is this what we have to look forward to with you two at all our future parties now? All this PDA shit?"

"Fuck off," I muttered.

"You—hold that thought." He held his hand up, his attention turning to the left of the room. "I'll be back." He stalked off, and I followed his line of sight to see Imogen leaning casually against the wall, drink in hand, her gaze fixed on his. He reached her, snatching the drink from her grip and practically throwing it down on a table. Then he was crowding her against the wall, and they were kissing.

"I guess they've sorted their shit out now," I mused aloud to Raine.

"Looks like it." She smiled, then turned back to me. "You never answered my question."

Lifting her to her feet, I stood. "Let's get out of here. I've got a date with Poison Ivy."

FORTY-TWO

RAINE

I stripped off my top and shorts inside Carter's truck, telling him he couldn't look at me. Even though it'd been a massive detour, he'd insisted on stopping back at his house for "supplies," so I'd taken the chance to run into my own house and grab my mask. The one Carter had originally given me.

Without the atmospheric lighting of Fright Night, the park felt empty and foreboding, and I shivered. After I'd pulled on my mask and boots, I locked everything inside the truck except for a tiny key ring I had, which had a flashlight and personal alarm. Despite Carter's presence, I wasn't about to go running through the park without some kind of protection. Not that it would do much. I shivered again, second-guessing my decision to come here, before I shook off that thought. Carter wouldn't be far away.

"Raine." Carter was suddenly looming over me, his huge, strong body against mine, and I completely relaxed. He wouldn't let anything happen to me. "Stay in the shadows. There are people in the skatepark." His low murmur vibrated against me, and I nodded. Pulling me into his arms, he kissed the top of my head, before releasing me. "They might not know we're playing, and we don't want the police involved."

I snorted at that. Yeah, trying to explain that I wanted my boyfriend to chase me around in the dark and make me scream might not go down too well with the police.

"Ready? I'm gonna give you a head start, then I'm coming for you."

I nodded again. The same feeling of adrenaline, threaded through with the tiniest amount of fear, fizzed through my veins, and I smiled. "I'm ready."

"Good." He lifted his hands, and I realised he was putting on his own mask. Not just any mask. *The* mask. The one he'd worn at Fright Night. "Looks like we both had the same idea."

Flicking a switch, the LED lights came on, and I shivered at the sinister slashes covering his eyes and mouth.

He spoke one word, in a low, menacing rumble.

"Run."

I did.

CARTER

She shot away from me, and I grinned. Behind her mask, I'd sensed the thrill of fear in her, the way her breath had come in short, sharp gasps once I'd put on my own mask. My girl knew I was coming for her, and her reaction to me had my cock responding instantly.

I adjusted myself, playing football drills in my mind,

because yeah, running with a hard-on was not fun. After waiting for a moment, I started prowling after her, my pace slow and steady as I allowed her time to get away, always keeping her in my sights. She raced around the side of the floodlit skatepark, staying deep within the shadows, hugging the chain-link fence that ran down one side. I increased my pace, easily keeping up with her as she bolted straight for the graffiti wall, avoiding the area where the few skaters were. She slid round behind the wall, and I smiled, slowing down again to give her time to catch her breath and build the anticipation.

As I reached the wall, I stopped, listening. Her uneven, panting breaths carried through the still night air as she tried to stay hidden.

My footsteps silent, I moved along the wall and then eased my body around the back, on the opposite side to her hiding place.

I could make her out, peering around the corner. Her breath was still coming in pants, but I could feel the excitement coming off her. She loved this. The fear, the thrill of the chase, then the moment when I'd strike without warning.

As I moved closer, I slowed my footsteps, my breathing even, coming right up behind her.

"Boo." I whispered the words in her ear, low and menacing, and my arms came around her, one gripping her waist, and the other, her throat. A scream escaped her mouth, and I slammed my hand over it, on top of her mask. She struggled against me ineffectually, and I held her in place. "Oh baby, you can't run from me. I'll always find you." I loosened my grip around her mouth and spun her to face me, pressing her up against the concrete wall. In the sliver of light that fell across us, I could see her eyes behind her mask, huge and glimmering as she stared up at me.

"Now you've caught me, what are you going to do with me?" Her words came out all breathy and lustful, and I smiled.

"Whatever I want." After pulling off my mask, I lifted hers and dropped it to the floor so I could see her face. Gripping her throat, I lowered my mouth to hers, and she opened for me. She tasted of whatever cocktail she'd been drinking at the party, sweet and delicious. I lost myself in her kiss, grinding myself into her, as she tugged my head lower, trying to pull me closer.

I trailed my teeth down her neck, as my hand cupped her pussy, the evidence of what our little game was doing to her already obvious from the soaked material. "My little trickster. You tricked me, right here."

"I'd trick you again, if it meant we'd end up like this," she murmured softly. She trailed off on a moan as I dragged my fingers roughly along her wetness.

"I'd let you trick me twice. You're mine now." Using my free hand, I slid the straps of her leotard down her arms and tugged it all the way down her body so she was bared to me.

"I—stop teasing me, now. I want you." She was panting now, as I sucked one of her nipples into my mouth. I brought up my other hand, coated in her arousal, and pinched and tugged at her other nipple until she was crying out. I moved my head to take that nipple into my mouth, tasting her.

"You taste fucking delicious, Rai."

She moaned, fumbling for the button of my jeans. I plunged two fingers inside her, and she gasped, her hand stilling on my jeans. I added a third finger, slowly pumping in and out of her, her wetness coating my hand. As my free hand moved to grip her throat, a low, needy sound escaped her lips. "Carter."

"Hmmm?" I returned my mouth to hers, swallowing her moans as we kissed frantically, and my movements became faster, as I moved my thumb across her clit, pumping and scissoring my fingers until she fell apart in front of me, her whole body trembling. I broke away from her, staring at her glassy-eyed, unfocused gaze as she came back down from her high.

"You're so fucking beautiful when you come." Seeing her there, her head thrown back, all flushed and breathless, made something that I didn't dare to put a name to swirl in my chest. I couldn't think about that, not yet. Especially not with the fact that she was going to be heading off to university away from Alstone. It was going to be difficult enough having a long-distance relationship without my feelings for her getting even deeper.

Fuck. Who was I kidding?

Pushing those thoughts away and concentrating on the girl that was right here in front of me, I placed my fingers over her lips, reminding her of the first time we'd done this. "Open up." She opened and I slid my fingers into her mouth, feeling her tongue swirl around my digits, imagining it was my cock.

Her hands went back to my jeans as I held her to me. "I love your cock."

I grinned. "My cock loves you."

She groaned, and I could see her cheeks flush in the dim light. "I didn't mean to say that aloud."

"I know you didn't. But now you have, so why don't you go ahead and show just how much love you have." Releasing my grip, I pushed her head down, and she sank to the floor in a crouch. Her hands made quick work of my buttons, and then she dragged my jeans down over my hips.

"Mmmm," she moaned, palming me through my boxers. My eyes rolled back in my head, her firm, confident touch sending a jolt of electricity straight through me. She freed me from my boxers, running her thumb over the crown of my cock, smearing my precum across the tip.

"Rai. Baby." I couldn't get any more words out, as she took my dick into her mouth, flicking her tongue on the underside. At the same time, she gripped my balls and lightly tugged on them, and my hands went to her hair, holding her in place as she sucked my cock.

Fuck.

I'd never get enough of her mouth on me.

As she took me deeper, she looked up at me, her pupils blown, and I felt the familiar tightening. Fuck, no. I wanted to come inside her. I pulled her head off me, and she stared at me, startled. "What's wrong?"

"Nothing's wrong. You've got me so worked up I was about to come in your pretty little mouth, but I want to come inside you."

Her expression cleared, and she rose to her feet. "What are you waiting for?"

After a moment's hesitation, I said the words I'd been wanting to say from the moment I'd first had her. "I want to go bare inside you, skin to skin. I want to feel all of you. Right here, right now. Is that okay? I'm clean."

She bit her lip, then nodded. "I really want that. I'm clean, too. I mean, you know that. It's only ever been you."

"It will only ever be me." I lifted her into my arms, kissing her fiercely, before I thrust up inside her. "Oh fuck. This is amazing." Her pussy fit me like a glove, tight, wet, and hot around my throbbing cock, no barriers between us.

She moaned in agreement, and I thrust again. "Harder, Carter. Fuck me so hard I feel you tomorrow."

I growled and pushed her back against the wall, fucking her without mercy, her cries echoing through the space. "Oh fuck, I'm so close," I panted, trying to hold on. Shifting my arms, I angled her slightly, and she cried out.

"There! Don't stop, please don't stop." I felt her pussy contract around my cock as her orgasm hit hard and fast.

Her orgasm triggered mine, and I came so hard, I swore I saw stars.

When I came down, my breathing returning to normal, I pulled her carefully off me. She winced slightly as I lowered her to the ground. "Are you okay, baby?" I brushed her hair back from her face.

"That was amazing," she sighed, her rosebud lips curving into a smile.

Fuck. A thought suddenly occurred to me. "I didn't bring anything to clean up with." T-shirt it was, then. Ripping it over my head, I sank into a crouch in front of her and was hit with the best sight ever. My cum, running down her inner thigh. "Fucking hell, Rai, look at you, here, my cum all over you. No one else will ever see this sight, not now you're mine."

I balled up my T-shirt and carefully cleaned her off. "What will happen after the summer?" Her quiet, sad whisper cut through me.

The same question had been playing on my mind, but I couldn't stand the thought of her getting upset about it. It was down to me to reassure her, to make her see that we were going to be okay. After helping her back into her costume, I rose to my feet. "We'll make it work. I don't want to lose you."

"But we're going to be at opposite ends of the country."

Her lip trembled, and right then, I understood exactly how much I meant to her, because the expression in her eyes reflected the way I was feeling.

"I won't lose you. Plenty of people make long distance work. We can do it. You're not just a fling to me, Raine."

She buried her face in my shoulder, clinging onto me. "I hope so. You're going to have so many girls throwing themselves at you all the time, though. I can't expect you to wait for me. You need to enjoy your time at university without worrying about me."

"Raine, don't you get it? I don't want anyone else. You're the only one I want. No one else."

A sigh escaped her lips, and she gripped onto me more tightly, her nails digging into my back.

"Come on. Let's get home. Your aunt's doing a night shift, right? Let's get showered and maybe we can try out the restraints I ordered."

"Restraints?" Her head shot up, a glimmer of interest chasing away the sadness in her eyes.

"Yeah. You heard right."

"Do I get to tie you up?" Her voice was playful as we made our way back through the park towards my truck.

"Nope. These are strictly for me to restrain you."

"And what are you going to do when you've got me at your mercy?"

"Whatever I want."

RAINE
EPILOGUE

TWO MONTHS LATER

My hands trembling, I turned the letter in my hands, the Southwark University crest taunting me. I slid my fingernail under the edge, easing it open, and pulled out the sheet of paper. Tears obscured my vision as I read the words.

Delighted to inform...transfer successful subject to final results...full confirmation and information package to follow by email and post...

I'd done it. I'd managed to switch from my original university to a degree course in textiles at Southwark University in south London. Carter and I would be an easy train ride apart. Since I'd become his girlfriend, I no longer had the burning desire to escape from Alstone that I once had. My priorities had changed. Carter was everything to me, and I didn't want to gain everything and lose him in the process. This was a compromise—I got to do the degree that

I'd been working towards all this time, but I'd be close enough that we could spend every weekend together, plus time during the week, depending on our class schedules.

It was scary putting myself out there, but as Lena kept reminding me, I had to push myself out of my comfort zone.

Now, I had to break the news to Carter.

Walking through the hallway towards the cafeteria, I breathed in and out deeply, clutching the letter in my hand. I knew Carter wanted me, but there was always the tiniest doubt in my mind. Would this be too much? Would he be happy about what I'd done? I paused in the doorway, just watching my gorgeous boyfriend on his table at the centre of the room. He was seated casually on the table itself, long legs propped up on the chair in front of him. He'd taken his school blazer off, and his sleeves were rolled up, exposing his strong forearms. His presence dominated the space, confidence radiating from him as the group surrounding him hung off his every word.

As if he sensed me, his gaze swung upwards and locked onto me, and a huge grin spread across his face. He crooked his finger at me, and I swallowed nervously, moving over to him.

"Hey." He swung his legs off the chair when I reached the table, tugging me in between them and gripping me lightly around the waist. "How's my favourite girl doing?"

"Good," I whispered. The letter was still clutched in my hand, the paper crumpled between us.

"What's up?" He cupped my chin. "What's—" Then he

must've noticed the crinkling of the paper because he reached between us and pried the letter from my fingertips. I stood, the nerves rooting me in place, as he silently read the letter.

When the silence stretched, I swallowed hard, then spoke. "Carter? Say something, please."

He finally raised his eyes from the paper. "What's this all about? You're giving up your dream degree course?" A flash of anger appeared in his eyes, and my stomach rolled.

"No. It's not... The location doesn't matter. The course is almost identical. I only picked my original university because I wanted to get as far away as possible. But now I have you, I thought... I wanted to be close to you... I'm sorry..." My voice faded as I dropped my gaze.

"Rai." He tilted my chin, forcing me to look into his eyes. "Fuck." He scrubbed his hand across his face. "Are you sure this is what you want?"

I nodded. "Completely. My priorities have changed, now."

He stared at me for the longest time, the gold in his eyes sparking as he held my gaze. "You know I love you, right?"

"What?" My shocked whisper was echoed next to me, as Xavier, who was eavesdropping and not even being subtle about it, stared between us both.

Carter's lips curved into a blinding smile. "Yeah. I love you. You. Raine Laurent." Suddenly, he was standing up and cupping his hands around his mouth, shouting out for everyone to hear. "I love Raine Laurent!"

"Carter, sit down now!" I hissed, my face flaming as every single person in the cafeteria turned to stare at us. I ignored the laughter of his friends around me, sinking into the chair and hiding my face in my hands.

Then, he was gripping my hands and prying them away

from my face and tugging me into his arms. "Sorry. I couldn't resist. I want everyone to know how much you mean to me."

I melted a little at his words, allowing myself to relax against his body. Throwing my arms around his waist, I stood there holding him as he stroked his hand up and down my back. As I grew calmer, I forgot about the attention of the other students and focused on what Carter had just said.

"You love me?" I drew back and stared up at him.

"Yeah. A whole fucking lot."

I smiled. "I love you."

He gave me a wide grin. "I know." Then he kissed me, before taking a seat in the chair and tugging me into his lap. Picking up his phone, he scrolled through his emails. "I can't believe you did all this. And you know what the weird thing is?" Pushing the phone in front of me, he tapped on the screen. "Look. I've been emailing Newcastle University to see about transferring there once my first semester in Alstone College is over."

Reading through the email, my eyes widened in disbelief. "You were going to do that?"

"I'd do anything for you. The thought of us being so far apart...I didn't want to lose you."

"You won't. And now, you don't have to worry. I already looked at the trains between here and my new uni, and there are loads every day. Not only that, just think of the weekends we can spend together in London."

A gleam came into his eye. "Yeah, maybe I could get season tickets for Chelsea." I groaned, and he laughed. "Just kidding. Maybe just one or two games."

"I can deal with that. I can even deal with the season tickets, if it means I get to spend time with you."

As he kissed me again, I didn't even care that people might be watching us. The person I loved, loved me back, and I no longer had to face the prospect of being apart from him.

CARTER

Standing on the pier with Raine, I watched her as she stared down the beach, her gaze distant. "You look like you're thinking very hard, there." I pressed a kiss to her head.

"I was just remembering." Her voice was soft. "The fortune teller. Aunt Marie. I-I met her down there, on the beach."

"You did? You never told me."

Turning, she tilted her head up and met my eyes, her hair glinting with golden threads, highlighted by the last of the sun's rays. She was so beautiful, and all mine.

"I actually forgot about it. It was that day that Xavier soaked me with his car, remember? Anyway, I was just thinking about the riddle she said. It went, 'both light and darkness lie ahead. Your path is shrouded with hidden dread. The question that you need to ask... What is hidden beneath his mask?' Then she added this whispered bit that was a little creepy—she said 'Find out... before it is too late.' At the time, I wondered if she was talking about you, but now I'm thinking it was about Dylan."

She huffed out a laugh, trailing her finger across the railing as the sun finally sank below the horizon. "Silly, though. Right? She can't really know what's going to happen."

I paused for a moment before answering. "No. How could she? She's just good at reading people."

"Yeah, you're probably right." She sighed, before laughing again. "Oh, I forgot the weirdest part. She had a talking bird with her. Did you know birds can talk?"

"Yes, I know," I said dryly. "That's Picasso. Aunt Marie's raven. He's…kind of annoying, for a bird. He has his uses, though." I thought back to the night when she'd disappeared with Dylan. As much as I disliked that bird, I couldn't forget how he'd appeared from seemingly nowhere and spurred me into action.

"I thought he was cute." A grin appeared on her face. "Although he did appear to be kind of judgemental."

"Yep, that's Picasso. Anyway, enough talk about the raven." I slanted my lips over hers, kissing her until she was breathless. "Fuck, I love you."

Her eyes shining up at me, she smiled. "I love you, too."

"How about you show me just how much?"

She raised a brow. "What do you mean?"

A slow smile crossed my face. "Do you remember where we parked my truck?"

At her nod, I licked my lips, letting my gaze rake over her body. I watched with satisfaction as she flushed, her pupils dilating, before I lowered my voice. "I'm in the mood to catch myself a little trickster."

Her eyes widened, and an answering smile curved over her lips. "You are, are you?"

Bending my head, I took her lobe between my teeth, feeling her shudder beneath me. Releasing her, I let the anticipation build, her body thrumming against mine, ready to fly. Then, pressing my mouth to her ear, I rasped the word she'd been waiting for.

"Run."

As I took off after her, a wide, satisfied grin formed on my lips as I closed the distance between us. I fucking loved this. Loved *her*. She was made for me.

Life was good.

We had our whole future to look forward to together, and I couldn't wait.

THE END

THANK YOU

Thank you so much for reading Carter and Raine's story!

Feel free to send me any and all abuse/love/comments, and spoiler-free reviews are always very appreciated 🤍

Want more from Alstone High? Get Kian and Preston's standalone story now at http://mybook.to/ctl

Interested in more from Cassius and Lena? Start The Four series at http://mybook.to/tlwt

A note on Picasso, the talking raven...

Ravens can talk! Check out this video on YouTube for an example.

Becca

xoxo

ACKNOWLEDGMENTS

The first person I thank has to be my husband, because you not only put up with me locking myself away to write, but you let me use you for the character of Chris, who is arguably a colossal dick.

Claudia and Jenny, darkside for life. Chair legs and all.

My betas, you are awesome and I love you! Ashley, Claudia, Jenny, Megan and Sue. And my street team and ARC team, we didn't have long to promo this but you worked magic!

Thank you to Cassie for the most epic cover ever, I love it so much! Thank you also for talking me out of buying a carpet cleaner at 3 a.m. Thanks to Sandra for editing, and to Sid for your proofreading skills! And thank you to Ivy for pretty much ensuring this book was finished. To all the authors that I'm lucky enough to know, your support and encouragement means a lot to me.

To Enticing, and the bloggers, bookstagrammers and readers who took a chance on Trick Me Twice - I really appreciate you all.

And I have to mention my friends that put up with me basically disappearing from existence, to the point where they essentially forgot what I looked like. I owe you all drinks. Lots of drinks.

Thanks again for reading!

Becca xoxo

P.S. Thank you insomnia, for tipping me over the edge of craziness and allowing Aunt Marie and Picasso in.

ABOUT THE AUTHOR

Becca Steele is a USA Today and Wall Street Journal bestselling romance author. She currently lives in the south of England with a whole horde of characters that reside inside her head.

When she's not writing, you can find her reading or watching Netflix, usually with a glass of wine in hand. Failing that, she'll be online hunting for memes, or wasting time making her 500th Spotify playlist.

Join Becca's Facebook reader group Becca's Book Bar, sign up to her mailing list, or visit her website https://authorbeccasteele.com

Other links:

- facebook.com/authorbeccasteele
- instagram.com/authorbeccasteele
- bookbub.com/authors/becca-steele
- goodreads.com/authorbeccasteele
- amazon.com/Becca-Steele/e/B07WT6GWB2

ALSO BY BECCA STEELE

The Four Series
The Lies We Tell
The Secrets We Hide
The Havoc We Wreak
A Cavendish Christmas (free short story)*
The Fight In Us
The Bonds We Break

Alstone High Standalones
Trick Me Twice
Cross the Line (M/M)
In a Week (free short story)*
Savage Rivals (M/M)

London Players Series
The Offer

London Suits Series
The Deal
The Truce
The Wish (a festive short story)*

Other Standalones
Mayhem (a Four series spinoff)*

Boneyard Kings Series (with C. Lymari)

Merciless Kings (RH)

Vicious Queen (RH)

Ruthless Kingdom (RH)

all free short stories and bonus scenes are available from https://authorbeccasteele.com

Lightning Source UK Ltd.
Milton Keynes UK
UKHW010809300822
408024UK00002B/580